Cunning
VOWS

USA TODAY BESTSELLING AUTHOR
T.L. SMITH
KIA CARRINGTON-RUSSELL

Hello there, lover, did you miss me while you spread those other pages?
Sincerely,
Your book boyfriend.

Warning

This book contains sexually explicit scenes and adult language and may be considered offensive to some readers. This book is intended for adults ONLY. Please store your books wisely, where they cannot be accessed by under-aged readers.

Blurb

Cunning, lethal, and resilient were just a few words men have used to describe Anya Ivanov. Some would use words that are far worse. The head of questionable auctions just so happens to have the eye of a very ruthless businessman, River Bently.

River knew she was his the moment he saw her. And he was more than patient, giving her time to realize he wasn't going anywhere. Even if he was imposing on her territory, he was there to stay.

The only way to spend time with Anya is if you have the money to pay for her company.

He very much could.

He would pay every last dollar she demanded in order to be in the same room as the woman everyone is afraid of. He doesn't see a woman who could cut him down to his knees. No, he sees a woman who he would gladly get on his knees for.

CHAPTER 1

Anya

"**I**s that the right spot, miss?" I shake my head in frustration. Nothing is working. Not even his mouth on my clit. Clay notices the shift in my mood, but Vance continues to work his mouth on my breast.

"What about here, miss?" he asks as he tugs on my nipple with his teeth.

"Just stop. Both of you, stop. It's not working." I push them away, and they back off obediently. Both sit naked at the end of the bed, waiting for either approval or another command from me. Just as God intended it to be.

But let's be real, God has no place in this room. Only fucking.

Even that's not working as the distraction it was intended to be.

Reaching for my phone, I check my messages, hopeful the private investigator has sent me a useful update.

Fucking nothing. No sign of my twin brother, Alek.

It's driving me mad, so fucking mad, that he up and left without a word. He would never do that. We're twins, but more than that, we're best friends. I do everything for him.

I trust no one in this life. Except for him.

So why did he leave me without a single trace as to his whereabouts?

"We could try again, miss," Clay offers, always eager to please me. I look up to see Vance nodding in agreement.

I never thought there would be something that could sour my libido, but the thought of my brother is most off-putting.

"Go, do whatever you do when I'm in here."

"We do you when you're here." Vance winks. He won't get a smile out of me. No man does unless I want something, but it eases my tension ever so slightly to know how eager these two are for me. At my beck and call whenever I please. It's powerful, and something I very much like the taste of.

Doing as they're told, they begin to put their clothes back on. Vance and Clay work for me in more ways than one. They have been here more lately, due to my neediness in an attempt to distract myself.

My brother left me in the lurch.

Because there is no possible way he got killed or abducted. Alek is way too smart for something like that to happen... way too deadly for it as well.

But it's been weeks with no contact or sighting.

All business dealings have been left to me, but it doesn't bother me, since I handle most of the business anyway. But... I'm used to having him around. All our lives, we've had each other. We were in and out of foster homes from the age of four until our final one at seven, when we were placed with a wicked older lady who dabbled in illegal things. She was also Russian, and her accent gave us a tiny glimmer of what home might've felt like with our parents before they abandoned us. But there was no love, only sharpening us as tools to be used in her dirty dealings. One thing I will give the old bitch is she made us who we are, and our business is just as cutthroat. She never took shit from any man, just shaped the rules and made a shitload of money in the process.

I thank the old bitch, but I also hate the hag.

Meredith showed us calculated cruelty when she should have shown us some sort of love. She ensured we were to never call her Mother or Meredith, but instead insisted on Chief. I call her old bitch in my head and sometimes call her Meredith just to piss her off.

The Chief is a cunt.

Rolling out of bed, I reach for my red silk robe and throw it on before pressing call on my phone.

It rings.

And it rings.

And it rings.

He never picks up.

But at least it rings. Right?

It asks me to leave a voice message.

"Alek. Alek, you better fucking call me back. Call me back!" I end the call and throw my phone on the bed.

I'm frustrated with not knowing Alek's whereabouts. Not that I would ever show the tiny sliver of weakness I have in my armor. But sex is the only thing I ever have to depend on to release that tension. Well, it's the one I most enjoy. It's powerful, the way men will drop to their knees and beg to worship me. It's always when I feel my most powerful. Of course, I can kill people, which offers an entirely different release, but that's more my brother's thrill then mine.

With Alek gone, it means I also have to handle his contracts and negotiations, which doesn't usually faze me. But we've had a rather persistent newcomer lately, one who I have to meet with soon, and I have very little interest in doing so.

However, this particular man has certainly grabbed my attention, and not in a good way. He blew up one of my favorite shops that sold rare jewelry collections. It was the moment he seriously grabbed my attention.

I've since had my people gather everything they can about the elusive River Bently.

Walking to the bathroom, I rake my fingers through my red hair and put it up in a tight bun before I start on my face, applying makeup and red lipstick.

It's mechanical. I've done this every day from the age of fifteen. Polished. Regal. Beautiful. I have to be all of these things to remain cunning in my role since I mostly deal with businessmen. I use it to my advantage. If a man looked down on me for being a woman, he still wanted to fuck me because of it. And that is *always* their weakness.

But no one would ever own me.

No matter what they offer or how hard they try.

I drop the robe on the edge of the white clawfoot

tub rimmed with gold, then walk back into my bedroom. Two white floor-to-ceiling pillars frame my king-sized bed with a gold headboard. The beautiful chandelier glitters from the remaining sunlight that slips through the bay windows as sky turns to dusk. I slip through the wall behind my bed to the two-level closet.

My hand drifts along the glass display of all my recent jewelry collections as I contemplate what I might add to my outfit this evening.

For my clothing, I know exactly what I'll wear. I reach for my signature tight red dress, which has a slit up the side high enough to give a peek at my under-wear. If I wore underwear, that is. I idly stare at my jewelry cabinet as I slip on my designer heels.

"I think I'll wear the rubies today," I say to myself, because I'm the only one allowed in this room. My collection of pretties is for my viewing pleasure only.

When I leave my room, Clay and Vance wait outside my door, dressed in their custom black suits.

"Who am I meeting tonight?"

"His name is River Bently." Clay reads the name from his phone as we walk through the halls, and my staff make sure to avert their gazes to the floor when I stride past.

My men guide me to the front doors, where a car

awaits us. Vance holds the door open as I slide in, and they both follow, sitting on either side of me. Clay continues once the doors are closed, always cautious not to speak of business matters in front of others. You never know who might betray you.

"He's a tycoon known around the world for running drugs and guns. He's been mostly on the West Coast but has recently come to the East. He requested a meeting with you and your brother. You both declined said meetings until he blew up one of your shops," Clay says and then looks up from his phone. "Then you tried to find him to kill him. He's smart, though, and has managed to either kill or avoid anyone you sent with a message for a meetup," he finishes.

I remember this asshole vividly. Not because I've met him but because he's left an unflattering taste in my mouth.

"I don't think it's a good idea for you to meet up with him," Vance advises.

"Yeah, well, he's threatened to fuck up some of my gun shipments, and I don't play when it comes to business," I tell Vance. Not that the guns were ever my forte since Alek always handled them... before he went missing.

"We know, miss, it's just without Alek here..."

"Are you saying I can't handle things without my

brother?" I snap. "Listen closely. Neither of you are my partners. Just because I let you play with my body does not mean you have any hold over me *or* have any say in how I conduct business." I glare at them through narrowed eyes. They both nod and look down.

Loyalty. That's what these two are good for. Plus muscle. And maybe to make me come as well—that's a bonus.

My men are silent for the rest of the drive, and I find myself unlocking my phone screen on multiple occasions in the hope Alek has called or sent a text or *something.*

Thinking of Alek will only be a distraction to tonight's meeting.

"River?" I ask them, and they nod. "How many men tonight?"

"Ten so far on-site." I nod as we pull up to a restaurant. Clay opens my door, and I get out and brush my hands down my red dress.

This man wanted my attention.

Now he has it.

But he should've been wiser not to flag me down in the city that I all but own.

When I step into the restaurant, the hostess recognizes me immediately and directs me to where I'm meeting the infamous River Bently. I want to roll my eyes at having to come here in the first place.

I'd contemplated walking straight in and placing a gun to his head. But that would be a lot of work to cover up, considering the number of witnesses in the restaurant. I'll just have to decide what to do during our exchange.

The nervous hostess walks ahead of us and guides us up a few steps to the area for private groups. The second level is cordoned off and only hosts a large table with a lavish spread of dishes on it, and several men seated around it.

I spot him right away, sitting at the head of the table with a glass of amber liquor in his hand as he watches me ascend the stairs. I take in his dark sandy hair, pushed back and styled. He's dressed much like everyone else in the room.

The hostess is gone before any of the men addresses her.

"Gentlemen, there is a lady present," the man at the head of the table says.

Pfft. Lady.

Who the fuck does he think he is to be able to do that? My heels click with every step until I stop at the opposite end of the table. Everyone puts down their cutlery, and all their gazes fall on me.

Being looked at by men has never affected me. They either worship me or want to fuck me. Or possibly want to kill me. Whatever, I couldn't care less. Men don't intimidate me.

"Anya, if I may call you that, please take a seat and have some food." He waves to the spot next to him. I pull out the empty chair before me at the opposite end of the table. Everyone exchanges uncertain glances but says nothing. I cross my arms over my chest and lean back as I size him up defiantly.

A server nervously comes over and pours me a glass of wine. I ignore it as I cross my legs and lock eyes with the devil at the end of the table.

The table is silent, and I wait.

I've never been great with pleasantries.

"I thought, what better way to make introductions than at my new restaurant? Please, order anything you wish," he says.

Interesting. He's settling into my city far too comfortably for my liking. The server stands beside me expectantly and is surprised when I wave him off. He looks at the end of the table, waiting for permission before he turns and leaves.

"To say I'm disappointed your Aleksandr isn't with you would be an understatement." Everyone around the table seems to shrink at his voice. "Is it true he has a fear of touching people?" I bite the inside of my cheek at his words. My brother is not *his* business. "Anya, come on now. We can talk."

"Do you care to use your manners and introduce yourself?" I glare at him. He smiles and nods, as if it were some kind of signal. But to whom? My men are standing behind me; I know it's not missed. His gaze slides from me to the man seated next to me. The one I haven't paid a lick of attention to before I realize now how intently he's looking at me.

"Sorry, Anya," the man at the end of the table says as he walks past a few of the men obediently sitting quietly. It dawns on me then. This man is no one important. I realize my blunder when he stops beside the man sitting next to me.

Striking. That's the first word that comes to mind to describe him. Cold autumn eyes stare back at me, a mixture of blue and hazel, and he has dark hair, almost black in color. He wears a button-up shirt rolled up to his elbows, showing off the tattoos skating up his arms and hands. There's a ring glinting on his finger in the dim lighting of the room. And he sits there watching me, tapping his fingers contemplatively as he does. The man I thought was River bends to speak to him in a hushed tone before both of them look at me. The one seated next to me puts both of his elbows on the table and leans forward. I stay where I am, waiting for him to speak.

"Anya." His voice is like silk that slips all over my body. He lifts his hand and offers it to me. "River Bently. Pleased to meet you." I look at the man behind him, who I assumed was River, and see him slip back to where he was. Just like that, the men at the table start talking again, but it feels like we're the only two in the room.

So this is River Bently.

I expected someone scarier.

Someone less... attractive.

He's most likely someone who uses his looks in the same regard that I do.

Glancing down at his hand, I make no move to touch it. Does he really think I plan to shake his hand?

Yeah, that's not going to happen. I may not be like my brother and have issues with touching people, but I will not be giving this smug asshole the satisfaction of even a handshake.

No, he will not be touching me.

Ever.

CHAPTER 2

River

L ethal. That's one word I would use to describe her.

Breathtaking would be another. Porcelain skin, bright red hair, and plush red lips.

I can tell she's cunning. The glint in her gaze insinuates nothing is missed as she calculates her next move.

I don't fall easily for pretty women, though, and I have a feeling Anya Ivanov is used to getting what she wants when she wants it, and I have no doubt her looks help in many ways.

"Did you think it was smart to trick me?" She waves a perfectly manicured hand toward the end of the table where my men sit. When I want to get an idea of who someone is, and I know they don't know what I look like, I position myself where I think they will sit. Not for one second did I think she would move to sit next to Michael.

One of her men standing behind her leans down and whispers something in her ear. She lifts a red nail and shakes it at whatever he says before her dark-green eyes focus back on me.

"I want to make it very clear, River." She draws my name out, and my gaze can't help but dip to her lips. "I don't take kindly to threats."

"So I hear." I nod, considering she's already sent someone to try to kill me. That didn't work out so well for them. But I did blow up one of her favorite shops, so I don't take it personally.

"If you do such things again, I will have no problem retaliating. And it won't be as simple as a shop getting blown up." Her lips morph into a perfect smile. Deadly. "I'm not sure what you know of me, but I tend to like to crush the body parts of those who betray me." She leans in closer to me and adds, "With my heels."

I have heard many things about her.

She is just as lethal, or maybe even more so, as her brother.

Perhaps that's because it's unexpected from such a beautiful and bewitching woman.

"Noted," I say, to which her mouth twitches, not satisfied with my answer.

"It's best you do." Her hands press against the top of the table as she goes to stand. I reach for her hand but don't touch it, sliding my own along so our fingers almost brush. I imagine touching this woman right now would end up with a lot of guns pointing in this room, specifically at my head.

"Stay. We still have business to discuss." I offer her a bewitching smile, much like the one she offered me only moments ago.

"Have you paid your cut?" she asks with her nose pointed high in the air.

"My cut?" I ask her, confused.

"To talk to me, you shall pay me."

Oh, now we're getting somewhere.

"And what would be the price?" I ask, playing into her demand.

"One million dollars. All cash."

"Done. Now, sit." I watch as her tongue moves across her teeth, and she stands, pulling her hands away. Now she seems pissed for another reason entirely. This woman is unsatisfiable.

"No man tells me to sit. Actually, no man tells me to do anything. You also seemed confused that by agreeing to purchase my time, it's on your terms. If you require a meeting, get your people to send payment, and we can talk. For now, you have taken way too much of my time already."

I'm not so much shocked as I am impressed. I'd heard rumors of the captivating redhead, but witnessing it personally is an entirely different experience. I'd come to town to solidify previous business dealings with her brother, Alek, who seems to have gone missing. But now, I'm intrigued by the change of siblings. Fascinated even.

Most people I wouldn't simply let walk out without giving me what I came for, but instead, I find myself saying, "Goodnight, Anya Ivanov." Her name leaves my lips as she turns and saunters away. She doesn't so much as look back as her two men flank her, a little closer than necessary, in my opinion.

"Wow, she's more than what they described," Michael says, still standing behind me. I often use him as a decoy to pretend to be me in meetings such as these.

"A Russian beauty, that one," Derrick adds. He's another one of my men, seated beside me. I don't voice my opinion on her one way or another, even though I wholeheartedly agree with Derrick.

The rest of the table is filled with clients. I prefer to

manage them all at once so I don't have to go out of my way for any particular person.

The energy in the room shifts as soon as she's gone, and everyone enjoys their meals and drinks. Michael pulls out the chair and sits where Anya was only moments before.

"Will you actually pay for her time? Considering why we're here, don't the Ivanov siblings owe *you*?"

Picking up my glass of scotch, I hold it in my hand before I swish the dark liquid around contemplatively. It's true. But by Anya's response, I'm under the firm belief her brother might've left her in the dark about our dealings. Although a debt is to be paid, I can't help but be intrigued by how Anya manages her own business. I wonder how she'll squirm under pressure. I can't really imagine it at all.

The Ivanovs are known in New York, and are deadly by themselves but also in who they're associated with. I was given fair warning to tread lightly before stepping into town, especially around the siblings.

"We shall see. We aren't in our territory right now, so until we know whose ground we are stomping on, we play nice."

"If you say so." Michael seems unsatisfied by my dismissal, but I don't give a fuck. He has no say.

"I do, and what I say, goes," I finish, ending the conversation.

He averts his gaze, and I lean toward Derrick. "Find out everything I need to know about Anya Ivanov."

"I gave you quite a thorough portfolio of the siblings. Is there anything specific you'd like to know?" he asks. Derrick is my go-to man, and he excels in finding secrets and profiling individuals.

"Everything. Even down to how she likes her coffee made."

Derrick seems surprised but nods. "I'll work on it immediately."

Good. Because, as of tonight, anything and everything to do with Anya Ivanov is now my business.

CHAPTER 3

Anya

One week after tolerating being in the same room as River for the first time, I'm sitting out front of one of my luxurious homes. I have several residences, all catering to different engagements and businesses. I'm particularly fond of this one since it hosts one of my favorite auctions.

Being in the underworld for as long as we have, almost nothing is off-limits. And every auction has a time and place. Like tonight, which has finally ended, the last of our patrons leave with items they couldn't so easily acquire elsewhere to satisfy their tastes.

"Pleasure doing business with you," Mr. Fox says with his man carrying a briefcase.

"We look forward to your continued business

during the next auction," I say without a smile. Because I don't smile and will only offer minimal pleasantries.

His gaze roams down my body but only briefly. His complexion turns pale as Clay steps closer into my space and looms behind me. Mr. Fox all but runs down the stairs to his waiting car.

"I don't need you to mark your territory," I chastise him.

"My apologies," he says.

I'm used to men like Mr. Fox. The thing they don't realize is, I charge them an extra million as an increase to their membership for glances like the one he just bestowed on me.

I admire my brick mansion, which often reminds me of a home one might read about in a fairy tale. That's what drew me to it at first. It was different from all the boring white homes in the nearby neighborhoods. And mostly, I enjoyed the large chimney and black roof tiling.

It was the first mansion Alek and I purchased before even buying our own personal homes. So it holds a special place in my dark heart. But without Alek here, it feels almost foreign and lonely to me now. A transactional place of business. It's lost all the charm that I appreciated it for in the first place.

Kicking my heels off, I glance at the driveway to see a set of headlights coming my way.

Who the fuck is coming up my gated driveway? I remain standing on the porch as it gets closer. Vance walks out of the front entrance and leans over my shoulder.

"It's River, miss. He was at the gate and said he had your money and didn't plan to leave until you saw him. Shall I stay?"

My nose naturally points higher into the air. I thought I made it abundantly clear that I would only see him under my terms. And I still have no intention of giving him the time of day. It's obvious this man is superbly stubborn or stupid and needs to be taught simple etiquette while on my turf.

"Leave." I wave Vance off, unimpressed he let River through the gate in the first place. Clay, however, I allow to remain by my side.

The sleek black Porsche comes to a stop in front of the porch. The car door opens, and a black-booted foot meets the driveway, then its match does the same. It takes a second before he fully comes into view. He shuts the door and turns to look at me. His hair is dark, so dark that I wonder how he got such beautiful autumn eyes that are so opposite his hair. His face is tan, and his full lips open as he says my name.

"Anya," he says, as smooth as melting butter. I don't reply as I note his empty hands, no money in sight. *Is that not why he came?* I don't have time for people who insist on wasting my time.

"Nice house." He nods to the house as he steps closer. I don't like how he invites himself onto my property or the way he acts as if he has a right to be here.

I stay where I am, two steps up from where he is, where we're at eye level, then he places one foot up onto the next step. When I arch a challenging eyebrow, he takes the hint and doesn't take another step.

He offers a charismatic smile that doesn't reach his eyes. I look at his shiny boot as he speaks, making it apparent that I find his shoes far more interesting than him. "We need to talk business. I've given you time to return my numerous invitations, and I've been respectful in your territory. But my patience grows thin."

"Respectful?" I scoff, still looking at his shoes as he takes one more step up, now leaving only one to separate us. He stands over me now, but it offers no intimidation. I only wish I kept my heels on. I cross my arms over my chest and finally look up at him. This man doesn't know a lick of what respect is. If he did, he would have never come. Not here, not tonight. And not on our turf at all.

"Yes, I am a guest in your kingdom, and I would like to become a business partner."

"Business partner?" I question. "I don't have business partners. I do have people who wish to work for me, though."

That arrogant smile once again blossoms on his lips. "Oh, I've heard stories about those who work for you. But also those you work in conjunction with, for example Dawson Taylor."

I narrow my gaze. My dealings with Dawson are an exception. As he runs the largest escort business in the area, we struck up a deal where we facilitate his virgin auctions and receive a cut for minimal work and effort. But only a few know of our agreement.

River seems pleased with himself. "Would you not call him a business partner?"

"No, I would not. The only business partner I have in this is my brother," I tell him.

My fucking brother, who refuses to answer my calls after leaving me in the lurch. I know he listens to my voice messages because it would be full by now. I wouldn't be able to leave any more, which means he's deleting them. He knows I know this. So I think it's his way of telling me, without actually telling me, that he's alive. That doesn't make me any less pissed, though.

"Yes, I'm aware. So where is your brother?" River locks eyes with me, and I wonder what he sees.

Can he hear my thoughts? Because there's no way anyone can read my expression. Does he see a broken, tormented woman trying to find her brother or a strong unmoving businesswoman? Not that his opinion matters to me. No man's opinion ever has. But I wonder with River.

One would almost assume that, like most men, he has a problem with dealing with me instead of my brother because I'm a woman. I've had to teach many in the past how that's their mistake. And if rumor alone hasn't been enough for him, then maybe this man is all looks and no brains.

The thought brings a venomous smile to my expression.

"You don't really seem to be the type to take orders from a woman... Lake, was it?" I say his name wrong on purpose.

His jaw tics, and he takes the last step up closer to me. Now, if I want to look at him, I'll have to look up. I don't. Instead, I look down at his cock—the only attribute I appreciate in a man.

"No, I guess you can say I'm not that type of man.

But I *am* the type who doesn't take orders from anyone. I'm someone who will play nice until it's no longer necessary, Tanya." My lip twitches at his misuse of my name.

"I don't like you," I tell him, straight up.

"I have a feeling you don't like many people, so I'm not offended," he says with a smile.

"Miss," Clay calls from behind me at the front door. River's gaze darts to him, as if only noticing him for the first time, but is quick to move back to me. I wave Clay away, and I hear his footsteps retreat back to stand beside the door, and I face forward again.

"A wave of your hand and men do your bidding," River observes. "Let me tell you something, Tanya." He pauses, as if he is waiting for me to correct him.

I don't.

He should know better.

And that alone is a strike against him.

"I think women are good for one thing—"

"Where is my money?" I interrupt before he can finish.

Because it's the only thing we might be in agreement about: the opposite sex is only good for one thing.

One of his hands scrubs at his jaw. "I don't like you, and I think you are surviving in a man's world."

"Luckily for you, the world doesn't turn on a man's opinion," I shoot back. "Now, give me the money and then fuck off. I'm tired and I'm ready for bed."

"Do you talk this way to all your partners?"

Taking a deep breath, I wonder if I should kill him now. I mean, then I could at least get some sleep, right?

"I've told you, you are not, nor ever will be, my partner. Now, drop the fucking money at my feet and leave."

He kicks up a smile. I expect him to snark back—I almost look forward to it—but instead, he takes a few steps back, his gaze never leaving mine, and it's somehow mocking and condescending. I want to punch him right in that immaculate jaw of his and wipe the smug expression from his features.

River reaches for a bag in the trunk of his car and casually carries it over, as if he has all day. He drops it at my feet. Clay steps forward and picks the bag up for me. I'll be fucked if I'm kneeling in front of this man. When Clay brings it to me, I unzip the bag, reach in to check the contents, and when I see the money, I zip it up and take the bag. Then I turn straight for the door, Clay and Vance standing to cover my back in unison.

"Now we talk business," River adds, as if I've missed some part of the transaction.

"Now I go to sleep." I don't bother looking back or waving goodbye as I walk into the mansion.

"Anya." He says my name correctly this time, and a smile tugs at my lips, but I don't give him the satisfaction of looking back. I know Clay and Vance won't let him pass through. I drop the bag inside the door, purposely tearing off my clothes before my men close the door behind me.

This isn't my main home, but at times, I'll use the facilities here, just like now.

Naked, I walk toward the spare room without a care in the world. Except one. The only one that's tormented me these past weeks. I press call on Alek's number, and after a few rings, it goes straight to voicemail.

"You left me to deal with everything. Fucking left me!" I scream. "He's annoying, and you should be here dealing with him. He thinks because I'm a woman that I am less, but I guess he doesn't know me. Maybe I'll blow up his pretty little car. Do you think I would prove my point then?"

I wait for a response, even though I know one will never come. Usually by now Alek would reprimand me to keep a cool head or encourage me to teach them a lesson. And although he is a man of few words, I miss his presence. I miss the calm and ease he always put over me since we were children.

But that's not now. Something is shifting. This River guy brought a different energy with him. I've dealt with plenty of new blood on my own. Alek and I are a team and a unified front in most of our decisions. But it looks like I'll be dealing with this one on my own.

I hang up, knowing he won't talk back. It's a voice-mail after all. I sigh.

People ask for him, and I can't keep them at bay forever. I don't want to be alone in this business. For all its perks, we only pursued this because we had each other.

River is a nuisance. Ever demanding and arrogant.

I have to shake him.

But I know someone like him will not give up so easily.

Neither do I.

CHAPTER 4

River

She has sass, that one. More sass than any other woman I have ever fucking met.

I want to strangle it out of her and watch her gasp for air.

Yet, I'm also amused. If I wanted, I could use brute force, but I find myself rather enjoying the show that is Anya Ivanov. A diamond amongst the day-to-day grind of business dealings in the underworld. She's as captivating as she is hard, and I can't help but find myself intrigued.

The first week, she outright avoided any contact from my men, and especially from me. Anya is a slimy creature to get ahold of. If not for the fact she attends her auctions almost every time, she's a hard woman to keep track of.

This week, I was ever so lucky to receive only one text, returning my multiple calls and messages. I stare at it again, almost in disbelief that she has the balls for such a forward reply.

> Anya: I'll reach out when I'm ready and can tolerate your presence. Wait patiently like a good boy. It will most likely be forever.

There was no query about how I obtained her number or email address. No mention of the money she'd taken from me. Nothing. And calling me a "good boy" really pisses me off.

Anya Ivanov is fucking bold and has bigger balls than most of the men I've met to leave me hanging on a thread like this.

I smile as Michael walks into my office.

"Not sure what you're smiling about since it looks like you lost a million dollars. It's been over two weeks, and she hasn't returned any of your calls or agreed to meet up with you," he states.

Being too rash will create problems in unknown territory, but I also have plenty of other business to take care of while in town, which doesn't solely depend on a she-devil giving me the time of day.

I ignore Michael. He might work for me, but he

always oversteps the mark to think we're anything closer than boss and employee.

He pops open the latches to the case he brought in, and opens it. I take a swig of my scotch as I admire the new gun model in the red, velvet-lined case.

"How many?" I ask him.

"They can make as many as you need, like usual. Depending on your client demand, of course."

I smirk. This beautiful little baby will make me a fortune. Because my clients always want what I have to offer. And who doesn't like shiny new toys?

My phone rings, and I expect to see "Redhead Devil" appear on the screen. It's not, though. It's an old associate I haven't seen or heard from in a long time.

Despite my disappointment that it's not a certain Ivanov spawn, I answer. I'm in a good mood from my recent acquisitions.

"Will. You're still alive," I say in greeting.

"River. You know, most would say 'it's good to know you're still alive.' Or at the very least 'it's good to hear from you,'" he says with a thick English accent.

"Semantics. Why are you calling? An issue with your latest shipment?"

That's doubtful because there have never been issues with my shipments. Everything arrives on time like clockwork. The only time anything would go amiss is if there's even one dollar short in payment. And there is no coming back from that. *For them.* I'm known for my cutthroat nature for a reason.

Which is why I find Anya peculiar. She doesn't fear how quickly I could attack her empire. Doesn't understand the magnitude of how she should be catering to my every whim and begging to please me. Yet I find myself playing into her hand, curious as to how she'll play her next card.

One truth is obvious—the absence of her brother is an issue.

"No issue with the guns you sent through. Just felt neglected since I haven't seen you personally on the West Coast for a while. That, and I heard through the grapevine you're in New York. Was curious if you were surviving out there, especially with the Ivanov twins."

"You listen to too much gossip," I chastise with a lazy smile.

"It's why assholes like you hire me, isn't it?" he replies.

Will is one of the few people I do like. I'm certain Will isn't even his real name, but I've enjoyed our dealings over the years. I wouldn't go as far as to claim him as a friend, but he is one of a few who I answer calls from.

"Yeah, about that. You called at the perfect time." I pause, considering. Derrick had already exhausted his intel on the Ivanov siblings. He's served me well in the past, but something about these siblings makes it very difficult to dig up their history. And tracking Alek has been nearly impossible. If he's not dead, the fucker is clever in covering his tracks. But why leave his sister behind? I wonder if I can use her for ransom. But even then, how would I do that if I don't know where to send the ransom note?

"I need you to find the brother," I order.

Will laughs, and I feel my temple pulse. "You know that a few feelers are already out there, right? Rumors are that his sister has been hiring a multitude of people to find her brother and coming up short. To be honest, I was just calling to see if you'd survived her alone, considering her ruthless nature. I heard that some dickhead double-crossed her on a piece of jewelry, and she put her stiletto through his temple. The thought kind of turns me on."

My jaw grinds. "*I* can put a stiletto through your skull if you'd like."

Will laughs. "Whoa there, I don't think you would look very good in heels. And it sounds like someone might be falling under the little witch's spell already, huh? Tell me, is she as beautiful as they say? I've seen photos, but surely, she has a fault."

The only fault Anya has is her untamable personality, but lucky for her, I like to break things in.

She is by every definition beautiful. "Whatever photos you have of her, burn them. They don't do her justice."

He lets out a whistle. "Are you sure you want the brother back? I've heard they're very protective of one another. Sounds like you might have a little infatuation?"

"I'm here for business, Will." I cut off that topic of conversation, exhausted by his insinuations. He always pokes for a reaction.

He laughs, and I can't help the smile that spreads over my own face as I bring the scotch to my lips. This dickhead has too much free time.

"Whatever you say, lover boy. In that case, my fee to find him will be double. Multiple people are already looking for him. Information like this is expensive and hard to come by."

"You're the best, are you not, Will?"

"Yes, I am. I'll find him."

CHAPTER 5

Anya

"Miss, his men have come around three times this week already," Clay says, more insistent than usual. I offer him my best eye roll as he hands me my red leather jacket.

"We have an auction tonight, Clay. You know I can't be fucking around wondering if I've upset River Bently. I couldn't care less about that fuckhead."

The truth is, I read every message and email he sent. And deleted them. Because he's a fuckhead. I've never known someone so bold to continuously demand my attention without understanding the repercussions.

Clay simply nods as I shuffle into my jacket and look into the mirror to reapply my red lipstick. I look hot tonight. It's no surprise since I do for every occasion. I run a hand over my tight bun, ensuring no hair is out of place.

Some of my top buyers are in attendance tonight, so everything needs to go smoothly as usual. I remain unseen with Clay and Vance in a private room until only a few minutes before the auction begins. This is so I can scout those who are in attendance and show my appreciation as I sweep the room, yet not leave enough time for someone to think they're an exception to private dealings and can speak with me.

I have no need to converse with anyone here. After all, they're here to purchase unique packages only.

A knock comes at the door, and my eyebrows furrow at the intrusion. Vance and Clay exchange a look before Vance checks the security camera.

"River is here, miss."

I feel the tic in my temple jump. *This guy.*

"Shoot him," I say, tired. That's one way to deal with this thorn in my side.

"Miss," Clay ever so lightly reprimands, "if you were to shoot someone at your own auction, it won't go well with the patrons."

I sigh, tortured by their lack of understanding of my dry humor.

"It was a joke." I shrug. But not really. I want nothing more. "Kick him out."

"I can't. He paid to be here. He plans to bid," Vance says.

I bite the tip of my nail and murmur, "Sneaky bastard." *Who does he think he is?* The only ways to receive an invitation to our auctions is through private screening by Alek and me *or* only a few privileged members are able to invite one guest every decade.

I ponder whose pocket he filled just to be here, but I'm also mildly impressed he could corner someone to do it within two weeks.

"The auction starts in ten," Vance says, cautious around what commands I might have. Because if I did tell them to kill River now, they would.

While I don't emcee the auctions, I am always there to make sure they go as smoothly as possible. And this is already a complication I would rather not face tonight. So I won't. I'll do as I've always done when it comes to River Bently. I'll ignore him.

"He's gone, miss," Vance reports. That was faster than I thought. Maybe I do have some charm after all. "He's sitting at his table."

Or maybe not as much as I'd hoped. I'll be fucked if I'm going to let him intimidate me at my own auction. He's more of an annoyance I simply can't swat away.

"The auction stops for no one, even a fuckhead," I say dismissively as Vance opens the door.

I follow my men out to the large, dome-shaped seating area. Our lady auctioneer stands in the middle of the podium and is the center of attention. I have worked with her for over five years now, and pay her very generously. Might I say I even like her. I don't like many people, but she gets the job done and doesn't fuck around or take anyone's shit. And you have to be able to get your job done here and not think of the wrongs we are doing.

She's wearing the pearl necklace I recently gifted her. A smile dares to lift the corner of my mouth as I admire it.

As my men escort me to my table, I look around the room. I note servers walking around amongst the many familiar faces. When one server bends over, their ass cheeks peek from beneath the short skirt. It's all very intentional. Especially at my auctions where I sell sex.

However, if anyone were to lay a hand on one of them, they'd be kicked out immediately. This room is reserved for those who can refrain from impulse. Well, until they secure the winning bid for their item of choice at the auction.

I dabble in a lot of things, but the auctions are one

of my favorites. While Dawson specializes in virginity auctions and we take our cut, it doesn't mean we don't sell other types of sex. In fact, it's what were known for.

We have men, we have women, we have men who are now women, women who are men, anyone and everyone. We respect them all and give them what they want. But we also protect them by giving them the means to live out their fetishes and fantasies. In return, we make a lot of money.

I watch as the auctioneer calls our first offering to the stage. It's a woman with long legs and raven-black hair. I know her story. She's a sex addict but refuses to work at a brothel. I didn't find her; she found us. She's a regular here and very respected. She has on a black wrap dress, and she walks in circles around the auctioneer as she describes what she's after—a man who is willing to fuck her every day for two weeks straight. Looking around the room, I see a few men smile and nod approvingly.

Before I drag my gaze back to her, I spot River sitting at his table. He pays no attention to the beautiful woman on stage because he's watching me. A slow and steady smirk touches his lips as we lock eyes. I'm unable to look away. Those eyes of his are mesmerizing even from a distance. I wonder, if I plucked them out and put them in a glass jar, would they still have the same effect?

Probably not.

Could I sell them for a fortune?

Most likely.

We stay in this heated staredown, neither of us moving first. The bidding continues around us, and when a winner is announced for the raven-haired woman, the next person comes on stage. I'm about to break contact when he suddenly stands, his eyes never leaving mine as he makes his way over to where I am. My chin angles slightly higher as he comes to a stop in front of me. I can sense Vance's and Clay's restlessness behind me. However, they remain stoic and have their hands clasped in front of them.

Even with my heels on, River towers over me, but I'm not one bit intimidated. I'm just pissed off by the way he looks at me. As if it's some honor to have drawn his attention.

I hate him.

"Pleasure to see you again, Tanya." He smirks, and I grind my teeth at his use of a name that is not mine. I say nothing, just stand there with our eyes locked. "You don't greet people?" he asks with a hint of sarcasm. "You've been avoiding me even after I paid my dues," he says, and again, I say nothing. "What does a man have to do to get your business?"

"You have a business, if I'm not mistaken," I finally say. He steps up a little closer, and smelling his musky cologne sparks my senses. Fuck, he smells good. Pity the man wearing it is an asshole.

"I do; a very successful business, which seems to be impacted by a certain redhead with an ill temper."

"She sounds like a hoot," I bite back.

"More problematic than most," he's quick to shoot back. "But one thing that can be agreed on is money. This is now impacting my money, so I wonder what other avenues I might have to take."

"Is that a threat?" I ask.

He smiles, then leans in and whispers near my ear, "No, dear. It's a promise." He pulls back and looks over his shoulder at the stage.

I sneer and turn my back to him as Clay pulls out my chair.

River cocks up a smile, as if expecting my rude dismissal. I watch the stage for a minute, trying my hardest to ignore him before shooting a foul glare in his direction.

"You plan to bid?" I ask him.

"Isn't that what we're all here for? But my tastes are a little more fine-tuned," he says, looking down at my breasts. It unfurls a certain amount of satisfaction through me, and I hate it immediately. "How much for you?" he asks.

I throw my head back and laugh. His gaze is on me as I wipe away genuine tears. This fucker is more deranged than I gave him credit for. I calm myself and stand so we're only inches apart, our bodies almost touching. Those cold autumn eyes seem amused.

"You couldn't afford me, Lake. Now, go and sit down, or I'll have you escorted out for not bidding." I take a seat again and cross one leg over the other as I stare at him pointedly.

Unfazed by my guards who stand close by, he rests his hand on the table and leans into me. I don't move.

"It's such a shame, Tanya. The only thing I can imagine right now is those flushed cheeks of yours as I bend you over this table and stuff you full with my cock."

My jaw clenches, and my nails dig into my arms as heat floods my stomach, the visual more stimulating than it should be.

He then casually leans back with his hands in his pockets, that arrogant smile cocked as he takes a few steps back and turns for his table.

Fucking asshole.

CHAPTER 6
Anya

Vance and Clay follow me to my private room during the auction intermission.

I'm fucking furious.

River won a collective vase with erotic paintings on it that took me months to curate, and I have no doubt the fucker doesn't even know or appreciate its worth despite purchasing it and throwing a wolfish smile my way.

I don't know why it irritates me that he purchased it, most likely because it impedes my ability to kick him the fuck out for not bidding.

When I get into the room, I pace back and forth.

That man is so insufferable.

Why is he even here? I understand being determined to reach a new market, but isn't being rejected multiple times enough to make him take the hint? What else could he want or need? Or is he outright stupid and stubborn?

This man needs to be taught a lesson.

He thinks he can buy me? Like I'm an object he can own and put on display?

I mean, I did take his money, but that was payment for being near me. Not many get that opportunity unless they're bidders in the auctions, and even then they don't speak unless spoken to.

"Miss." I look up as Vance steps toward me and drops to his knees. Clay comes up behind me, and his hands curve around my breasts. I sigh into their touch, doing everything I can to get one certain fucker off my mind.

Sometimes you just need to have an orgasm to clear your head.

It's the best therapy, really. And I highly recommend it.

Vance hikes my dress up, exposing bare flesh because I never wear panties, and lifts my leg over his shoulder before his mouth descends on my clit. I've trained them well enough to know I need a change of pace to unwind. Which their mouths usually provide. Clay's hands disappear under the top part of my dress as he squeezes my nipples, and I lean my back against him. I can feel his hard length through his trousers, and while I sometimes fuck them, I don't need to. I like this level of worship, control, and power.

Vance inserts a finger into my pussy, and his tongue makes perfect circles around my clit, exactly the way I like it. Just like I taught them. And while they don't always get it done perfectly every time, they try. Each time, it gets better and better. Vance slides another finger in as I hear cheering from the other side of the door, and I know my star of the auction just walked on the stage.

She's a newcomer, and I knew the minute I saw her, the customers would be very happy with how she looks. She has that perfect hourglass figure with large breasts, a large ass, and long blond hair that falls in waves down to her ass. Pink, supple lips and a baby doll face.

Men like to dominate, and she gives off that innocent vibe they can't seem to say no to.

I let a moan slip through my lips and turn my head. When I do, I notice the handle of the door turning. When the door swings open, I lock eyes with River as he stands there, his mouth in a firm line as he watches.

Vance goes to move his head, but I grip his hair and push him straight back down. Clay instinctually goes to move, but I growl out, "Do *not* stop."

I can sense the friction between my men, but they do as they're told. River's hooded gaze drinks in every moment. And I thrive on it. Let him see firsthand the only purpose a man has in my life.

I'm not a woman to be fucked with, only fucked. And certainly not by the likes of someone like him.

I pay no attention to him but am eerily focused on his presence in my peripheral.

"Am I interrupting?" he finally asks.

"Considering this is not a room that you were invited to, yes," I say lazily as I try to focus my attention back to my men. How good they usually make me feel and how I can get my next hit. Especially considering the man I'm frustrated with now stands in this very room.

"Thirty million," River says, interrupting again.

"That's a reasonable amount if you plan on watching the entire time," I say, trying to focus on Clay and Vance, but I can only focus on *him*.

It's fucked the whole mood because while I'm like this, looking for my release, he's the last person I want to be thinking of.

I let out a frustrated growl. Clay moves his hands from my breasts, and I push Vance away, righting my dress. Now I'm pissed that he interrupted something that could have made this night better.

"Leave," I tell Clay and Vance. They seem confused.

"Miss, for your safety—"

"I can look after myself," I remind them as I take two steps over to my bag and pull out a gun. I casually cross my arms and arch an eyebrow. "Don't become target practice."

They nod and leave, giving River an inquisitive once-over.

"You seem to seriously misunderstand your invitation here," I say, frustrated with that still eager thrumming at my core. I'm unsatisfied. Still thirsty. And left only with this man, who's the bane of my existence.

"Thirty million is what I will give you."

"Thirty million?" I scoff. "You think I don't make that in a night? That your money is sufficient enough to what, have a stake in my business?"

"No, you didn't let me finish." He stretches his neck from side to side, and I hear it crack. It gives me satisfaction to know that my clipped responses infuriate him just as much as he does me. "Thirty million for you to lift your dress and let me taste you."

I stare at him. He's dead serious. I then glance at the gun in my hand. Decisions. Decisions.

"Will you leave me alone after that?" I ask.

"I don't think you want me to leave you alone,

47

Anya Ivanov. I think you want me to pull your hair and force you into a submission you've never known."

I cackle, the laughter foreign. *Submission? Me?*

He's deadly serious.

Looking down at my heels, I smile as I step closer to him, holding the gun behind me to look as innocent as possible. Although River thinks he's in control, I have the power. And it's intoxicating to know I have any hold over this man.

"You think my pussy is only worth thirty million?" I scoff.

He eyes me, and I see the dangerous man lying in wait for the first time. I see the calculations that run behind those lucent eyes.

And despite my better judgment, I want to see what pushes him over the edge. What is the undoing for this peculiar man?

River Bently is dangerous, and most people fear him.

But he's never met someone like me before. I'm sure he has never paid that amount for a woman, and he probably never will again.

Business aside, I have to beat this man.

To obey and serve.

For some reason, I want to break River Bently.

CHAPTER 7
River

Sex on a motherfucking stick. That's what she is, and she knows what she wants. How that makes my cock rock hard, I will never fucking know. I'm a victim of my own desire and I want a taste of her. And unlike other men, I have the means to get anything I want. Even if it costs a fortune.

I didn't intend to walk in on her, but when I heard her moan, my curiosity got the best of me. And I'm glad I did.

"Thirty million," I say. Fuck, I'd almost give her my life savings at this point.

Shit, I'm not thinking right. It's my cock talking, but the moment I saw Anya with her men, it unfurled a very primal need to dominate and claim her. I came here for business, and this is anything but.

No, I just want to taste.

I can focus on the business at hand after.

"Tell me, River." Her velvety smooth demeanor is beautiful in the way that she owns the room. And what makes her so cunning is that she knows she has this power. She owns it.

"So you do know my name?" I smile at her. She flutters her lashes at me in confusion and then realizes she just slipped up. But it doesn't rattle her in the slightest. Our little warfare game is happening, and I can't help but be almost charmed by her audacity.

"My men service me in the ways I need. Tell me why I would let you touch me. Who even are you?" She eyes me up and down, her gaze dragging over every inch of me, pausing at my hard cock pressing against my black trousers.

She licks her lips, and it does something to me. We can deny it all we want, but we find one another attractive. Anya might be used to being in control, but it doesn't take away her womanly curiosity.

And if I want a woman, I will make her mine.

And she wants to compare me to her two lackeys. She wouldn't need a second man in the room if I had my way with her. She'd be so perfectly filled.

"I can be your worst fucking nightmare or your

greatest victory." I smile at her. Either way, she'll be mine. She just doesn't know it yet.

"Thirty million for a taste?" Anya licks her red-stained lips, intentionally drawing me into the fantasy of what that mouth and wicked tongue could do.

"For what's between your legs. A taste of that." I nod to her dress, and she smirks.

"Hmm." She ponders my offer thoughtfully while tapping the barrel of the gun on her lip. A benevolent smile blooms, which is sinister in itself. "Deal. Transfer it now, and I'll give you a taste."

I pull out my phone and hand it to her. She enters her details, and I click send. Once she checks her phone and sees the money is in what's one of her many illegal accounts, her smile grows wider. "A deal is a deal, and while I hate most people, you strike an interesting bargain," she says as her hand moves down her dress till she reaches the hem and lifts it. I watch as it reveals her thighs and then she slips a finger between her legs. I see her pussy, and she slides her fingers through her folds, her eyes on me before she pulls them away. She takes the final step between us that brings us toe-to-toe, and lifts her hand up. Elegantly, she puts her finger that was between her legs to my mouth and slides it between my lips.

Heaven.

I suck her finger, my tongue curling around every edge, my eyes fixed on her. Anya licks her lips, and I don't even think she realizes she's doing so as she watches my mouth. All of a sudden, she pulls her finger free and takes four steps back to casually lean against a table and smile at me.

"Pleasure doing business with you. Now, please get back to the auction or you will be escorted out."

I realize what she just did.

Seduction is a dangerous game, and I'd willingly offered to pay her thirty million dollars for a taste of her.

It was worth every penny.

I go to speak, but she raises her eyebrow. There's irony in the power this woman thinks she holds over me, considering the circumstances and money her brother owes me.

Despite it, I offer a cocked smile instead, because I've not yet finished my dealings with Anya Ivanov.

No, this has only just stirred something entirely unholy inside me instead.

"See you later, Red. I'll be having more than just a taste next time," I say.

She beams a smile at me. "If you think bankruptcy looks good on you, then be my guest to try."

CHAPTER 8
River

I continue licking my lips, memorizing the taste of Anya. I stare at the glass of scotch, bittersweet from not yet having a sip so I don't wash the remains of her away so quickly.

Dawson Taylor sits across from me in a bar owned by Crue Monti, head of the Italian Mafia. Dawson's business is the sex industry, with both legal and not-so-legal endeavors. I've known both men for years now because any person who decides to dance in this dark part of the city always needs guns.

"Crue couldn't make it, huh?" I ask, finally resigning myself to take a sip.

Dawson watches the women at work, mostly because they work for him. He's always kept a keen eye on his staff and their safety. Something not many care about, considering his industry.

"Nope, all married and loved up, I'm afraid. They're expecting their firstborn soon, so he's been glued to her," Dawson says matter-of-factly.

A chuckle escapes me as I pause the glass at my lips. Who would ever think men like Crue and Dawson would find female counterparts? And what also seems like genuine affection in their tone when speaking about them.

"You just came from the auction, didn't you? You clearly didn't piss Anya Ivanov off, considering you're still breathing. You didn't tell her I'd slipped you the invite, did you?"

I laugh and shake my head. "No, Dawson, I didn't rat you out."

"Anya isn't someone to be trifled with. Although I have the right to invite whoever I want to that auction, you owe me big time."

"I still offer protection to your staff on the West Coast, do I not?" I counter.

"So long as you don't ruin my business here," he warns.

I like Dawson and always have. For all his pretty-boy appearance, there's a deadly tycoon beneath.

"You know she's absolutely crazy, right?" Dawson

continues. "You seem to be taking this lighter than you should be. You've already been here for over a month, but you're still not entirely welcome."

"What can I say? I find her personality and curves charming."

He laughs, bewildered. "You're smitten, and you haven't even seen the full crazy of her."

"What type of crazy are we talking?" I ask, because I want to know Anya inside and out. Maybe then I'll discover why I'm so intrigued by her, and be able to get her out of my system.

"You know she doesn't take partners, right? She has her bodyguards to eat her out and fuck her when she wants it."

"Yeah, I kind of walked in on that," I tell him, to which he raises a brow in surprise.

"Just casually walked in while she was...?" he asks.

In a compromising position. I then paid her a lot of money to have a taste. But I wasn't telling him that.

The silence alludes to enough because he throws his head back and laughs a full belly laugh.

"The look," he says between laughter. "The look on her face when you asked would have been price-less." He shakes his head as the laughter dies. "I'm shocked she didn't throw a knife at your neck. Or, I don't know, gouge out your eyeballs? She does like pretty things."

"Are you telling me I have beautiful eyes, Dawson?"

"Fuck off. I'm warning you she's more than any one person can handle," he warns. "Finish up with your dealings and go back to the West Coast."

Backing down from Anya is not an option. But it does derail me from my original course of action by coming here. "When have I ever not been able to handle my business?" But truthfully, I'd expected to meet and deal with her brother, Alek. This should've changed nothing, yet somehow has.

"You think what you do to ruin competitors is bad. Well, the twins fuck up anyone who so much as looks at them the wrong way. I once walked in on both of them covered in blood, 'playing' with a man while he was hanging from the ceiling by his hands. And let's just say, he survived. Because they are that good. They know where to cut and how to cut to draw the pain out. And if you're on their radar, then you're in serious shit."

"I think I want to marry her," I tell him in awe. Perhaps it says more about me being attracted to such an unhinged and lethal woman. I can't deny the feeling that she was made perfectly for someone like me.

"Have you met her?" he asks in disbelief. "You really want more than what she gave you?"

"I fucking want it all," I insist.

"Well, we can't say you haven't been warned," Dawson adds, shaking his head as if I'm the crazy one.

"You know me, Dawson. Do you really think for a second I couldn't handle her?"

He waits a moment too long before saying, "River, I get that you run a very successful business because people know not to fuck with you, but she will never be that person. *She* will fuck with *you*. Take every cent you have and let you bleed out but won't kill you just so you know who took it."

"I plan to marry her," I tell him. "She can bleed me dry."

"You really don't know what she's capable of, then," he chastises.

"I'm certainly keen to find out. She'll be mine within the month," I tell him confidently.

My second in charge, Michael, shifts uncomfortably behind me. I can tell he thinks otherwise of mixing business and pleasure, but the knowledge that I have the upper hand this whole time stays true because Anya still doesn't realize what serious strife she's in.

"I still advise you leave the city within the month before she retaliates. You can't start dealing on their turf without their permission. Even if you do have interested prospects."

I shrug casually and take another swig. "I came here to deal with her brother. Unfortunately for her, he's left some loose ends on our business transactions. It looks like I have no choice but to make her pay for that instead."

"You plan on blackmailing Anya Ivanov?" Dawson shakes his head in disbelief.

"Blackmail is a strong word. I prefer the term persuading. Charming even."

Dawson scoffs before he takes a sip himself. "You're as good as dead, man."

I enjoy the challenge. I didn't know what to do with the sister at first. But now I know exactly how I want to handle her. I wonder how she'll take to being cornered, most likely for the first time in her life.

With the added benefit of her brother's whereabouts still unknown, she must be going stir-crazy. And I can't wait to add fuel to that fire. How disastrous can the wrath of Anya Ivanov be?

CHAPTER 9

Anya

"Alek, I can't keep doing this. Fucking answer me! Why are you not answering me? Do you even care if I live or die?" I scream into the phone, furious. It's been too long now since I've heard his voice, provoked him, or asked for his opinion on something. Yet I can't help but continue calling, no matter how mad I am. I'm just waiting for him to answer to finally hear me out and tell me what the fuck he's doing.

"Vance pulled a tracking device from the car yesterday, and a week before that, River paid me a lot of money for something he thought he could have." I laugh into the phone, almost deranged at this point, considering how bizarre the circumstances.

River has messaged me every day, all of which I've

ignored. I can't deny the tension that builds in my core at his erotic promises.

I sigh, feeling defeated and distracted. "I wish you were here. I wish you could tell me why I hate him so much yet find him insanely attractive. And you know me, Alek. You know how much I hate most men, that apart from you, they are only good for one thing, and that's making me come. Fuck, I don't even know what I'm doing anymore. Can you please just call me back and come home? You've left me with a serious work-load." I hang up, and think to myself... *and I miss you.*

I thread my fingers through my long red hair, which is rarely down, as I sit at my desk with what seems to be endless paperwork. I *hate* sitting at a desk. I look around my library/office, and although I once enjoyed the beauty of it, now I just hate it. I'm used to Alek sitting behind the table and me sitting on the long sofa as we discuss things while sifting through our business. Well, it's mostly me talking, but I feel his absence so heavily. And I'm seriously pissed about the pile of work he's left me.

How much longer am I supposed to deal with him not answering?

I sometimes think it would be easier if I knew he was dead.

Alek and I haven't ever done well being apart. It's

one of the reasons when we were in foster care we were always placed together. I had separation anxiety. I would scream and cry the house down. But when he was near, I would be calmer.

He does that for me. Calms me without even having to do anything.

My therapist told me if I keep relying on him, I'll never find happiness or seek it somewhere else.

I quit therapy that day. I don't need that kind of negativity in my life.

My life now is a mixture of money and violence, though Alek always handled the violent part more so than me. I'm good with money—doubling it, making it more than where it started from.

I'm a goddess at it, not to be mistaken for a god.

Women are better; it's just facts.

I love women, I do, even though they aren't my biggest cheerleaders. Women help to generously pad my bank accounts. And violence? Well, guns and drugs are the icing on the cake.

"Miss, your tea, as requested," Clay says, bringing in a silver tray with a porcelain china teacup and pot. I notice the housemaid peeking through the double wooden doors. The kitchen staff never approach me directly, handing my food and beverages to my men. When I was a teenager, I thrived on how staff cowered in my presence. As an adult, it's tiring and amounts to too many spilled cups of tea.

I adjust my red silk robe and don't miss it as Clay's gaze drops to my fluffy pink slippers.

"You've been working on this for hours, miss. Perhaps you should get some sleep," he says gently as he places the tray beside me.

"And expect my empire to run itself? What a happy la-la land that sounds like, Clay," I snark. He doesn't bite back. He never does. Neither does Vance. I sigh and slump back into my purple velvet chair, and rub my eyes.

My men know how to please me, and at times, they make suggestions that would mirror someone who cares. But I know better than to believe they actually do. And with Alek's disappearance, I'm now managing the workload of two. We both remained busy, so keeping up with everything is becoming tiresome. Not that I'd ever let anyone see the cracks in my facade.

The worst part of it all is I haven't had time to shop. Like, fuck, what's a girl have to do for a little bit of time to spend her fortune on all the pretty things the world has to provide?

Clay pours me an aromatic fruit tea. "Perhaps you might be able to ask The Chief for some help."

I scoff and kick my legs up, placing my crossed,

slippered feet onto the mass of paperwork. "And have the old bitch meddle in my affairs and remind me how useless I am? No fucking thank you."

I pick up the teacup, embracing the tea's fragrance and warmth before taking a sip. Clay's phone buzzes, and he glances down at it. Impartial to the news he just received, he looks up at me. "Vance has brought back the man who tried to rip your brother and you off. How would you like to proceed?"

Can't a woman even enjoy a cup of tea in peace?

But instead, I say, "Bring him in."

This fucker wasn't hard to find, and after ripping us off to the tune of ten million on an artifact, I'm not at all impressed. People don't fuck with us and get away with it. Ever.

I grab the gun out of my top drawer and casually sling myself out of my chair. I appreciate the softness of the plush white carpet and my fuzzy slippers.

When Vance greets me at the open doors, holding a man who has a sack over his head and his hands bound, I tsk him to take three steps back, away from the plush white carpet in my office.

"This is the guy?" I ask Vance. Clay is standing behind me with teacup in hand.

The housemaid who was peeking in only minutes

ago is nowhere to be seen. Good. I'm not entirely sure she could stomach what she might witness.

Vance answers. "Yes. Did you want to negotiate or—"

I lift the gun to the man's hidden face and pull the trigger. The sound echoes, and his body drops to the floor. Vance's jaw tics, most likely a thrill of adrenaline pumping through him from the closeness.

"Make sure the blood doesn't leak onto the carpet, and I want the wooden floors scrubbed. I don't have time for shit like this," I say as I turn and grab the teacup from Clay. "Because I have paperwork!" I yell, deranged, waving the gun in the air. "Don't disturb me for the next three hours."

I hear them mumble behind me as they close the two large wooden doors and are no doubt dragging the body away already.

My brother and I might've once had fun in a situation like this. Alek, mostly, since he usually deals with these types of things.

But right now, I find nothing fun or thrilling about it.

Autumn eyes come to mind, and I push down the thought of River's imposing gaze.

CHAPTER 10

Anya

R iver's back. I can't decide whether he is a sucker for punishment or just plain stupid.

We're at another auction in another mansion. This one involves guns. Not your average buy one, get bullets free either. No, this involves black market guns in bulk. And they always do extremely well. Though, I must confess that Alek always ran this auction, and this is the second one I've watched over while he's been gone. Despite the change, none of the patrons dare inquire about his whereabouts, but I know gossip has spread about his disappearance, which pisses me off even more. Because my personal family affairs are of no concern to them.

Considering the already bad mood I find myself in,

I walk around to where River is seated and lean down next to him and whisper in his ear.

"How did you get in?" He turns to me, his mouth barely an inch away from mine, and he smirks. His full lips lift, and I have to remember why I hate him.

Clay and Vance stand behind me, and I know they don't like him, particularly since they've warned me to stay away from him and to not give him my time for the million dollars he paid weeks ago for a chat.

"Why hello, Anya." River says my name with a slight drawl at the end. I flick my tongue over my teeth as I stare at him, waiting for him to answer my question.

The bidding has started, and it's getting higher and higher. Usually, it thrills me to anticipate how high it might go. To think about all the beautiful things I can buy with the proceeds. But I'm certainly pissed that he's here and doesn't seem to be bidding at all. Who the fuck gave this guy access to my auctions?

"I'll tell you exactly why I'm here over a drink, perhaps?"

"I don't drink," I tell him, and his brow shoots up in surprise.

"Why is that?"

"I prefer my judgment not to be impaired," I tell him honestly. "It's how drunken mistakes happen. It's how people fuck the wrong people." As I say it, my gaze flicks back down to his lips. He licks them, and I know he can tell I'm thinking about them.

I want to strangle him for getting under my skin so much. Why does he just keep popping up like he owns the place? And why haven't I appropriately dealt with him like I would anyone else?

"Smart, but one glass never hurt." He stands, and I pull back as he towers over me. "Shall we, so we don't interrupt?" He nods to the showcase on center stage as bids continue to increase.

"Considering I'm about to have your sorry ass escorted out for not bidding, I'll walk you there myself. Wouldn't want the door to hit you on the way out," I snark.

He kicks up an arrogant smile but proceeds to follow me anyway. Clay and Vance walk on either side of him. Very few of the bidders give us their attention.

We walk out into the hallway and toward my private room. Out of all the mansions we own, this is my least favorite. It's boring, with brown tones and dreary paintings and trophies on the walls. It suits well to the theme of items sold here, but without Alek in it, I find nothing nice about the place. It's an eyesore, really.

"Wait outside," I instruct my men. They briefly

glance at each other but say nothing as they stand on either side of the door, staring down River as he steps inside first. I follow him into the private room and close the door. This room is just like the rest of the mansion—basic. Functional. *Empty.*

"How did you spend my money?" River asks, walking to the bar in the corner. I couldn't be fucked telling him not to have any of Alek's liquor.

"Which money?" I ask him since he's paid me twice.

"The last lot."

I smile as I pointedly glance at my hands, flashing my new jewelry.

"You like expensive things," he notes.

"I do," I say, looking back up at him. He's staring at my hands, which are covered in Cartier. "Stunning, really, don't you think?"

"I agree," he replies, but he isn't looking at my hands when he says it.

My core floods with heat again, and I hate how my body betrays me around this man.

"Let's get your proposal out of the way, shall we? You paid me one million dollars for my time to hear you out. So I will. Then I'll happily reject you and send you out of town. If you're not gone in two weeks, you'll leave this city in a body bag," I say sweetly.

He cocks a smile as he pauses to take a sip of his scotch. I lean against the table and brush my hand over my red leather dress, still entirely aware of his gaze that rakes over me.

"Surely, thirty million would suffice for me to taste again?" he says slowly, his gaze fixed on me.

"Taste again?" I ask, surprised in his change of topic, considering I just threatened his life. "Ha." I comb my hand over my sleek hair that's pulled back in a tight bun.

"You'd turn me down?" He puts a hand to his heart as if I've offended him.

"Is that what offends people these days? Really?" The threat lingers in the air as if it was never mentioned, and that pisses me off. Because River Bently clearly doesn't see me as a threat. I begin to rummage through Alek's top desk drawer, curious about what objects I might be able to use as a weapon, until I pull out a letter opener.

"For the love of God, Red, please don't let it cross your mind that you're going to try to stab me to death with a letter opener," River says with an exasperated tone.

I place the tip of it against my finger. "It's more effective than you'd think. And stop calling me Red."

He chuckles with a cocked eyebrow. "I shouldn't

be surprised that you've already used one on some-body. Did they make it out alive?"

I shrug casually. "I don't know. Did they ever find the body?"

He laughs, and I'm surprised and transfixed all in one. "I've been curious ever since I was told you were crazy."

Some might be offended by being called crazy, but I love it. Thrive and bask in it. It means I'm unpre-dictable, and people fall into place easily around unpre-dictability.

"Curiosity often kills the cat."

"Lucky I'm more of a dog person," River replies dismissively as he walks toward me and stands between my legs. I allow him that close, and he allows me to put the letter opener to his jugular.

He seems unfazed as he puts the glass of scotch down beside me.

"Be careful. You can't touch what you haven't paid for," I purr. My body thrums for him, an unwelcome need eating me alive.

But I refuse to give in to the likes of River Bently.

When he becomes a little bolder and presses into me, his bulging trousers in line with the edge of my skirt, I press the letter opener firmer against his throat. It won't do too much damage, but if I were to get a little stabby with it, it certainly will. "Tell me why you're here, River."

His gaze dips to my cleavage, and it arouses satisfaction in me because he's still only a man. I paid a lot of money for these tits, so they better be the best. Enough to even bring someone like River to his knees.

"For you, of course," he says without hesitation.

"Why?" I ask again.

"I think I'm due my taste," he insists. In such close proximity, I can smell his cologne, and I hate how it challenges my focus.

"Yeah, about that. We didn't agree on how many 'tastes' you got. Now, you can leave if that is all you came here for."

"They're my guns, did you know that?" He inclines his head toward the door, indicating the auction room.

"Sorry, your what?" I ask, confused by his words.

"Those guns you're auctioning off in there are mine."

I freeze momentarily. There have only ever been a few times I've been caught off guard. In fact, I can count them on one hand. This is one of them.

"Are they?" I ask. Truth be told, I don't know where Alek gets them from. I know who I contact about them, and that's the extent of it.

"Yes, and as I said, I have played nice. I have given you your cut for me to work here, and I've even been working with your brother to give him guns." He picks up his glass and takes a sip of his drink. "So where the fuck is my cut?"

"Your cut?" I ask.

"Yes. Your brother usually pays on time, but not this time. I let the shipment go in good faith and as a favor to you. Because I knew you were good for it. Tell me I'm wrong, Red." I'm shocked. How did I not know this?

Reaching for my phone beside his glass of scotch, I scroll through my contacts for the gun smuggler and place the letter opener beside me. He remains where he is as he smugly takes another sip. His size widening my legs is a very difficult distraction, making me want to mount him.

The smuggler answers on the third ring. It sounds like he's just woken up. "Anya?"

"Who is the supplier?" I ask him.

"Well, it's a shipping—"

"No, who owns it." I cut him off. He pauses, as if unsure what to say. "Who am I buying these from?" I basically growl into the phone as River stands in front of me, sipping his drink and watching me with those fucked-up eyes.

"River Bently does," the guy on the other end of the phone says.

My heart falters for a moment. *Fuck.*

I hang up and look River dead in the eyes.

"How much does my brother owe you?"

He smirks, taking a last sip of his drink before he places the empty glass down. I hate how it smells on his breath. No, it's just him as a whole. This entire time, he's been fucking with me. I had no idea, and I don't handle being fooled very well. He casually brushes something from my shoulder, though I'm sure there was nothing there.

"A lot," he utters, leaning in and breathing in my ear. "I don't take kindly to late payments, but I could let this one slide for another taste." My nipples peak in attention at his closeness, and I can feel my breathing grow heavier.

Just a taste.

I don't like being backed into a corner, and suddenly that empty glass near his hand is awfully tempting. His hand drops to mine when I hadn't even realized my hand was already drifting toward it.

"This is not the time to get stabby, Tanya," he chastises.

"I was going to use the glass over your head first, then the letter opener."

His laugh kicks my heartbeat up a notch, and I'm certain I can feel its vibration slip straight to my core.

This man is dangerous on so many levels.

"How much do I owe you if I agree to a taste?"

"Technically, without the late payment, he owes me fifty million." He smiles and pulls back, and I feel the absence of his warm hand over mine. I have the urge to scrub my hands and body immediately, not used to the unfamiliar feeling that lingers.

He casually takes his empty glass and walks over to the bar as if he owns it, and pours himself another drink. I know my brother only likes expensive-tasting liquor. We're the same in that sense, a taste for expensive vices. Mine just so happens to be the shiny type. "Late payment is an extra million a day," he adds.

"How late is he?" Fuck, Alek, what have you done? *What have you left me with?*

"One month."

"Thirty million?" I ask, shocked at the amount. He nods.

"And then there's the matter of the last shipment. I never got payment for that."

"I have money," I tell him. Money hasn't been an issue for years.

"Oh, I know you have money. You've done very

well for yourself, Anya. I'm impressed. Even without your brother, you're doing well. But now I'm here."

"I don't accept business partners," I tell him.

"No, but do you know how late the payment is for the last shipment?"

My guess is it would be triple the amount of the last and would take everything we're making tonight to pay it off.

All of it gone.

Fuck.

I'll have to do another sex auction. Those always bring in good money. And it's easier than dealing with River.

"As I said, the latest installment could be waived for a taste, but the last lot..." He shakes his head.

"What about if I fuck you?"

His brow raises. "Don't you mean if I fuck you?" he counters.

I shake my head.

"No. No man has ever fucked me, River. *I* do the fucking." My hand goes to my hip. "You'll waive both late fees, and I'll allow you to touch me while I ride your cock, and we'll discover if you can make me come."

That arrogant smile kicks up again. "Be careful

what you wish for, Red. Addictions can be a dangerous thing."

I laugh at his insinuation. "The only thing I've become addicted to is sex toys."

He holds his hand out to me, gentleman-like, and I frown at it.

"Aren't you just going to fuck me here over this desk?" I ask.

"No, Red. I'm certain that somewhere in this seven-bedroom mansion, there's at least *one* bed."

I jump off the desk, unsettled by his intentions. I just want this over and done with. "You're not going to try to cuddle me or some shit, are you?"

He laughs as I lead him out the door. "I don't think you'd know what to do even if you were given affection handed to you on a platter, Red. But I'll fuck you every way, wherever and whenever I please. But first, I want to muffle your screams with a pillow. You know, being a gent and all."

"You assume already there will be a next time," I scoff as I walk between my men, who look confused. "Finish up the auctions. I'll be busy until the end," I instruct them, and besides, I've already made my obligatory appearance. "River, follow me."

CHAPTER 11

River

Anya doesn't look back as she leads me up the spiral wooden staircase, her posture immaculate and head held high. We walk down the hall, the sound of bidding in the distance as she opens the third door we come to.

It's a lavish room in size with a wooden bed and silk green blankets and pillows. The rest I don't care for because my attention is only on her. I'd heard a rumor that Anya has a room in every auction house because she often slips out during them to fuck her two men. The woman has an appetite, and I wonder if they were supposed to be here tonight instead of me.

Like I give a shit. If she needs two men to service her, she obviously hasn't found someone worthy to match her libido.

"You agree to removing both fees?" she asks, leaving the door open for me to enter but in no way friendly about it. When I close it behind me, I imagine she's rather disappointed that no one might casually stumble along it and be able to peek in.

"Remember that in this negotiation, I do the fucking," I say as I approach her and tip that defiant chin of hers higher. A smugness unfurls within me as I realize the small permissions this woman grants me to touch her like this. That her brother's disappearance has very much become my gain, and I'm not the least bit apologetic for abusing it. I reach for my buttons and begin to undo my collared shirt. "Now, drop the fucking dress."

"Men don't tell me what to do in the bedroom," she spits, and I love the burning rage in those green eyes. I want more of Anya. To bring that crazy to the forefront to see and bathe in all of her ugliness. Because something so beautiful must surely be rotten at the core.

"Yeah, well, you fuck men who are scared of you. I'm not one of those."

"We shall see," she bites out as she reaches to her side to unzip the dress. "Late payment will be voided?"

"Yes," I breathe as I trail my gaze down her body,

almost mesmerized. My cock is throbbing, torturing me with how many times I've already imagined this.

I *will* make this woman mine in every way, even if I have to break her in the process.

I simply need to brand her so deeply that she will never be able to leave my side.

My nostrils flare at the carnal urges and thoughts running rampant in my mind.

I've never wanted something so badly, yet for this woman...

"Only payment for the stock will be required?" she questions, and fuck me, she's purposely taking her sweet time with that zipper.

"Yes," I grit out, then swallow a dry lump in my throat. Fuck, I need to taste her.

"And have you paid for sex before?" she asks, and now I know she's outright teasing me, enjoying this power she has over me. She shifts her dress ever so slowly, letting it rest on her hips, revealing a lacy black bra. Her tits are so perfect, and it takes all my willpower to raise my eyes to hers. Those fucking eyes that flash wild sex through thick eyelashes.

"No, and I'm not now either."

Anya is used to men coming to her. This verbal warfare is just part of her temptation. Though I want every part of her, to go to her and take, I know I have to treat Anya differently from any other woman I've had before.

"But you are. You're paying a lot of money to fuck me," she says, looking almost confused. She's doll-like with those porcelain features. Bait to the little devil that lies within me.

"Taste, then fuck," I correct as I move to the edge of the bed and sit. My cock pressing against my trousers is excruciating as I watch her. "Are you telling me, Anya, that you've never thought of me fucking you?"

"No," she says flatly, and a part of me considers she might be telling the truth. Who's to know since she's lived a life of not giving anything away. But that's all about to change tonight. "I don't fuck men for the enjoyment. I make them do whatever I want. I like the power."

"Yes, your men." I nod to her dress, which is still resting on her hips. I didn't expect her to stall so much, but I also realize this is her game, her power struggle because I'm not falling to my knees for her like everyone else she's fucked. Fuck, do I want to, though. "Tell me, do you touch your men?"

"Wouldn't you like to know," she sasses as she

pushes her dress to the floor and turns around in a circle, showing me the goods. My god. As expected, Anya doesn't wear underwear. And that tattoo of hers is unexpected. But there are many mysteries to unfold tonight.

"I would, actually. Who do you fuck?" I say, my voice all gravel and thirst now. Fuck, if I believed in curses, I'd claim her as a witch.

"Myself." She smiles sweetly. "Now, do you plan to drop your pants or continue small talk?" she asks. I can't help the arrogant smile that spreads over my lips. Because I still refuse to give in to Anya like she expects. I raise my hand and indicate for her to come closer. This little she-devil will learn a lesson tonight. I'm not a man she will boss around. Ever.

Her nose raises higher, but she does as she's told and steps between my legs. I reach for her arm, and I can see the trail of goose bumps that follow. Smooth. Delicate. Soft. Still a woman despite that hard exterior of hers. My hand lands on her stomach and partially on the detailed tattoo.

"Medusa?" I ask, looking at the head and snake wrapped around her side.

"She's a warrior," she says, dignified. And so is she.

"Interesting," I reply as I graze my fingertips along

her pubic bone and lower. I watch her, her unyielding expression. The only thing that gives her away is the hooded gaze. The expectation and curiosity. "Tell me, Anya."

"Yes, Lake," she barks back, and my lip twitches at her use of the wrong name. Yet again. She's nowhere near to submitting to me. But I'll make her.

"Do you think I can make you mine?"

The moment I say it, her back straightens, and I can see, as well as feel, her body go rigid.

"No," she says without hesitation.

I trail my finger lower toward her clit. And it takes all of my restraint not to take my gaze from hers and bury myself within her. This is forcing more patience on my part than I've ever held with a woman before. But it's a lesson to be learned.

Her body naturally leans into me as I slide my finger between her folds. Whether she'll admit it or not, she wants this just as badly as I do.

"Really?" I ask. This will become awfully painful for her if her answer doesn't change.

"No, I will never be yours," she defiantly says, but her breath is clipped. Anticipation for my finger that's hovering at her entrance.

When I don't push my finger in, she seems frustrated as I bring it to my lips and taste her. Fuck, it's even better than the last time. I don't think I'll ever get enough of tasting her.

"We shall see," I say as I grip her hips and move her to the side before standing. I rearrange my painful erection before heading straight for the door.

CHAPTER 12

River

I hear her say something, but I pay no attention as I stride out of the room. That is until she's suddenly right behind me.

"I owe you nothing. Payment has been made in full." I turn around to find her still in nothing but the lacy black bra. Looking around, I see no one here, but that doesn't mean that people won't be walking out of the auction room very soon.

"Miss." Fuck, where do her men come from? Stepping up to her, I reach for her and lift her over my shoulder.

And she is very fucking light.

"Put me down," she seethes. But I walk, with my hands on her ass, straight back into the room. Her nails claw up my back to try to find traction, and I get an elbow to the side of the head. My cock twitches with the urge to pin her down and force her into submission.

Kicking the door shut behind me, I throw her onto the bed, where she bounces. I ignore my own carnal urges to pick up where we left off, but that would only be giving in to her and giving this tantrum-throwing brat exactly what she wants.

"Payment," she pushes.

"You just walked out there almost fucking naked," I growl, shaking my head. "All those men could have seen you." I don't take kindly to others seeing what I've already decided is mine.

"Yeah, and? What does it matter to you? I'm talking to you about payment. Now, answer me."

"Is that all that's important to you, sex and money?"

"Is there anything better?" She smiles as she says it. "Now, do you plan to fuck me or what?"

"I thought you said *you* do the fucking," I tease her. Fuck, how I want to slide into her and make her think of only me.

I bet I could own her, brand her so deeply that she'll never find another man who would compare. Not that I'd let her, but that's how badly I want her.

"Semantics." She waves at me and unclasps her bra,

dropping it to the floor. "I prefer a man on his knees," she adds. I bet she does, and that's just how I like my women.

"Two jobs, one fuck," I say, trying to keep my eyes off her perfectly round tits. Fuck, they're perfect... and pierced. And a weapon I'm certainly not immune to. I bite the inside of my cheek until I taste blood, to stop from reaching out to touch them, and tell my cock to calm down.

Her expression drops. "What?"

"You do two jobs with me, and fuck me once, then your payments will be cleared."

"That's not what we agreed on." She narrows her eyes as her hands casually go to her naked hips.

Will I really be able to walk out of here? I don't want to give in, though. I don't pay for sex, even though that's technically what I'm doing.

But I'll make it my way.

"I changed the agreement."

"You can't do that. And why two? It's a fucking weird number."

"Oh, but I can. You see, it's you who owes me now, and I like to have you owing me." I smile at her and turn to toward the door. "And I can choose one, two, or twelve times because I'm the one making up the agreement. Get dressed."

I immediately regret only saying one time for the sex. I know the moment I have her, I won't be able to get enough of her, but for some reason, it sounded good at the time because it was stretching past this ever only being a one-night thing.

"No," she says, smiling.

"Well, I guess you're sleeping in here tonight, then, aren't you? Because I won't let you out."

"My men have seen me naked. Not that my body is of any interest to you," she says as she reaches for her bra.

"Yeah, you'll need to stop that. If I find out you so much as let one of them touch you again, I'll stop shipments." I smile at her. And I'll do so much worse too. She'll have to find replacements for her men because the current ones will be in body bags.

"You couldn't. We've had shipments for over ten years. We have a standing relationship..." She doesn't finish as I smirk.

"With me?" I finish for her.

She scrunches up her nose, then reaches for her dress and slides it on. To say I'm disappointed to see her cover back up is an understatement. But I'll let it go.

When she's fully dressed, I open the door to find

one of her men standing there while the other walks up behind him.

"If either of you so much as touch her inappropriately, I'll have you both killed." They eye me and then look back at Anya.

"My men don't take orders from you," she says as she crosses her arms over her chest.

"Well, they better learn really quick. Or I'll send pieces of them back to you." I push past them and hear them speak, but I make no move to stop.

Now, I have to somehow come up with a work date—a date that won't scare her.

I have a feeling normalcy is something she would be very scared of.

And I'm willing to go to extraordinary lengths for this woman.

CHAPTER 13

Anya

How dare he? Who does he think he is?

I spend the next two days wanting to be fucked, and my nerves are shot because I need a release. And he teased me. I am not a woman who takes to teasing, yet I let him do just that.

It makes me so fucking mad.

How did I not know he was the supplier, and why did he not tell me when he first arrived?

I crack my neck from side to side, looking over the final documentation in one of my offices; this one is in central Manhattan, and it's a particular favorite of mine. Consider it a front, if you will, for our many businesses. Usually, Alek would be standing behind me, but instead, I have Clay and Vance. The powerful man sitting across from me remains quiet as I sign off on the last piece of paperwork while we wait for the second man to arrive.

When I look up, Dawson is first to speak. "It's been a while," he says, looking around at the new painting I've hung. The room is simplistic, with dark wooden tones. He's seated on a black leather chair on the other side of my desk, and I'm sitting on what one might describe as a gold throne. Call me dramatic, but I like a power play.

And after the run-in I had with River, I intend to gain every bit of my power and dignity back. I didn't take him seriously before, but now I have no choice.

I take a casual tone with Dawson. We aren't friends. I tolerate him and Crue at best, as they do me, but we respect one another's businesses and how we co-run within the city. Dawson with his virgin auctions, and Crue, being head of the Italian Mafia, for keeping the riffraff out of the territory. We all have our role to play. But River being in town changes that.

"Yes, how is your plaything? All loved up, I guess?" I ask him. Dawson is a beautiful man, a stunning fucking devil. Though, what I've always appreciated about him the most is his business ethics. His auctions are known worldwide, and while mine are as well, his hold a different type of power.

"Yes, very. Honey is doing amazing."

"Why are we talking about my sister-in-law?" Crue asks as he enters the room. Crue is Dawson's best friend, and their wives are sisters. So sweet. I really don't care; I'm just attempting to be pleasant.

"And the lovely Rya, how is she?" I ask Crue, thinking of the fireball criminal lawyer he took for a wife. She's one of the best lawyers there is. I'm hoping one day I can get her on my team as well. And if my intel is correct, she's due to deliver their firstborn any day now.

"Stunning as usual," Crue says, taking a seat next to Dawson.

"That she is," I agree.

"Considering my lack of free time, I'm assuming you haven't called us both for no reason," Crue says, adjusting his black dress shirt.

I'm reminded why I tolerate their companionship, because they don't fuck around and get straight down to business.

"River Bently, aka the current pain in my ass, who for reasons unsaid I can't immediately kill, is inserting himself into the city and dealings for his guns on the East Coast."

"You called us in to discuss River?" Dawson asks, but he doesn't seem entirely surprised.

"You don't seem surprised. Is that because, by chance, you gave him entry into my auctions?" I drop my chin onto the back of my hand as I stare at him. But Dawson is one of the few men who don't become uncomfortable under my cutting glare.

He casually shrugs with a charismatic smile. One I'm sure that melted his sweetheart. She and I are opposites.

"Some of us have friends, Anya, and I owed him a favor. Regarding business, he's good at what he does. And being in business with him has provided a long-running profit for you and your brother, if my information is correct."

Motherfucker. How did Dawson know about the supplier before I did? But I'm not surprised. I'm not even mad, really, that Dawson gave him access to my auction, considering it's in the contract. And Dawson's right; I'm also certain River would've found another way in no matter what.

"Have you dealt with him?" I ask Crue.

"I've had dealings with him in the past. He's easy to work with, and his guns are always top quality. And, as Dawson said, he's good at what he does."

The problem I face is the agreement River's put in place to pay off my brother's interest. If I have to go with him for two business meetings, then we look like a united front. People come to *me* for meetings, not the other way around. And if River and I are associated, then people will assume he's bought into our territory. I need to weigh the options as to which offers the greatest gain. Either I bring him in and permit him free rein to do business dealings for a cut or I dispose of him permanently. But I don't want to tarnish our name by not honoring a business deal.

Dawson breaks me out of my thoughts as he says, "He's been asking a lot about you." He seems to be looking for some kind of reaction. When I don't give him one, he adds, "He's paid you?"

"He has," I say bitterly. Sure, the fucker gave me a million dollars for a conversation, but due to unforeseen complications, we have surpassed that stage. Not that I would tell either of these fuckers that.

"And that means...?" Dawson lets the question hang.

"I may let him in," I say, hating every bit of it. I'm literally backed into a corner. Not one I intend to stay in for long. But considering putting an outright hit on him is out of the question, I need to be cunning in other ways.

Despite my hatred for the man, there may be a lot of money made if I play my cards right. And that's the one thing that I'll put above my indifference of a person. What money can I make in the process?

"From what I've heard, it's been well over one million that he's paid you. Someone even mentioned ten million."

Gossips. The lot of them. Dawson and River have probably spoken, but I'm not the least bit curious about what, especially if it includes me.

"Buy-ins are getting more and more expensive." I smile.

"Keep it clean. We don't need unwanted attention," Crue adds.

I scoff. As if I'm going to let any man tell me what to do. And it's slightly hypocritical of him to say that. "That's funny coming from you. Did you not shoot your wife's boss in the head?"

His jaw tics at the reminder. It's not like he can kill him again, but with the look in his eyes, he would if he could.

"He took videos of my wife. Of course I did," he says simply.

"So you're saying, if it comes to a loved one, then it's acceptable?" I sarcastically ask.

"Speaking of loved ones, where is Alek?" Dawson inquires. It's a hard slap back into reality. "Not that we don't love dealing with you, Anya, but it's been months. Where is he?"

That's the same thing I'd like to know.

Where the fuck is my brother? And why isn't he at least returning my calls?

I look at my phone. My screen saver is a picture of us when we were just kids. Neither of us is smiling, but it's the only one I have of us from back then. We didn't have parents to keep memories of us. It was just us. So when I found this at my foster mother's house, I took it and kept it and added it to my phone. It's an image only I can see with facial recognition, because I'll be damned if I let anyone see any type of weakness.

While those days were hard, knowing that I've had the same person all my life, even from the womb, I think has somehow gotten me this far.

And I hope it will continue to do so.

But now it leaves an empty space in my life. And a deeper unanswered question—why did he leave me behind?

Whatever his reason to leave, did he really not think I could help him? After everything we've built together?

"Has he run away?" Crue asks, and I don't know how to answer that. I don't know what he did. And I hate that, the not knowing. Imagine having someone in your life constantly and then one day they're gone. I'm not referring to a life partner. I'm talking about someone I shared a womb with, for fuck's sake. That is a different thing altogether. No life partner would ever come close.

At least that's what I tell myself.

Maybe it's different for Alek. He doesn't really like to talk much as it is, and I'm the person he talks to the most. And even then, he uses as few words as possible.

"I doubt it," I say.

I try my hardest to push the uncertainty down. I won't show weakness, especially in front of these two men. But I owe them at the very least, the answers I can give, considering in their own silent way they've also supported me during this time.

Had I been in their shoes, I would've come for their business the moment I saw an opening. Then again, it'd take an entire army to take me down. It hardens my resolve to know they measure me as such.

"You believe he's alive?" Dawson asks.

"Yes," I say without hesitation.

"In danger?" Crue asks. I want to laugh. Alek in danger? Alek could kill all of us so easily. He is the most lethal person I know. And I know a lot of evil men.

"Never," I say.

"I believe you. I doubt Alek could be in danger," Dawson says. "My men still haven't found information on his whereabouts."

I let out a slow sigh. It's the most I can manage to hide the exhaustion behind the mask. Both of them have feelers out, in addition to mine, and still nothing.

I wish I could say I'm surprised that not even the best have yet found Alek, but in my eyes, *he* has always been the best.

"Thank you for looking into it," I say. An uncomfortable tension ripples through the room, and I hate the words on my tongue. My jaw tics as I straighten my back and lean into my throne. "If you hear of anything, let me know immediately. Until then, I'll sort out the River Bently situation. But I'm not letting him in so you can make this into some kind of boys' club."

Dawson chuckles as they both stand. "Let me assure you, Anya, that none of us think our balls will compare to the size of yours. Boys' club or not."

"What a vulgar thing to say to a lady," I retort, but I can't help finding amusement and appreciation in his words.

I watch them leave, then check my phone. There's a text from River.

> River: I've been thinking about
> those perfect tits of yours all day.

I exhale a sigh. Is this really the fucker I'm considering letting in?

Absolutely not.

I need to find a way for River to accidentally trip and fall into the path of a bullet fired from one of his own guns.

CHAPTER 14

River

"Something blue. She's a bit of an ice queen, you see," I say to the woman showing me Cartier's most recent collection.

She offers a flirtatious smile. "I think she'll be very grateful that you had her in mind while picking these out."

We can disagree on that. However, one thing I know my woman loves is a shiny jewel.

"We have a rare Paraiba tourmaline set that just came in. Let me go get it for you. I think it might be perfect for your intended lady," she coos before she dismisses herself.

If it's rare, I know Anya won't so lightly turn it down. Depending on whether she already has three sets of it.

"Forgive me for saying, sir, but it's strange to see you in a jewelry store," Michael says as he looks over the items with a lack of interest. He certainly terrified the staff until they saw how eager I was to buy.

Another woman comes over. "Oh my, your champagne looks empty," she says to Michael, offering him another glass, one he happily takes, then stares at her ass when she walks away.

"Behave," I growl under my breath. "And I'm curious about this part of Anya. These shiny jewels she enjoys. I want to brand her in every way. So why would I get one of my men to choose that in my stead?"

Michael carefully places the glass down and casually leans against the glass case. One of the staff seems affronted by the movement but says nothing. "I'm just trying to understand our mission here. We came here to get your money and negotiate better rates for the guns, didn't we? As well as gain permission to sell directly to certain buyers here on the East Coast. I'm confused as to what part Anya Ivanov has in all of this. Are we not here to do business with her brother?"

"Anya is just as capable to do business with, if not more so," I quickly say, shooting him down with a stare. "And it just so happens that I've found myself besotted with the Ivanov sister, and I intend to marry her."

A tic jumps in Michael's jaw. "Don't you think that's a little bit of a stretch? The woman's clearly in-insane." He stutters when I glare at him.

"An insane woman who one day you'll be taking orders from, so you better learn to watch your tone with a lot more effort than how you speak to me. Or are you looking for unemployment before we reach that timeline?"

"No, sir. Sorry I spoke out of line," he says quickly.

"Here it is," the woman says cheerfully on her return. She opens the white box to reveal a set of blue encrusted diamond earrings. She proceeds to open another two boxes, revealing a matching necklace and ring. "It's a beautiful set. Do one of these items catch your eye?"

I stare at the ring, almost wanting to choke on my own laughter. If my mother knew I was seriously looking at pursuing a woman, let alone considering a ring for her, she would have a heart attack. Perhaps I need to put Anya to the true test by meeting the future in-laws.

"I'll take them all," I casually say as my phone begins to buzz in my pocket.

The woman's eyes widen, but she offers a bright smile. "Of course. I'll pack them for you immediately."

I answer the unknown number.

"River, it's been a while," the man on the other end says. I recognize the voice. We've spoken a few times over the phone already and met in person once. "I heard you were in New York for business, and I'm interested," Igor says.

"Igor, it's unlike you to call personally. I usually have to deal with your second in charge. To what do I owe the honor?"

"Well, let's just say my middleman saw the new item you had on display at the Ivanov auction. I heard it was a one-off. But since you're in town, I was interested to know if maybe you have more. I'm willing to fly in from Russia to negotiate business."

My smile grows as I hand over my credit card to the woman. I'd done underhanded deals in the area before but always in small numbers and cautiously to ensure the twins never found out. Considering the circumstances now, I have free rein to do as I please. Within limits, of course. I don't want to give Anya a reason to put out another hit on me.

She might've already tried that once, but if she were to do it now, while in debt to me... that would be very bad for her business. We might not be good people, but one thing we are good on is our deals. If not, then you end up as good as dead.

"I might be interested," I say as I shuffle the phone

between my ear and shoulder. "Send me the place and time you'd like to meet. I'll make arrangements to be there."

The timing couldn't be any better. It's come so easily that I can organize a little date with the she-devil herself as well.

CHAPTER 15
Anya

Rummaging through my brother's belongings is as boring as watching paint dry. Because despite his immense and expensive whisky collection, Alek doesn't splurge on many things. His house staff have hidden themselves away after my intrusion, and I've been throwing his shirts from hangers in fits of rage ever since.

Vance stands at the door as Clay walks in with a pot of herbal tea. All of my favorite flavors are in Alek's kitchen because I made it so. Clay sets the tray down as he quietly says, "Miss, this is the fourteenth time you've searched for a clue in your brother's home. I don't think there's anything here. Perhaps you should get some rest."

"Luckily, I don't pay you enough to think," I snap back.

He says nothing more as he carefully pours the tea. I sigh and want to crumple to the floor, not that I ever would in front of anyone.

I take one of Alek's shirts, bring it to my nose, and inhale, the remains of his cologne still there, bringing my thundering heart to ease. I know he's not dead. But what if...?

No, not Alek. Never.

But why would he leave me behind?

Was I not enough to trust with his secret?

Was I a nuisance instead of someone who could help?

I shake my head, knocking the insecure thoughts out. They have no place in my world. I refuse to go down some dramatic rabbit hole, questioning my brother's loyalty and opinion of me.

After standing, I take the cup of tea and sit at the end of Alek's bed. Looking around his room, I realize how bland it is. Well, if I'm comparing it to my own lavish tastes. The only painting on the wall is one of a ballet dancer. I never quite understood his fascination with the eyesore, but I'd allowed it since it was something besides neutral tones like the rest of his house.

Clay drops to his knees and removes one of my heels as he begins to massage my foot. I sigh in relief as

I look between him and Vance. I know they don't care about me; I'm just a paycheck to them. I wonder, however, if I didn't have them during these months, whether I would've lost my mind entirely. Most likely not. I would've managed as I always do.

His strong fingers move up my calves as he kneads the muscle, and it stirs an entirely different demand from me. I haven't fucked in days. Although my men don't listen to River, I don't want to risk him sticking to his word if they touch me. And I think he was deadly serious in his threat.

"That's enough, Clay," I say, then take a sip of tea, becoming far too carried away by my desperate need to get off. "Both of you, leave the room."

They curtly nod, and I watch as their burly figures leave. I walk over to the side table and place my tea down as I open my phone and look at the image of my brother and me when we were kids. I call the most recent number—Alek's.

It rings.

And it rings.

Until it hits voicemail.

I sigh before the avalanche of pent-up rage releases. "Alek? Where the fuck are you? I'm going crazy here. And more than my usual crazy self. Do you know what shit you've left me in? River is basically blackmailing me to fill your shoes and pay the debt you left. I either let him buy in and permit him to do business or I kill him. And if I kill him, I'll probably get myself into more trouble. Besides, killing is usually your job.

"Where the fuck are you? I can't stand this man. All he wants to do is own me! Like every other fucking man in this world. But this one has a serious screw loose." I let out a deranged laugh as I look at Alek's empty bed. The absence of him growing larger and larger.

There isn't meant to be a world without Alek in it. We were always in this together. I always had him to depend on. He was the only person I had to talk to.

And now he's gone.

"Alek, what the fuck is happening? Do you need me to help? I can help! You know I can do anything. Just fucking call me back! And I'm tired! Hurry the fuck up and get back home!"

I hang up, but as quickly as the anger built, it washes away into something else. I feel empty. Alone. Isolated. Just like when we went through foster care, I'm unable to control my fate or reality. But at least I had Alek. We had each other.

Something wet runs down my cheek. Shocked, I put my finger on it. I'm in disbelief, so I turn to face the mirror near the side table. A tear. *Me? Crying?*

"You've got to be fucking kidding me," I say to myself. "Fuck no. We are not doing this." I wipe it away defiantly. I can't remember crying since... since we found out about our parents abandoning us. I was quick to learn no one liked a crying child. Or a crying adult.

My phone buzzes, and I unlock it, rolling my shoulders back and forth, certain I have a knot in there.

Fuckface: *Tanya, good news. I have a business meeting. Be ready at seven for our date.*

I blow out a hot breath. This motherfucker. I press against my temples, reminding myself repeatedly that murdering him will come with consequences.

But when have I ever cared for about that before?

CHAPTER 16
Anya

W hy he wants me to go with him and meet with his clients is beyond me. Considering the circumstances, I really have no choice but to play by his rules until I figure out how to take control of the board. I'll do a lot of things for money, but I'm not grateful to Alek for fucking me over on this one.

Alek is still withdrawing funds from our account, and the motherfucker is doing nothing to replenish it. Mind you, a lot of the money sitting in there is his by right.

I don't care that he's taking money. I just need answers. I need to understand what's happening and why.

Even if I'm due to meet River for a business deal, I

never said I was going to make it easy for him. Fortunately for him, I'm well known for my smashing personality.

Getting dressed in my tightest red dress with a slit up my leg and no bra, I apply my red lipstick and slide my hand over my hair to make sure not one hair is out of place. I consider my jewelry carefully. *What do I feel like today?* I reach for the black pearls.

"Are you ready, miss?" Vance asks as I slip my designer heels on.

"As ready as always for fuckery," I say.

"Shouldn't you eat first?" Clay suggests.

I give him a wry look. "I thought I hired you to fuck and take a bullet for me. Not to become my nanny."

He says nothing and takes his place behind me with Vance. But now that he mentions it, I realize I can't remember the last time I ate. Perhaps yesterday? Maybe that's why my mood has soured immensely.

"But perhaps something small when we return won't hurt," I say. From the corner of my eye, I can tell he's trying not to smirk. *Idiot.*

When we step out onto the patio, I feel my top lip curl up into a snarl.

"Anya." River drawls out my name, and it's like

silk. Touching me in the softest of places, which only raises my hackles more.

My body is craving for touch. For release.

Fuckhead.

"Lake," I purr. He opens the car door for me with an arrogant smile playing at his lips.

"Your men aren't welcome," he says, nodding to Vance and Clay.

"I don't go anywhere without security," I tell him.

"No one will harm you around me, of that I'm sure," he says matter-of-factly. It's not that I don't believe him; it's just that I don't entirely trust him. For all I know, this could be a part of his grand scheme to overthrow me. River has balls, but I don't know if any man is that bold. No one has yet dared try.

"Am I just supposed to take your word on that?" I scoff. "I didn't agree to no security. I agreed to go on your jobs as some type of fucked-up payment. You understand I run my own jobs as well, right?"

He considers me as I refuse to get in his car, my arms folded over my chest.

A tic in his jaw jumps as he lets out a frustrated breath. "You can follow at a distance but always stay back. My buyers get skittish easily," he tells them. They look at me for confirmation, and I nod.

"How does it feel?" he asks as I climb into his car,

surprised that he has good taste in vehicles. This car is different from the other one I've seen him drive. I don't know cars, but I know the touch and smell of luxury, especially when I'm sitting in it. He waits for me to answer him, leaning into the car.

"How does what feel?" I deadpan. I don't have time for this fucker's riddles.

"To have powerful men at your disposal?"

It irks me, the way he says it. Vance and Clay are powerful men, but I don't take kindly to the tone and mockery he makes of them. Only I'm allowed to objectify them in that way.

"I don't know, you tell me," I throw back at him. Does he think it's any different because I'm a woman? That he doesn't have men beneath him who do what he says and when. Maybe he's simply jealous because at least I fuck mine. Did fuck them. Will again. Whatever.

"Touché," he replies as he shuts the door and walks around the car.

I roll my shoulders back, internally praying this is a quick meeting. If it's not, I can't guarantee what I might do on an empty stomach. And with the lack of sleep... well, some might call me a little crazy.

"I bought you something," River says after closing

the door and settling in the white leather seat beside me.

"You shouldn't have," I say dryly, and I mean it. I love gifts more than the next, but not from this fucker.

"Open the glove box."

When I don't move, he leans over and opens it for me. Inside is a red box. I know its classical branding from anywhere. Cartier. One of my many favorite jewelry designers. I don't want presents from this man. I am, however, also a woman with little restraint when it comes to shiny things.

When I reach for it, he pulls it closer to himself, so it's just out of my reach. "Promise me, Anya, that you'll be good tonight. A deal is still a deal."

I fold my arms over my chest. "You should be grateful I'm allowing you to make direct deals in my territory. It's not me who should be on their best behavior, asshole."

His smile kicks up at the "asshole" as he hands me the box. I snatch it from his hand, taking a second glance at his arrogant smile. The way he grips the steering wheel is too perfect. Too deadly. And I want to kill him for it.

I sigh as I pull the ribbon and reveal a stunning set of earrings and necklace. Paraiba tourmaline. I shift them from side to side, mesmerized. Fuck. I love them.

"Are they to your liking?" he asks.

I'm quick to box them up and place them in my clutch. "Aren't we supposed to be somewhere, Lake? I want this over before nine. I need my beauty sleep and all," I say with a sharp smile.

"Most women say thank you."

"I'm not most women."

"That you are not," he says as he starts the car, and we roll down my driveway. I peer through the rearview mirror to make sure my security isn't far behind.

I play with my black pearl ring, finding far more interest in it than any conversation River might attempt with me.

Surprisingly, he doesn't say anything either.

Reaching over for the touch screen, I consider in what way I might be able to torture this man.

Alek and I were raised on classical music. The one time the old bitch found me listening to pop, she snapped the record and banned me from shopping with her for a month. It was fucking torture.

Considering he's a man in his thirties, I wonder what would be his type of living hell. I hide the devilish smile as I type in Mariah Carey "All I Want for Christmas." I lean back and pretend to enjoy it, watching River from my peripheral.

"I'm surprised you know a Christmas song,

114

considering it's the season of giving. Do you even know what that means, Anya?" he asks with a raised eyebrow.

I shift in my seat and prop my chin on the back of my hand as I lean back. "I'm well known for my 'giving.' It just so happens I deal a cruel hand."

He smirks but makes no remark about the song, which pisses me off even more. I lean back over and play the Backstreet Boys.

"Classic, really, wouldn't you say? Which was your favorite?" he asks, deadly serious. But I know he's fucking with me.

"I prefer men, not boys," I chide.

What else, what else?

I switch to Britney Spears.

"I feel like you and Britney would have much in common," he remarks.

Oh, fuck off.

I switch the music off and peer outside the window. We're definitely not going into the city. Instead, we're surrounded by trees and ample plots of land. It begins to rain, and I sigh at the eerie pitch-black outside.

River laughs, and it fills the car enough to put the hairs on my arms on edge. I hate how my body so easily reacts to him without my consent.

I'm going to lose my fucking mind if I have to stay in this car with him much longer.

"His name is Igor, and he flew in to see what kind of deal I can offer him," River says, and it offers a mild type of calm to my nerves. Business I can focus on.

"Flew in from where?" I ask.

"Russia," he says casually.

I turn to him fully now, but he pays me no attention. I still entirely believe that River is a fuckhead, but I've come to learn that he's a very intentional being. I can't help but wonder if he's taking me to meet with a Russian client because of my own heritage.

While our birth parents are both Russian, Alek and I were born here and only lived in Russia for three years before moving back to the States. It wasn't long after we turned four that our parents fucked off and left us behind, giving us the jolly old time of being bounced around in foster care. No matter what, it was always Alek and me against the world. Then it was just our luck that we ended up with a lady who is also Russian, which is where I think we kept our accent from. But my knowledge of the Russian language is minimal, at best, so if he's expecting some kind of translator, then he drew the short stick.

"Have you been back to Russia since your parents brought you back?" he asks, and a cold shudder runs through me. I hate that it feels like he can read my mind. That without words, he knows where my thinking has gone without knowing a lick about me. Then again, he probably had someone rake as much information about Alek and me as possible. Flattering.

"Let me guess, you have a little file on me and think you know everything about me?" I snark.

"No, Anya, it's called polite conversation. You are Russian, aren't you?" he says.

I look out the window again, my nose pointed high in the air. "I don't do chitchat." Silence fills the air, and I find myself adding, "I am. Russian, that is true."

I've always been proud of who I am, even if I had to fight to become her.

"Maybe you'll know him," River suggests.

"I doubt it," I say, bored as I play with my rings. Why is this drive taking so fucking long? I check the rearview mirror, and the boys are still following.

I then twist, squeezing my tits together so he has a perfect view down my dress. I smile sweetly when his gaze flicks between me and the road.

"Anya," he warns with a growl, and it runs shudders up my arms. A curiosity spreads through my core, and I bite my bottom lip.

"So when do you plan to fuck me?" I ask.

I just need to let this guy stick his cock in me once, right?

His gaze lands on my cleavage once again, and I notice how his grip tightens on the steering wheel. He grabs his cock to shift it uncomfortably. A womanly pride runs through me. Men are all the same, and so easy. I'm not better than a man with my sexual demands, and that's why it always works in my favor.

"As beautiful as you are, I won't be fucking you tonight, Red," he says.

I huff and throw myself back against the seat.

"That big Russian man you were talking about sounds like he might be my type. What did you say his name was? Igor?"

River's hand slides over to my leg and squeezes with a bruising grip. Any other man I would've slapped away, but I'm curious. Will he still be able to say no to me after touching me?

"Anyone who tries to touch you will end up in a body bag," he growls.

"And they say romance is dead," I coo. "I'm not wearing any panties, by the way."

"Christ," he breathes. "You're never wearing panties. And you're sadly mistaken if you think this is all it takes for me to drop to my knees for you, Anya."

I grin. "The visual is a delightful thought, though,

isn't it?" I ask as I feather my hand over his. He catches my wandering hand and clamps it to my leg.

"You have no manners. You know that, right?"

"Manners don't get you anywhere in life, but being ruthless does. Now remove your hand. We're not doing this hand-holding shit."

He flashes a wicked smile. "Do you really think you can make me listen to those god-awful songs without consequence, Red? You will sit through the torture as well."

I try to pull away again, but the force of his hold doesn't lessen. I huff and look out the window again. But I can see our reflection, and I notice how much bigger his hand is than mine.

I hate it.

A constant reminder of how physically bigger men are. The reminder of a time I couldn't always defend myself. And although I don't feel like River is a threat when I should... it reminds me of how small I am in comparison.

A woman.

With more obstacles in this world than River has ever known.

He's just one more obstacle that I will overcome.

I can't fucking wait.

CHAPTER 17
Anya

When we pull up, I see five men all smoking and leaning against their cars. River gets out of the car first and walks around to open my door. When I get out, his hand slides to my lower back as he leads me toward the group of men. I grit my teeth at his possessiveness but allow it.

My security dropped off tailing us about ten minutes ago, at least that's what they've made River believe. They'll be far enough away to go undetected, but both are extremely talented with a sniper rifle.

I make sure not to step in any of the puddles from the rainfall that evidently happened before we arrived.

All the men turn to me, but Igor speaks first.

"Hello," he says to River in a very thick Russian accent, but he keeps his gaze on me.

"This is Anya Ivanov," River says, introducing me.

"Russian?" the man says to me. "Privet." He nods.

"Privet." I greet him back. He goes to say something else, but River cuts him off.

"English, if you both wouldn't mind," River commands.

Igor looks at me and nods before he says to River, "Of course. I wasn't aware that we would have guests." And I've been around enough pissing contests to know that I'm not welcome simply because I'm a woman.

"I wasn't aware this was your meeting to dictate who comes and goes. Do you want the guns or not?" River replies as he lights a cigarette, and I do all that I can not to sneer at it. *Disgusting*.

Igor considers this, but there's really nothing to contemplate. A man like him wouldn't have flown all this way, with a security team of four men, if he didn't want this business. "You know I like what I've seen."

"Forty million for the lot." River smiles at him, but it's not a friendly smile. If he even has one of those. It's more of, *who the fuck do you think you're talking to*.

"Hmm." Igor muses while he takes a puff of his cigarette. His gaze slides to me again as he gives me a once-over. "You aren't related to Aleksandr Ivanov by any chance?" he asks me, ignoring River for the moment.

"My brother," I confirm. He nods and smiles. His men whisper something.

"Not just a pretty face, then," Igor remarks. River's hand presses into my back, and I know it's a warning to "be good." My gaze hits his, and his autumn eyes are screaming exactly that. Why do I give a fuck if he loses forty million? Or perhaps it's a reminder that Igor might be fishing, looking for a bargain or weakness within River to favor this deal.

Igor continues. "Your brother was back home not long ago, looking for a girl." I go to step forward, but River takes hold of my arm. It's on reflex. It's the first amount of valuable news I've heard since the day Alek went missing.

A girl?

My brother?

Impossible.

"How do you know it was him?" I ask Igor. He looks back at his men and says something in Russian. I can't pick it all up, but I got the part about him wearing gloves.

"Strong man, wears gloves, and hates to be touched," Igor says.

"When?" I demand.

"Two weeks ago," Igor replies casually, smiling to reveal a gold-plated tooth.

"Who was the girl?" Because that's the most unlikely part of this entire story.

"River," Igor says to River, ignoring my last question. "I don't care to entertain your fling any longer. I'll accept your forty million in good faith that I will be considered the first choice in your next collection."

"Fling?" I scoff.

"Anya," River warns.

"No." I jerk my arm free of River. Fuck this guy and these men. I've played nice for far too long. "Do you not know who I am? Whose fucking city you're in?"

"Apologies if we've offended you, miss," Igor says insincerely.

I laugh hysterically. I'm hungry and pissed. The last fucking thing I needed on my plate was another asshole thinking he has some entitlement to fuck with me in my own city. The men look at one another.

"Miss?" I reply rhetorically. "Oh, now come on, Igor. That just won't do. My name is Anya Ivanov, and don't forget it."

I raise my hand, and, suddenly, a bullet is shot straight through the eyes of the man standing next to Igor. With a wicked smile, I pretend to blow out smoke at the tip of my fingers. Perhaps I forgot to mention how exceptional my men are with long-range shooting.

Igor's men explode into action, pulling out guns and aiming at me, and my carnal smile only grows as I open my arms wide, daring them to fucking try. "You're in my fucking city!" I shout. A reminder to them and River. "And you will play by *my* rules and bow to a woman while doing it. Do you fucking understand?"

Igor holds his hand out to ensure his men don't shoot, and River's stepped closer to me now. How chivalrous, but I doubt he'd really take a bullet for me. Or maybe he will. Maybe even he is no exception to my charm.

"Now, tell me. Who was the girl?" I ask again, and this time, any politeness is dipped in venom.

Igor looks at River, who I can feel is glaring at me. But I don't care. He should know the risks involved in taking me on. If he did his research better, he would know that being quiet and a "good girl" are not qualities I possess.

"You killed my man," Igor accuses without heat.

"You underestimated me. Why? Is it because I'm a woman?" I ask him.

He seems mildly amused. Now he looks at me like

he would've if I were a man. Much like he respected River, he now holds the same impression of me.

I don't play when it comes to power.

I *am* power.

"Yes, I do think I judged you for being a woman. Next time, I will know better," Igor agrees. "He was chasing some dancer. That's as much as I know."

A dancer?

Why?

I raise my chin and step out of River's grasp. "Finish up your business. I'll wait for you in your car. Move it along, I have things to do." River's jaw clenches, and I purposely walk out of his range so he can't reach for me. Because the way his gaze burns into me, I know he wants to pull me into him, and I don't know if it's to punish me or fuck me. Both are fine with me if they're mixed together and clear my debt.

When I walk away, I overhear Igor speak. "Dangerous game you are playing with a dangerous woman there, River."

Who knows? Perhaps out of the two, Igor's the smarter man.

I slam the door shut behind me and curse feverishly in Russian. I want to kick and tear apart the interior of his car, but I know it'll do very little to remedy my frustration.

Fuck. Fuck. Fuck.

I pluck my phone out of my clutch on the bottom of the car floor and hit call.

"Come on, Alek, pick up. Please," I say quietly.

Ring.

Ring.

Voicemail.

I explode. "You're in Russia? Really, Alek? Are you still there, or have you just jumped to the next country while having a fucking holiday?"

I expect a chastising comment, but I'm left with his cold rebuff that's wounded me more than anything else I care to admit. I bite my bottom lip as I look around. It's dark, and the only light is from the cars. River is still speaking with Igor and his men.

"A dancer, Alek? You're chasing a dancer?" I scoff into the phone. "You didn't even tell me about her. We tell each other everything. How could you leave me for a woman? You left me in the lurch with debts, and now I have to spread my legs to pay for them." I hear myself and laugh.

"Wow, I never thought I'd be complaining about sex. Alek, this is fucking torture. River says he wants to fuck me to wipe your debt clean, but he won't actually fuck me. I'm on fucking edge because I can't sleep or eat. And I'm not being fucked! This is all your fault!"

Now I'm just rambling, maybe even going insane, as I talk into the phone as if Alek is actually listening. I hate that it offers me some kind of comfort, a luxury I'm not too familiar with. Only ever with my brother.

But River's seriously gotten under my skin. I can't read him or understand the pull I have toward him. I enjoy sex because of the power it gives me over men. I need to solidify that with River because he's the only man thus far who has made me feel like my power is slipping ever so slightly.

Through the rearview mirror, I see River approaching the car, and immediately squash my thundering rage. My feelings toward him are not Alek's fault, but it feels good to blame him anyway considering all the other shit he's put me through lately. Now, it feels like I only have a few more moments with Alek. Even though he's not here with me now. I know he's somewhere out there, listening to these voice messages eventually.

"Alek, please just tell me what's happening. I have to go because tall, dark, and brooding is walking over. Oh, by the way, I hope we don't have anything to do with a guy named Igor because I kind of killed one of his men. Okay, bye."

I hang up as River opens the door and sits in the driver's seat, a cigarette hanging between his lips. I wind down my window, snatch it out of his mouth, and throw it out. "Smoking's fucking disgusting."

"Do you really want to push me to the edge tonight, Anya, after the stunt you just pulled?" He glowers as he twists in my direction.

I drop my bottom lip. "Wishing you didn't splurge on those jewels for me since I've been such a bad girl?"

He smiles, a lethal edge to it as he grabs my cheeks and squeezes. "You keep dropping that bottom lip like that, Red, and I might be inclined to cut it off."

I smile in return. "As if you'd fucking dare when you dream of these lips around your cock every night. And besides, need I remind you that I have a gun pointed at the back of your head? Now, fucking drive. I'm hungry and want to go home."

River's smile widens and then his eyes light with frightful amusement as his tattooed knuckles flex on the wheel, his one singular ring shining from the interior light.

I have the feeling he's about to do something crazy.

I'm all for crazy.

CHAPTER 18

River

I have to remember that I don't want to throw her out of this car, even if she has an attitude problem. Her smell fills the small space. It's like she's suffocating me without even knowing the power she has over me.

And I'm fucking livid, and not even at her, though I should be after that little stunt she pulled. I'm furious with Igor and his men. How they treated her. I didn't say anything because I know Anya can stand on her own two feet. But it doesn't sit right in the subtle way they threatened her.

My hands grip the steering wheel so tightly, I think I might actually leave indents of my fingers in it. I still haven't even put the car in drive. The silence in this suffocating car is grating on my nerves after my meeting with Igor. I look in the rearview mirror, and see them laughing and enjoying their cigarettes in what was a successful business deal.

Do I give a shit about forty million? Not really. Not if it means Igor might be tempted to come back to New York and find Anya for some vengeance for his man.

I'm not thinking clearly, but this woman does something crazy to me.

"Still want to take me on your second business meeting?" she dares to ask. Always pushing me. Forever trying to get on my nerves. And it's fucking working.

What's forty million? I paid almost that just to have a taste of her. I can let a forty million deal go if I know it means no one will come after her. She can handle herself. I know that. But I can't stop my raging possessiveness.

"How good is your boy's shot?" I growl out.

A promiscuous smile reaches her lips. "The best." And a silent plan forms between us.

"Leave Igor to me," I say. Kicking open the car door and opening my trunk, I pull out a rifle.

Michael is going to chew my ass out for this, and I don't fucking care. He doesn't make the rules. I do.

The first security guy drops to his knees with a

clean shot in his forehead. In my peripheral, I see Anya's arm out the window, her hand in the shape of a gun. When she pulls her thumb down like a trigger, the next guy drops to his knees.

The third man is too late to pull out his gun as I blow out his brain, soiling the side of his car. Igor goes to pull out his own gun, but I already have the rifle pointed in his direction.

"What is the meaning of this?" he spits. "All for a pretty little cunt?"

Whatever my expression, I can tell it's probably half crazed because his eyes go wide.

"You ever threaten to come after her again, I will find you and do far worse than what I've done to your men."

He holds his hands up slowly in surrender, confused as I walk up to him and put the tip of the rifle to his head.

"Why do you care? We're just doing business," he says, shocked at the turn of events.

Wrong answer.

He's a man who still doesn't understand that he's about to meet his maker.

"So is this," I say, stepping back and pulling the trigger. His overweight mass pushes into the side of his car. I won't run the risk of Igor returning and targeting

Anya. Unfortunately for him, I'm the only one allowed to chase her.

I sweep my gaze over the bodies, a tendril of adrenaline coursing through my veins. It wasn't enough. Who could be the next person to come for her?

I internally slap myself. Anya is not a damsel in distress, and if I ever voice this out loud, she'd chop my balls off. I know she can look after herself.

It doesn't make me any less inclined to step between her and any risk.

Fuck, I really have lost my mind, and all I had was a *taste* of her.

When I do fuck her... I know it'll bring me to my knees.

I throw the rifle back into the trunk and slam it shut.

"Feel better?" she asks out the window.

"Call your men to clean up the mess," I demand as I walk around to her side and open her door.

"Why?" she asks with her arms folded over her chest. That tight dress pulls on my last fucking nerve.

"Because your men started it." I drop my gaze to the phone in her hand. "Call."

She rolls her eyes, and if that's not enough to be punishable, I don't know what is. She presses a few buttons on her phone before she says, "The cleaners are ten minutes out. It will be taken care of."

I have no doubt her men are capable. She is as vicious as she is beautiful. A cleanup crew at her disposal is expected. I bet Clay and Vance never remained more than ten minutes away, and it's an entirely different team she calls for clean-up. She clicks her tongue. "You have blood all over your face."

She pulls out a red handkerchief from her clutch. "Clean yourself up."

"Lift your dress," I command.

Her eyebrows lift, and she laughs. "As much as I enjoy blood sports, you will clean yourself first."

I place my hands on the edge of the door and lean in so I'm only inches away from her face. "Then clean it for me since this is your fault."

"*My* fault? *You* were the genius who thought bringing me here was a good idea."

My jaw tics, and she sighs as she lifts the handkerchief slowly to my face and wipes. Our gazes never leave one another. My heart pounds from the adrenaline, and I need a release.

I need *her*.

No, if I give in to Anya Ivanov now, I will lose her. But, fuck, do I need something.

"Care to tell me why you went all Rambo on

them?"

"No," I growl. My hands are wrapped so tightly around the edge of the car that I'm doing everything in my willpower to have restraint. This beautiful fucking she-devil in my car. Her perfume melting into it. She's driving me crazy.

"I'll show you my tits if you tell me," she teases.

"You'll show me them anyway," I growl.

She laughs, but I notice the constriction at her throat first. "Can't you just imagine me slamming into your cunt against the car right now? Being so deep that you can scream as loudly as you want out here."

Her green eyes flash with want as she looks up at me through thick eyelashes. "I scream loudly wherever I am, but let's be real. It's not like many men can make me scream."

My tongue licks over my lips as my cock grows uncomfortably in my trousers. Her gaze drifts to my crotch, then those devastating eyes shift back to me.

Fuck this woman and the spell she's cast on me.

"Give me a taste, and I'll tell you."

She rolls her eyes. "You and your tasting. What do you think you are, a fucking connoisseur?"

I grab her cheeks, squeezing so those fuckable lips are my entire focus. "You eye roll me one more fucking time, and there will be consequences."

Her gaze promises sex. Everything about this woman oozes sex.

She drops the handkerchief, and her hand pulls down on her dress, revealing those perfectly pierced tits.

My cock needs to be buried deep inside her. But if I fuck her, I know I won't have enough of her. It means our agreement will be over in a blink of an eye, because if I'm in her only once, I won't be able to contain myself. And then we're done. But if I can limit myself—no, torture myself—to just a taste, it might take the edge off.

I release my grip as I drop to my knees. I don't care if the fucking ground is wet from the rain. This woman has me so wrapped around her pinkie, and in the way she stares at me, she fucking knows it.

"If I'm a connoisseur, then I specialize in sweets because your cunt is the sweetest thing I've ever tasted."

At this angle, her gaze pierces through the dark night with only the interior car light acting like a halo around her. But she's anything but angelic.

I lean into her, licking over the bars pierced in her nipples. A small moan escapes her as she watches me, but her hand slowly reaches out to grab my shirt and pull me closer.

I'm not the only one who's been holding out, it would seem.

Good.

I suck on her perfect nipples, gripping her thigh tightly to anchor her, as if any moment she might go up in smoke like she never existed.

"You owe me one truth," she says with a tight breath.

I spread her legs and keep my hand on her chest to push her back. She holds the edge of the leather seat and dashboard as I smirk at the welcome of this short dress and, of course, no panties.

Fucking perfection. I push her dress farther up so her bare ass rests on my leather, and dip my tongue between her folds. So fucking perfect.

"You're already wet for me, Red," I say as I taste her.

"Stop speaking," she says as she feathers her fingers through my hair and pushes my head down. I'm more than happy to oblige as I devour every bit she gives me. I insert a finger, eliciting a moan from her and then a second as I pump into her.

I slide my hand from her tit to her throat and hold her in place.

"Fuck," she says as her head rolls back, and she gives in to me little by little.

My cock pushes painfully against my trousers. I'm creating my own misery. But I know for Anya, sex is simply transactional. She's someone who loves the high of it, the power play, and it's not something I'm willing to give her yet because I haven't made her mine. And I'll be fucked if I'm letting this she-devil slip through my fingers.

I'll bind, gag, and trap her in a basement somewhere before I let her go.

"Let me ride you," she demands, and goes to move, but I keep her in place by my hand at her throat.

Oh, Anya, how I would like nothing more than to watch that perfect body of yours bounce on my dick.

Fuck, I'm getting more addicted with every taste.

This beautiful fucking woman is so used to men being on their knees for her, but I doubt she's actually felt anything past physical attraction and domination. I'm hellbent to be her first and only she'll feel anything deeper with. I'll make her beg for it.

I pull away and bite her inner thigh. Another moan escapes her with one more lick, savoring the taste of her.

Her eyes fly open as I retract my hand from her throat and get up from my knees, my pants now wet.

"What the fuck? You can't be serious," she hisses. "Get back on your knees *now.*"

I graze my thumb across her sharp cheekbone in admiration. I want to gag her on my cock, use those sweet lips for what they were made for.

"Igor would've come for you eventually. That's why I shot him. I think it's fair you owe me a proper date since I turned down a forty-million-dollar deal for you."

She slaps my hand away, a wild fury taking over. She's sexually frustrated, and it gives me satisfaction to know she took my rule seriously.

No one else is to touch her.

No one but me.

"I don't owe you shit. I also don't need you protecting me or my honor. I can handle myself, Lake." She grabs her clutch and shoves me out of the way as she adjusts her dress.

"I wasn't defending your honor. I was securing my chance of having more tastes of you, if I'm being honest," I tell her. "Can't do that if you're dead, now, can I?"

"That's fucking presumptuous, thinking you can have a taste whenever you please," she snaps.

I cock an eyebrow with a smug smile. "I do believe I was between your legs less than a minute ago. Now, get back in the car."

Any tension from earlier has eased, and I stand

back and enjoy the beauty that she is while she's a seething, venom-spitting she-devil.

"Fuck you. I did what I came here for," she says as she begins walking away.

"Get in the car, Anya. I can drive you home. You can't very well walk all the way there."

A set of high-beam headlights silhouette her perfect figure, and I curse myself. I should've known her guards would be close, but I hadn't even noticed them creeping up.

"Get in the car, Anya."

"Bye, Lake. I hope you have a collision on your drive back home." She flips me off.

I can't help but smile as I place my hands in my pockets.

Under any other circumstances, I would've killed the closest person to me if a forty-million-dollar deal slipped through my fingers. But, somehow, I find far more value in watching Red walk away pissed off.

"Good night, Anya," I call out.

She slams the door without so much as another word, and I find myself laughing.

When was the last time I've had this much fun?

Have I ever wanted anything this badly?

CHAPTER 19
Anya

Was it a date?

I mean, he did kiss me, just not on those lips.

So was it a date?

I shake my head. Am I out of my ever-fucking mind? I don't do dates.

Not since I attempted my first one at sixteen, and when he tried to come into my home, Alek broke both of his legs with a bat. I didn't tell Alek that I'd actually invited him over so I could explore my raging teenage hormones. Then I learned the value of sex. Not dates. *Sex.*

And that fucker marked me on my inner thigh. *No one has ever marked me.*

Then he so easily left me high and dry with no

fucking care in the world. Why is it so hard to fuck this man? Anyone else would've caved in already. I would've gotten what I want, and this blackmail bull-shit would be behind me.

I let out a frustrated breath, pick up a pen, and aim for the new blue china vase I had imported. I throw it as Vance walks in, and it lands right on target.

"An impressive shot as always, miss," he says.

"Obviously," I say as I spin myself on the chair to do a full circle. I'm sick of sitting at this desk. I'm tired of these new constraints. I'm most certainly going out of my fucking mind as I try to find Alek and under-stand River.

It's filthy to think that I'm thinking of Alek and River almost equally as much.

"A package has arrived for you," Vance says, and I come to a stop and clap my hands together once.

Oooh, I do like presents.

He places a red box before me and goes to walk out without a further word.

"Vance." He stops and turns around.

"Yes, miss?"

"Any luck with the investigator?" I ask. He shakes his head. I do all that I can not to slump into my chair. Despite the shit show with Igor, he'd given me a lead. I've since asked my investigators to focus on Russia.

"Nothing so far," he says.

I sigh. "Can you request some tea to be made?"

"Yes, miss," he says, nodding and leaving as he closes the door behind him. Again, I'm empty and alone in this vast space. I narrow my gaze on the present, which is the only thing taking that loneliness away. Reaching for the package, I tear it open, revealing my favorite brand. Another Cartier jewel for the collection. I smile as I stare at the pretty red box, but then I remember I didn't order anything. Lifting the box's lid, I find a card.

The way this snake will wrap around your wrist is how you wrap around my fucking willpower.

X

River

I fight the smile that attempts to curve my lips. No, I'm not giving that motherfucker forgiveness after he left me high and dry last night... but this is certainly speaking my language. Especially with the beautiful new addition of the earrings he bought me.

Smiling, I open it to find a watch I've seen online but never in person. The band is a serpent that wraps around the wrist and is encased in diamonds. The head holds the clock, and I smile as I put it on and admire it.

Beautiful.

A knock on the door interrupts me and my expression drops. *What now?*

"Come in," I say as the large wooden doors open to reveal the old bitch herself.

I stand behind my desk, surprised. "Meredith?"

"You've certainly gotten comfortable if you think you can continue ignoring my calls," the old hag says, well dressed in a designer suit. Her almost-black hair is wrapped into a tight bun. Those piercing blue eyes are as lethal as ever. If it weren't for the faint hint of the wrinkles around her eyes, most wouldn't guess she's a woman in her late sixties.

"Things have been busy. It's unlike you to visit. Are you about to kick the bucket?"

She offers me a look that expresses she has no intention of ever dying. "Why, so you can spend the inheritance on more shiny things?" she says as she looks at the box on my desk. I don't know why, but I don't want her to know it's from River. The old bitch doesn't need to get any more in my business than she already tries to.

"If memory serves me correctly, you were the one who started me on 'shiny things,'" I remind her as I step around my desk to meet her in the center of the room. We both take a seat on the long sofas, a wooden coffee table between us.

She looks around the room. She's only ever been here once before. All other times, Alek and I went to her. It's unsettling to have her in my home because of that fact.

This was in many ways my oasis. When someone like the old bitch makes her way in, you live in uncertainty that she might burn it to the ground simply because you like it. I know this because she raised me on the same mentality.

"Your waitstaff are slow," she reprimands as she pulls out a cigarette and lights it with a gold lighter with a dragon engraved into it. I sneer at the disgusting habit, and hate that she does it in my home.

"They'll be here with tea shortly."

In many ways, I was grateful to the old bitch for fostering my brother and me. But it doesn't mean we weren't broken in or molded to her standards. Any questions or longing we might have had about our parents were quickly dismissed.

I had hired a private investigator in my teens to search for them. When Meredith found out—not that it took her too long—I was heavily reprimanded.

Longing, she had taught me, was a weakness.

Despite the ordeal, the investigations came up empty.

"When were you going to tell me about Alek?" she growls out.

Ah. That makes sense as to why she's here.

Clay walks in with a tray of tea, followed by Vance, who has a tray with an assortment of biscuits and sandwiches.

"You still have these two, huh?" the old bitch asks, blowing smoke into the air. "Well, at least they survived longer than the last ones. Means you're being more careful."

I offer a curt smile. "You can't very well still be holding against me the two security guards who were shot dead when I was seventeen, can you? Especially since the people who shot them were after you, not me."

Her head tilts higher as she watches them place the trays down and quietly leave the room.

Clay is peering in as he closes the door, as if offering me sympathetic support. My men can push back the world and most who arrive at my residences. The old bitch is not one of them.

She picks up her tea and takes a sniff. "Well, we've always had very different tastes, haven't we?" she says as she puts it back down. I have the feeling this will be a very short visit, which suits me just fine.

"In some things, yes," I agree. But in many ways, this is the woman who molded me in her own likeness. Some things I took as strengths, and others I discarded as she tried to mold my personality as well. And, well, we all know how unbreaking and riveting that is.

I take a sip of tea, appreciative of its balance. "Alek went missing over three months ago. I have investigators searching for him, but all of them are coming up empty."

"Three months?" she scoffs.

I try to downplay it as much as possible. I might be grateful to the old bitch, but my loyalty has and always will be with Alek. She will always come second to that.

"Why am I only finding out about this now?"

I casually shrug.

"You will lose the attitude. I'm asking you a question," she reprimands.

I eye her. My brother and I were not raised with love. We learned quickly about consequences, respect, negotiation, and manipulation. We were given tools to build an empire, ruin lives, and make money. Right now, I feel like a child again, learning that lesson. This old bitch is the only one who can make me feel so small, and I suppose in ways, that's what a parent does, isn't it? Constantly lecturing and checking in?

"I have it handled," I say.

"Three months says otherwise." She stands. "I'll have my men search for him as well. Do you not realize how weak this makes you look?"

"I can assure you, the auctions are still thriving even without Alek and—"

"It's been three months. What do you think it will look like in six months, Anya? It's better off if he's announced dead than simply missing."

Sharp pain erupts in my jaw from how tightly I'm clenching it.

Her gaze softens ever so slightly. "You've always been too dependent on him. I've raised you to be a brutal and cutthroat woman. If he remains unfound, he is a loose end."

"How could you say that about your own son?" I say as I place my tea down and uncross my legs to stand.

The old bitch doesn't know how to show compassion or uncertainty. But the fact that she's here shows she's concerned. She also lives by the philosophy of cutting something off if it no longer serves a purpose, and the longer Alek remains away, the more she will think of him that way.

It's why I didn't tell her in the first place.

"I love you both dearly," she says, and I try not to laugh at the term "love." But we love in our own ways. "But we can't show any weakness, Anya. As a woman, you know that better than the next person. Find him so this doesn't become a bigger issue than it already is," she warns.

She turns for the door, and Clay opens it on the other side, letting her out.

No goodbye.

No hugs.

Just another lecture.

I bend over to pick up my tea and then walk back to my paperwork and stare at the new watch wrapped around my wrist.

Beautiful.

CHAPTER 20

River

"And you just shot him in the head?" Michael asks two days after the meeting with Igor.

I shrug, unconcerned. "Igor was a sole trader. A man of luxury with a lot of money. It's not like he was attached to the Bratva or anything. Besides, I won't have him threatening Anya."

I pull out my pack of cigarettes and stare at them contemplatively. I only smoke if I'm stressed or socially with a drink. The thought of Anya ripping it from my lips and flinging it out the car window brings another smile to my face as I put them back in my pocket.

Michael and Derrick casually sit across from me in my office, each with a glass of whisky in hand. Derrick has added to his findings on the Ivanov siblings, but I find myself bored reading over the file. Now that I can access Anya anytime I please, I find it much more interesting to discover things about her on my own.

"If I may, sir," Michael starts. "I'm starting to think perhaps your judgment is clouded when it comes to Anya Ivanov. Your intentions have changed greatly since we first arrived."

"Those intentions are mine to change. Might I remind you that you work for me? Both of you. I might allow you to have a drink with me, but don't forget the hand that feeds you."

Michael dips his head submissively. "Apologies, sir."

"My goal is very clear. I plan to stay and make Anya Ivanov my wife."

Michael's jaw grinds, but he says nothing. Good boy.

He hasn't been shy about his thoughts that my association with Anya Ivanov is dangerous, especially if it doesn't fall in our favor. But I have no intention of letting Anya go anywhere other than my bed.

The moment I met Anya I was in awe. I could've gotten straight down to business, but I wanted to watch her, mesmerized in the way she controlled a room and scared men just with that icy gaze alone. I knew then that I could worship a woman like that every day as well as treat her as my equal. She is the first and only woman who has ever measured up to something I hadn't even realized I was looking for until her.

"Is the house settled?" I ask Derrick.

"It's all in your name, and your belongings have already been moved," he says.

"Excellent," I reply, rather chipper. I've bought many properties, much like the penthouse I'm in now, but none of them excited me as much as my new purchase. I will make Anya come to me, and I have no doubt she'll soon find out how I'm further settling into her city and encroaching on her space.

My phone rings, and I pull it out of my pocket.

Will.

"What have you got?" I ask. The moment Igor mentioned Alek was last seen in Russia, I had Will focus on that location.

"Not the news you want yet. But I'm on his trail now," he says, rather smug with his British accent.

"I don't know why it's taken you so long already. I thought you were the best," I chide.

He chuckles. "Well, it seems like you found a slimy and clever prick all in one. But no matter how long he tries to go under the radar, he'll eventually surface. I just wanted to update you. I also hear you're creating a stir with his sister back home."

"Where, pray tell, might you have heard that from?" I ask.

He laughs down the line. "You underestimate me. You got it bad, huh? Never seen you seriously interested in a woman before. Unless there's something you're trying to get from her?"

I pause with the scotch at my lips. "I plan on extracting many things from Anya Ivanov. Which reminds me. Wherever you have your little gossip meetings, I want you to make it very clear that no one is to touch so much as a hair on Anya Ivanov's head. If they do, they will deal with me."

Michael and Derrick look at one another. They'll no doubt ensure the same message goes to my men.

Will whistles. "Wow, you've fallen pretty hard for the beauty, haven't you? But I'll make sure your message is spread loud and clear."

"It's not falling when I'm simply claiming what's mine."

"And does Anya know about this?" he asks pointedly.

"She will."

If I don't fuck it up and give in to my carnal urges first.

"Alright, lover boy. Good luck. And if you end up

ten feet under, know that I still expect payment. Chasing this fucker isn't cheap or easy."

"I'll transfer some money over now to boost morale," I promise.

"That's why you're my favorite," Will teases.

I hang up the phone and am surprised when I see a text message from my mother.

> Mom: Are you moving to New York permanently? Should I come visit soon?

The only woman I've ever permitted to tell me what to do is my mother. She might be naïve to what her son does for business, but it brings me pride to know I can cater to her every need for the rest of her life.

I wonder how my mother might perceive a woman like Anya. They couldn't be more opposite. I also can't deny the pleasure it will offer me to see Anya being introduced to any parent.

CHAPTER 21
Anya

I'm on edge. I haven't had sex for over a week now, and no matter how many times I use my toy, it's just not cutting it. Especially considering I'm in an internal war with myself because my mind keeps drifting to River.

It's late afternoon, and I just left a meeting in the city. I watch the people around the car, bored by their busy, insignificant lives.

Friends shop with elbows linked together.

Lovers hold hands.

Parents cradle their babies.

All of these things are meaningless to me.

At least as I was raised to believe. Since Alek's disappearance, I've found myself more curious as to what their lives might be like. I feel like someone looking from the outside in. All of these things I was raised to exploit and use as a weakness. Yet they all look happy.

I sigh and look at my phone. I'm busier than I've ever been, yet I've never been more bored with the mundane running of our empire. The shine of the diamond snake watch grabs my attention, and I smirk. Well, much to my irritation, there's one person who has made it less boring, as much as he is disruptive.

I untuck my shirt from the hem of my skirt and lift it past my tits. I angle my camera and poke out my tongue as I take a pic of my tits on full display. Vance watches me through the rearview mirror but says nothing as I send the photo to River. The sooner he gives in to me, the sooner I can push away this confusion and uncertainty he raises in me.

And I royally need to be fucked.

"Vance," I call out. "Find out where Mr. Bently is staying and take me to him."

He nods through the rearview mirror as I hit call on Alek's number.

Ring.

Ring.

Voicemail.

"Alek, what the fuck? I got my ass chewed out by the old bitch because of you. You need to come back home. She's not impressed, and I don't want to deal with her. She came to my house. You know how fucking weird that is in the first place."

When I look out the window, honey-colored hair catches my eye. I'm surprised to see Dawson and his woman, Honey, strolling along. She's laughing at something he says, and his smile in return... I've never seen him make that expression.

It fills me with loneliness because of the thought that I might be missing out on something.

Yuck. I shove that thought down. "Alek, you need to come home. I'm starting to go crazy, and not in my usual loveable way. Like in a weird-as-shit way. Like when you look at couples and babies and think it doesn't look too bad." I erupt into laughter. "Actually, fuck that, kids are still disgusting creatures. But something weird is happening while you're not here."

A somber thought crosses my mind. Something I've been in denial about since I found out Alek was chasing a woman. "Is that what you're looking for, Alek?" *Love?* I can't say the word out loud. It's not something that Alek and I have ever discussed or even know how to navigate.

"Are you looking for a companion?" *Was I not*

enough? We always have each other's back. But now something is changing, and I can feel it fracturing inside me bit by bit, and I don't know what part of me will remain. "I don't care about you withdrawing money or the shitty situation you dropped me in. *Please* just call me back."

I hang up, noticing the desperate plea in my voice. I brush a hand over my hair to make sure not one piece is out of place. Something is happening inside me, and it squeezes like a vise around my throat. I feel exposed, and without Alek, who will have my back?

I roll my shoulders back, internally laughing. No, I can do this on my own. Always have and always will. When I finally look up, I narrow my gaze on the familiar road.

"Vance, I clearly said I wanted you to take me to River's address, not back home," I reprimand him.

"Yes, miss. You see, the thing is..." he says as he turns into the driveway to the property beside mine. "Mr. Bently seems to have purchased and moved into the mansion beside yours."

My jaw unhinges. "How could he—" I snap my mouth shut. Because River Bently can do whatever the fuck he wants, that's why.

The steel gates open as we drive along the long hedges, and it irritates me how much River most likely expected this. I look at my phone and see he hasn't yet replied to my text message, which pisses me off. Considering how many texts he's sent me with nonsense about all the wild things he wants to do to me, and when I finally reply, not a peep from him.

Sharply trimmed hedges surround the three-story, light-brown mansion for privacy. In the ten years of living next door, I'd never been curious about my neighbors or their home. Now, I wish I knew the layout inside and out.

I see the edge of a pool through the hedges, and the Victorian estate presents itself with a beautiful facade. The front doors open, and he steps out. It's evening now, and his front porch light is on, showing him dressed in black slacks and a white T-shirt, his tattoos on full display, snaking up his arms.

Motherfucker was expecting me.

"I'll call you when I need you to pick me up, Vance," I say as I unbuckle my seat belt.

"Miss, I'll come with you," he insists.

"No, don't," I say as I watch River come down the stairs and toward the car. My men go everywhere with me. It's just how it's been for a long time. And it's always done me justice. But right now, I don't plan on going anywhere that puts me in danger. Actually, scratch that, I hope he fucks me up.

River opens the car door, leans down, and peers at me.

"Anya." He says my name correctly, and his gaze falls to my wrist. "I see you got my gift."

"Buy a girl diamonds, and you may very well get laid," I say to him. He eyes me before he steps back, waiting for me to get out of the car. I place one heel on the ground, followed by the next, and rise from the back seat. He closes the door behind me as I look over his estate.

"The house next door? Really?" I snark.

"Some might consider it a happy coincidence. Think of all the sleepovers we can have," he says, trying to spook me.

"Just so you know, the last boy who tried to climb into my window got both of his legs broken by a baseball bat," I warn, rather fond of the memory.

"Then whoever had the bat didn't do a good enough job, because I would've aimed for his skull," River says with a tight smile. When I look at him, I realize he's not joking anymore.

"Come. I know you're dying to know what my bedroom looks like," he says as he grabs my hand.

My gaze lands on his hand holding mine, but he seems unfazed by my icy glare. "I very well expect you to be a squatter living in your own home. A mattress at best."

He chuckles. "It'll take you a lot longer than that to send me into bankruptcy, Tanya, but keep trying."

I bite the inside of my cheek, hating myself for actually finding this fucker funny at times.

I can't help but stare at his back as I follow him into the house. Even dressed, I can see the outline of his muscles. River is a powerful man, and he exudes power from every pore.

The house seems only half full of furniture as he leads me through the main living space and guides me to the staircase. I find myself peeking around every corner, and when I glance up, I realize he's looking over his shoulder at me.

"I'm still waiting on the last of my furniture to arrive," he states.

I bite my bottom lip, trying not to laugh. "Sure, you are. Or maybe you had to sell it off for this pretty thing," I say, lifting my wrist to indicate the watch.

"Did it work?" he asks.

I shrug. "I've added it to my collection with all other items mortal men who fall for my trap have given me."

"What a mighty collection you must have, Tanya,"

he says dryly, and again, I find myself biting the inside of my cheek, amused.

He stops in front of a door and pushes it open, and I see a large king-sized bed in the center of the room. He walks in and sits on the edge of the mattress and kicks off his shoes as he looks at me.

"Why are you here?" he asks as he untucks his shirt and pulls it over his head, discarding it on the floor. I can't help but take him in. His chest is covered in tattoos as well. He has an eight-pack, and his muscles create ridges under skin. Vance and Clay are large men, both with different body types but both as equally as fit as one another. River looks more along the lines of deadly, where my men look scary. There's a difference.

He unbuckles his belt, pulls it free, and wraps it around his knuckles. When he takes his trousers off, I'm not surprised to see he doesn't wear any underwear.

"Anya." He says my name, and I realize I've been staring like a woman in heat. That's because I am. I'm fucking craving his touch.

River has the upper hand, and it's usually me who has the power in these types of situations. My body is rarely ever denied. I'm not used to this lack of control, and I think he knows that. Yet, here I am, without fully understanding why. To have sex with him so I can finally get rid of him, right?

"Why are you here?" River asks again, purposely making a show of the belt in his hands. A cold chill runs down my body. I want him just to scratch this itch.

"Why are you naked?" I wave a hand at him. He looks down at his body and his semi-hard cock. I avoid licking my lips at the sight of it. At the sight of all of him. River is a fucking pain in my ass, but God was generous when he built him.

"I was going to take a shower when you suddenly pulled up," he informs me. And I know he's fucking lying.

"You didn't reply to my text message," I say as I scan his room absentmindedly. "Thought I needed to remind you that a debt is still owed."

"I might've not replied but I certainly made the picture my screen saver," River says as he flashes a roguish smile over his shoulder as he strides to the bathroom. The light is automatic and comes on when he walks in. It fills me with a strange satisfaction that I can tease him from his screen saver every day. Also, with the knowledge that he'll shoot a man if he so much as peeks at his phone. Not that I care if anyone else sees.

He reaches into the shower and turns on the water, and I know he's taunting me. I stand there and watch as he gets in, stepping out of my sight. I take the opportunity to look around his room more thoroughly.

I find it strange that I'm a woman who takes control and dominates every man I meet. Yet now, in River's room, with his lack of effort, I feel stubborn still trying to make him come to me. Every man does.

I search the room and notice a photo frame on his bedside table with a picture of a child in it.

Does he have kids?

Picking it up, I walk into the bathroom and prop myself on the counter. I sit on it with legs crossed, enjoying my view as a mixture of water and soap runs down his body.

"Have you come to sing to me, Anya, or join me?"

"Who is this?" I ask. He wipes a hand over his face, his muscles flexing as he does.

"My niece."

"You have family?"

"My sister is dead. That's her daughter."

I look at the picture of them, my eyebrows knitting together. I think about the parents I saw today, happily playing with their children. The normalcy of lovers hand in hand.

What did I come here for? Sex. Why am I asking him about his personal life?

What the fuck am I doing? Why did I come here?

A chill runs down my spine, and suddenly I feel like I'm going to be sick. Surely, I didn't come here for... companionship?

I'm not a woman who would chase a man, ever. It's never been necessary. When I was old enough, I understood the power of attraction and knew I had it. So I used it. A woman has to use whatever is at her disposal to get where she wants in life. It's easier for men. I wanted to make it easier for me. So I did.

Is River doing that very same thing to me?

"Anya, what's going on in that beautiful mind of yours right now?" he says as he rubs soap against his body, and I know he's doing it on purpose. Every part of me is screaming to leave. But I need to ensure that I get exactly what I came here for. Because if I don't, then that means I really did come here for companionship.

I hike up my skirt and widen my legs. "Not much thinking at all. Just wondering if you're going to fuck me or not," I say as I rub against my sensitive bud with my pussy on full display.

His jaw tics, and his facial expression changes. It gives me satisfaction to know that although he might've been in control, naked and looking like a god, I can take that power back.

I rub myself as he watches, and his cock grows harder. "I need you," I say with an innocent tone.

A haunting laugh escapes him. "You don't need anything or anyone, Red. Not yet."

And it's the challenge in his tone, the exasperation that he still thinks I will ever become his, that makes me want to run for the door just as quickly. If I fuck him now and a second time, then the contract is mostly done. Right?

I hop off the counter and saunter to the shower. He watches my every move as I open the door and step in. My white shirt immediately becomes see-through, and his hand automatically trails up my outer leg as he pushes my skirt farther up.

I suck in a breath as we stare at one another, more intimately than I have with any other. I grab his cock, and the cord in his neck pulses at my touch. I'm not the only one who's been holding out.

"You could slip in those heels," he growls and pins my back against the tiled wall.

"You'll catch me, though, right?" I say innocently, and I can tell it's working magic on him. Someone like River needs submission. An innocent doe, which is the furthest thing from what I will ever be. But I wonder if I tell myself that to keep him at arm's length.

That startling realization hits me hard, but then his hand cups my pussy, and the worry falls away as he pumps me with a finger.

Neither of us looks away as we hold one another, trying to force the other to submit first. Trying to see who will break. I offer a smile and trail my fingers down his ridiculously chiseled stomach. Fuck me, it's divine.

I rub against his hand, riding that single finger, hoping he adds more. I need more from him. His gaze dips to my pierced nipples on full display under the white shirt.

He grabs my throat, and the painful pressure causes a pounding in my core. Fuck, I want him.

"I'm not going to fuck you, Red," he says, but I'm certain I can make him regret those words. Every man has fallen to their knees for me and given me exactly what I want, when I've demanded it.

River's grip shifts as his thumb begins to stroke my jaw, and the touch feels different. Intimate. Gentle. I don't let the uncertainty show on my face.

I fuck. That's it. And I currently have an itch to scratch, and that's all, I remind myself.

"Don't you want to taste me?" I encourage, trying

to divert his expression from how intensely he's staring at me.

His head dips, and I'm startled by the feather-light touch of his lips against mine. My hand freezes on his cock as his tongue pushes against mine, demanding. I'm swept into him momentarily, wanting to curl my hands through his hair and pull him in.

I push him away and almost slip in the water on the floor of the shower. He catches me by my elbow, but I'm quick to break free and stumble out.

Fuck, I need to leave.

None of this makes sense. I shouldn't be here.

A kiss?

When was the last time I let anyone kiss me?

River wraps a towel around his waist. "Anya?" He catches my wrist before I can escape. And for the first time, I feel a chill of terror run through me. Not because I'm scared of River but because of the way I feel myself changing around him.

"It was a mistake coming here," I say.

His eyebrows furrow in confusion, but he releases my wrist and lets me go.

When I take my leave, he calls out my name again.

I grip the edge of his doorway, my red nails wanting to dig in to keep me here. A part of me knowing it should run.

Feelings. Alek and I don't get them for other people. So why is my brother halfway around the world chasing a woman?

And when he does return, I may very well kill him for leaving me this long.

Because isn't that what I'm doing right now? Chasing?

I have never been apart from my brother for this long, and I'm mistakenly craving something I'm missing, and I'm looking for it in all the wrong places. Namely, River Bently.

I shake my head and push myself out of his bedroom and go straight down the stairs. When I reach the door, I hear his voice from behind me.

"Tomorrow, Anya, you owe me. I'll pick you up at three."

I don't turn back to look at him, because I know if I do, I'll walk straight back up those stairs and into his arms.

Not because I want a hug or a kiss, I tell myself. Because I want to fuck him.

And that's becoming a dangerous sentiment in itself.

"I'm busy tomorrow," I shout back.

"I'm picking you up," he shouts down the stairs.

"Don't pick me up before five. I have plans!" I yell before I slam the door behind me.

My heart pounds as I walk out, shivering cold and still wet. I send Vance a text and start walking down the driveway, never looking back.

What the fuck am I doing here?
Have I lost my fucking mind?

CHAPTER 22

Anya

"You seem quiet today, miss," Clay says as he looks through the rearview mirror at me.

"Everything's fine, Clay," I say dismissively as I clutch the black briefcase in my lap.

Everything is *not* fine. Last night, I didn't even recognize myself. I'd slipped up.

River is the enemy. He's sexy as all fuck, but he has no place in my world. Yet I naturally gravitate toward him, fooling myself that it's just for sex.

No, I can get sex anywhere I want.

So why did I go to him?

I push the mounting thoughts down. I don't need the complication of thoughts or feelings. I don't do feelings, and I don't chase men.

It's a debt to be paid. Once it's done, River will be

out of my life forever. Though, I'm not so sure of that now that he's bought the house beside mine. But I'm sure I can become the neighbor from hell.

And even after all the mental fuckery, I still didn't get laid.

"Clay, stay by the car. You scare the kids," I say as I step out of the back seat.

"Yes, miss," he agrees. "I'll be watching from here," he adds as he steps out of the car and stands beside the driver's door.

I look up at the worn-down building with bold letters that say "Orphanage." I've always hated this place. It reminds me of a prison, and in many ways, it was for my brother and me. We were handed through two foster families before the old bitch found us. Each one of them said we were too much to handle. Granted, Alek got violent at the last foster home we were in, but that place was beyond full of children. That man deserved every moment of the beating Alek gave him. When I was a teenager, I returned to his home, and he was the first man I'd taken satisfaction in killing for what he had done to me.

I would never fall victim to a man again.

My grip tightens on the briefcase as I cross the road. Same time, same day every month, I come here.

I'm not a good person, but there's a small relief

inside me knowing that all this money I've amassed might help a child in the same circumstances as my brother and I once were.

"Anya," Mikaela says expectantly. She's second in charge to Lucy, the woman who has run the orphanage for the last thirty years. "Punctual as always." She opens the door, and I cringe at the thought of stepping into a hall full of children.

"No, thank you. I'll just drop the money off here," I say as I hold out the briefcase to her, but she takes a step farther into the hallway.

"Lucy would like to see you briefly, if you have a moment," she says. I sigh and take my designer sunglasses off and prop them on my head. I handle men like they're a sport. Surely, I can handle the uncomfortable presence of children.

I slip through the door and follow her down the hall. It's quiet, and my heels click against the wooden floors. It feels colder in here than outside. So many things haven't changed here over the years, yet every time I enter, I can see the subtle updates made to the estate. No doubt from my "anonymous" contributions.

As I walk down the hall, I notice a pair of beady eyes peering at me through a door that's ajar. A young girl watches me. Because that's not creepy in the slightest.

I'm escorted through to the main reception area and on to Lucy's office.

I cringe at the sound of a child crying when I step inside. I all but fold into myself as Lucy rocks a baby back and forth. The sixty-year-old woman looks like she hasn't changed a bit. That doe-eyed affection fills her gaze as she bounces the infant around.

She looks up with a smile. "Anya. It's been a while since you've shown your face. It's good to see you."

"Pleasure," I reply dryly.

She lets out a little laugh, always having found amusement in my dry tone. Yet in some ways, it's oddly comforting. Despite my spoiled ways as a child, she had always taken time for me and my brother after our parents abandoned us.

"Would you like to hold her?" She offers me the child, and I use the briefcase as a shield.

"Allergic, actually," I say with disdain.

"Allergic to a baby?" Lucy scoffs and hands the infant over to Mikaela with a smile. I'm relieved when she takes her out of the room.

"You haven't changed a bit," Lucy says as she begins to pick up the few toys on the floor. She looks pointedly at my ring finger. "Still not married, I see.

I'm telling you, Anya, beauty only lasts so long. You need to lock a man down while you still can," she grumbles as she stands up again, her back stiff.

"Ironic, considering my foster mother has an entirely different opinion about my marital status." To the old bitch, marriage is a form of weakness.

Lucy seems grim at my mention of Meredith. I've always found irony in the way she seems to have an opinion of the old bitch despite handing us over legally to her. But it was better than here.

"You wanted to see me?" I ask expectantly as I walk across the room and place the briefcase with the cash down.

Lucy watches me step away from it with a warm smile. "As prickly as you are, Anya, you've always had a big heart. I hope you find someone you can share it with beyond your brother."

The mention of Alek draws short on my nerves, but I say nothing. She steps around the desk and pulls out the top drawer. I idly look at some of the pictures of children pinned to the wall and the scribbles of disastrous interpretations of elephants.

"I went through some archives two months ago and found some old photos of you and Alek. I thought you might want them," she says as she pulls out an envelope and hands it to me.

I furrow my eyebrows. "Do I seem like the sentimental type?" I ask as I take them.

She laughs again. "Anya, most people would say thank you."

My lips draw thin as I open it out of curiosity. Most gifts I receive are diamond encrusted, but I suppose it couldn't hurt to look.

I flip open the envelope to reveal four old and worn photos. I maintain my expression as a smile dares to form. A photo of me hanging off Alek with a big smile. He looks miserable. I'm missing a front tooth and almost want to choke on a laugh at how feral we look with dirt on our faces. A different time and place.

The next one is a photo of me screaming so audaciously you can see my tonsils, and Alek is trying to console me.

The third is a photo of me and a young girl yanking on Alek's arm, fighting over him. My eyebrows furrow. I vaguely remember the girl, and this particular moment. She didn't stay with us for long. My gaze dips to the child's foot and see she's wearing worn-out imitation ballet shoes.

"I don't remember this girl much," I say pointedly to Lucy as I raise the photo.

"Cinita? She wasn't here for long. Fostered out rather quickly, actually. I heard she became a dancer. I try my best to keep tabs on all my children who pass through here."

I tuck that information away. Could this be the dancer Alek is chasing? It's a slim chance, but I'm willing to go off anything right now.

"I'd love to know what you have on my brother and me now," I say with a tight smile as I push the photos back into the envelope and pocket them in my long black jacket.

Lucy's face seems grim as she quietly says, "Business owners, right?"

"Business owners," I agree. Lucy, for all of her nurturing nature, is also a highly intelligent woman. I have no doubt the moment the old bitch walked in, she understood exactly what type of woman she was. As expected, anything can be paid for. Hell, I make a living off it.

"Thank you for the gift, Lucy. And make sure you use some of the money to get your back checked out. It'll become a nuisance for your workers here if you can't pick up wailing children," I scold.

"Thank you for caring, Anya," she says from behind me as I walk out the door. "It's good to see you."

I walk out with my chin held high, noticing the same door that was slightly ajar is now fully open. The same girl peers around the edge of the doorframe. She's no older than I was when I first came to this place.

She stares at me and slowly points at the black glasses she now has atop her head.

I look down the hall and notice no one else is there. Curiosity gets the better of me as I come to a stop in front of her door and crouch down to her level. I hold my knees to try to make myself as small as possible.

"Did you put those glasses on because they look like mine?" I ask.

The girl offers a smile, revealing one missing tooth, and I can't help but offer her a small one back. A reminder of the photos I'd just been given; one in particular of me with the same missing tooth.

I pluck my glasses from my hair and look at them. I have a million of these anyway. I offer them to her. "These are Versace. Very expensive. Very beautiful. If I give these to you, you have to look after them."

Her eyes go wide. "Will I look like you in them?" she asks quietly and clings to the doorframe shyly, and another small part of me breaks. A reminder of the child I once was. A time when I, too, understood innocence until it was taken away.

"Even better," I whisper as I hand her the glasses. Because every part of me hopes that with the financial contributions I offer to this establishment, the only problem this little girl will face is whose heart she wants to break next.

I stand and notice Lucy watching from the end of the hall with a smug smile. My jaw tics as I hold my chin high and walk back out the front to be greeted by Clay waiting at the door.

"I told you to wait by the car," I scold.

"But then you went inside," he says unapologetically. I adjust the hem of my jacket but proceed to stride across the road, two steps ahead of him.

I fish out the envelope of photos. "There's a photo of a girl in here during the time we stayed in this orphanage. I want you to find out everything you can about her."

He says nothing as he plucks it out of my hand.

Every time I leave here, a small part of me feels like I've done at least a little bit of good in this world. This time feels different, though. And it's as unsettling as it is loud.

Fucking River Bently.

CHAPTER 23

River

I t's either a risk or stupidity taking her to another business meeting. I'm not sure which. What I wasn't expecting of my she-devil was her appearance at the orphanage. When she told me she wasn't available to meet until now, I had one of my men follow her. Out of curiosity, of course. Not that I'll mention it to her, because I'm certain hell will freeze over if I insinuate she has one kind bone in her body.

I'm discovering many things about Anya. Especially that her venomous tongue and steely resolve, as beautiful as they are, are also used as a shield to protect herself. And it's another thing I would never imply unless I want my brains blown out the very next second.

After last night and the kiss we shared, I now realize Anya is more precious than I gave her credit for. This woman has never had a lick of love or affection in her life. Although I'm not sure I can give it to her, I'm certainly willing to give it my all.

I never thought there would be a woman I'd cherish or want to literally give everything and anything to. I may not have all the answers, but I'll make it my mission to do whatever it takes to make her happy. Even if I go broke in the process.

I pull up to the curb of my new restaurant, and she lets out a frustrated sigh, seemingly unimpressed to be brought back here. I chuckle as I unclick her seat belt.

"It's not that bad, Anya. If you ate the food, you might come to realize you actually enjoy it," I say.

"I'd rather go through a greasy fast-food drive-through," she bites back.

I laugh again. "I doubt you've ever been through one of those."

Her lips purse, and I know I'm right. She'd dealt with the reality of living off bare essentials until she and Alek were taken in by their third and final foster mother, who is extremely wealthy. But this little princess hasn't "roughed it" a day in her life since.

I haven't been able to find very much regarding their birth parents. At four, they could barely spell their first and last names, let alone provide anyone with any pertinent information about their parents.

"It feels almost full circle bringing you back here since this is where we first met," I say when she doesn't continue the conversation. She's been prickly with me since yesterday. I knew she would eventually come to me, especially when she found out I purchased the mansion next door. One second, she was there asking about my niece, and the next, she locked up and vanished.

I'm certain it's because of that fucking kiss.

"Unless we're doing a drive-by on this shithole, are we getting out of the car or not?" she asks with her arms crossed over her chest. I laugh again and step out of the car as one of my men comes to collect the keys. Another one of my staff collect the keys from her two bodyguards who park behind us. I was lenient in allowing her to bring them, considering they would've found a way to come in anyway.

I adjust my suit and walk around to her side of the car and open the door, where she's still pouting. But gone are the days when she's opening and slamming doors herself. No, now she expects me to open them for her. Progress.

I hold my hand out to her, and she takes it and steps out. She's breathtaking. I will never tire of watching this beautiful woman in her tight dresses and skirts and icy gaze.

She tries to remove her hand from mine, but I tighten my grip as I thread my fingers through hers. The action doesn't go unnoticed by her men, who glance at one another skeptically.

"Yuck," she spits. "I didn't take you as the overbearing type."

"One of us has to make up for your prickly presence," I say, unfazed as I walk us through the entrance. The hostess greets us, and when her gaze lands on Anya, she turns a paler shade. Anya has that kind of effect on people. It fills me with pride.

The hostess escorts all four of us to the private space where my men are waiting. The chatter grows quieter as they nod to me respectfully but stare at her suspiciously. They know how dangerous she is and what happened with Igor as a consequence of him underestimating her. They advised I cut all ties and do my business in her territory without her permission. But it's not just her permission that I need; it's access to her auctions as well. I need to prove to her I can ensure they'll have a consistent income by partnering with me, more than just with a monthly auction. It's just a perk in addition to everything else I'm willing to offer her in the process.

Patrons fly or send people from around the world to come and bid at the Ivanov auctions. And she doesn't let just anyone in. She is very selective, and the only ones I know are Dawson Taylor and Crue Monti.

On top of that, I threatened if any of my men were to so much as attempt to lay a hand on her, I would not only kill them but their families and anything or anyone they ever loved.

Michael stands as we get closer. The table is already filled with food and liquor.

"This doesn't look like a business meeting," Anya says as I pull out her chair, which is next to mine at the head of the table.

"It is. Just be patient," I tell her.

She says nothing as she takes her seat. Anya's men stand behind her near the wall, looking stoic and broody as usual. The server comes over with more food and places it on the table as I reach for the bottle of wine and pour myself a drink. Grabbing the water, I pour her a glass and place it in front of her, remembering she doesn't drink alcohol. "What do you want to eat?"

"Why, do you plan to hand feed it to me?" she asks, lifting a perfectly manicured brow.

"Do you want me to?" Because I will if it means I

get to play with those lips. I've touched her other lips, so it's only fair I touch the other set, right?

"Give it a try. Let's see how many fingers I can remove with my teeth," she snarks back. I smile, transfixed by her. I want to bend her over and punish her. My cock grows uncomfortable at the thought.

I lean over and say against her ear, "Maybe we should finish where we left off last night."

Her hand slides over to my thigh under the table, and she offers a promiscuous smile. "You want me to fist your cock right now in front of all your men?"

Her hand is a feather touch against my cock, but it's enough to cause splitting pain through my jaw by how hard I clench it.

"Don't you want to fuck me, River? The contract's almost fulfilled. This will be your second meeting. Now all you have to do is actually fuck me," she says sweetly, but with a hint of venom. The atmosphere shifts, as it always does with this dangerous woman.

"Sir, we expect your guests to join us in ten minutes," Michael interrupts as I trail my fingers over her smooth skin, causing goose bumps to erupt in their wake.

"Thank you, Michael," I grit out.

Her gaze is hooded as she stares at me.

"I don't want to eat this," she says, gesturing to the plateful of food. "I'm hungry for something else."

"I won't fuck you yet," I say, because, fuck me, if she isn't everything I want. If I give in to her now, let her win this challenge, she won't return. If I let her think we're about nothing but sex and business, she'll be done with me once the debt is paid in full. I want to brand her as mine for the rest of her days, but this newfound discipline of mine is grating on my nerves, and she knows it.

"We'll see. Don't you have a secret little room here somewhere? Or should I just start stripping now?" She pouts as she begins to slide down her dress strap.

I snatch her hand and push back from the table. "We'll be back," I bark.

"But your guests—" Michael begins.

"Will wait," I seethe.

"Miss?" one of her guards asks.

"I won't be gone for long. Stay," she commands, with no complaint this time as I hold her hand and guide her out. We almost bulldoze one of the servers as I push past them and into the small office where the manager sits looking over invoices.

"Oh, Mr. Bently, is there something—"

"Leave," I say. He seems startled, but then abruptly grabs his things and hurries out of the room.

When I turn, I slam Anya against the door, her back hitting it to shut it only seconds after the manager has left.

Her hand goes straight to my belt as I place one hand on her hip and the other on her throat, tracing her sharp jawline with my thumb.

"No running away this time, Red," I growl.

"No sweet nothings," she says back.

The elasticity of my control snaps as I press my lips to hers. Anya's hand freezes on my belt. I can feel her reluctance. The hesitation in opening up to me further. But then I pinch her nipple, and she lets out a small moan. I dive my tongue deeper into her mouth, and slowly, uncertainly, her tongue begins to work with mine.

Her hand unfastens my belt as her kisses become feral, desperate even. Slowly, Anya is opening up to me, whether she likes it or not. There's a hunger driving us both insane.

She wraps my belt around the back of my neck, pulling me in tighter as I cock her leg on my hip and work my fingers against her already wet cunt.

Her lips rub against my cheek as she savors the feeling. This fucking woman.

"I want to see you," I demand.

Her eyes widen, surrounded by thick, dark lashes. "Open your legs wide and bend over the desk."

She tightens the belt around my neck. "I don't take orders."

"You do if you want that sweet cunt of yours eaten out and to be dripping down my fingers." I pinch her sensitive bud, and she hisses. "No sex."

She rolls her eyes, and I squeeze her cheeks again. "Stop being so defiant all the time, and let me break you into a million pieces."

I step back as she gives a pointed look at my cock bulging against my trousers. She licks her lips in anticipation as she shoves me to the side, and I take the belt from her hands.

I grab both of her wrists and put them behind her back as I bind them with the belt. "You better make me come," she bites back.

"I could say the same to you. Or is the only good thing that pretty mouth of yours is good for is yapping?"

She goes to say something, but I push her over the desk. Then I pull up her skirt and kick her legs apart. I lick my lips. Mother of God. This cunt. I hold her hips and momentarily slam my cock, that's still trapped in my trousers, against her. The shove shocks her, and she tries to look over her shoulder.

I can imagine it perfectly, thrusting my cock inside this sweet cunt of hers. "One day, I'm going to break you from the inside out."

"So you say. Why not just fucking do it?" she bites back.

"It drives you mad to know that I can say no to you, doesn't it, Anya?" And that is the biggest lie I've told.

"Is the only thing your mouth is good at is yapping?" she snaps.

I grin as I tug on her restraints, her hands bound behind her back as I drop to my knees and bury my face in her sweet pussy.

She moans and almost climbs up the desk as I pin her hands down to control her movement. The other hand I use to insert a finger and then pump inside her.

"Fuck," she moans as I work her, licking everything this beautiful woman is willing to give. Sex on legs. That's what she is.

My cock aches as I dive into her deeper with my tongue. Fuck, I could just give in to her now. I could just fuck her and put us both out of our misery.

A knock on the door interrupts us, but Anya is quick to scream, "Fuck off!"

I'm smiling as I continue to eat her out, pumping in harder and faster as I add a third finger.

"Fuck, it's been so long," she whines. It gives me satisfaction to know she's held out, and I reap the reward when she explodes on my lips. Her legs begin to tremble as she leans into me. "Fuck, River, you better finish this or I will fucking kill you."

I leave her pussy for only a minute as I bite her ass, and she yelps in pleasure. "I don't think you understand the precarious situation you're in," I say before I continue to suck on her clit and fuck her with my fingers.

She's quiet for a moment until waves of pleasure break free within her and her pussy muscles squeeze around my fingers. Anya squirts and moans as I taste everything she's offering until she goes limp. Even after her orgasm, I can't stop tasting her. Don't ever want to stop.

My cock aches, still pressed against my trousers. When I step away from her, I half expect her to run for the door, even with her skirt pulled up around her hips and her arms bound behind her back. But when she looks up, that lustful expression is raging.

I let her stand, then I grab her jaw as I kiss her. She might not like it yet, but it's sure as hell progress from last night when she fled because of it. "Fucking beautiful," I say as I bite her bottom lip and tug on it with my teeth.

"Sit on the chair," she commands. "And drop those fucking trousers."

I smile and pinch her cheeks. "So these lips aren't just ornamental?"

"You have one chance," she bites.

I chuckle as I round the desk and notice a small pillow on the manager's chair. I drop it on the floor for her and unzip my pants. "The belt stays around your wrists, though," I say as I let my pants drop to my ankles and fist my cock. She licks her lips at the sight.

"I expected it to be bigger," she says dryly, and I'm not so insecure to think that this isn't one of the biggest cocks she's seen. She still gets on her knees on the pillow and has a taste. The moment her tongue runs up the bottom of my shaft, my entire body goes rigid.

Fuck, how I've thought of her every night since first meeting her. Waiting for the day this poisonous tongue would be on my cock.

Anya is used to being the one pleasured. I doubt she's gotten on her knees for many men, if any. The thought of her being with any other man pokes an ugly, lethal side of me, and I grab her chin before she can suck on my cock.

"You will swallow every drop," I command.

She flashes a wicked smile, as if accepting the challenge, and when her lips surround my cock and that venomous tongue slides against my shaft, I know I've met my match.

"Fuck," I grit out as she bobs on my cock. I can imagine her, arms still bound behind her back, pussy pulsing around my cock instead. That sweet cunt of hers milking me dry. I want to fuck her so badly. I grip the armrests of the chair so I don't do exactly that. Maybe it's me who has to be tied up against my own urges instead.

Another knock on the door. "Fuck off!" I bark out, and can imagine the vein in my neck bulging.

I bend over slightly so I can grab one of her tits and pinch at the perfectly pierced nipple. She moans around my cock, and it's my undoing, as I blow into her mouth. Like a good girl, she takes her fill. My hips jerk as I cling to the chair.

I haven't come that hard in a long time. Then again, nothing compares to this. To *her*.

Anya licks at the tip of my cock, her lipstick slightly smeared and most likely all over my face and cock, but I don't give a shit. I grab her chin and bend over to kiss her. She freezes under the touch but doesn't pull away.

"See how good we taste together," I tell her, appreciating the curve in her posture with her hands still bound behind her back.

"There is no *we*. There is simply fucking. And this high school shit of holding hands and foreplay, apparently," she says with an unimpressed look.

I smile as I stand and lean over her, undoing my belt to free her. She rubs her wrists and then wipes her lips.

Another knock on the door. "Fuck off!" we say in unison.

I look at the wall clock and realize we've been in here for over thirty minutes.

She smiles sweetly. "Can I leave now?"

"No. We still have a meeting to attend," I reply, sweeping a glance around the room. Items from the desk have been knocked to the floor, the pillow discarded to the side, and my ass cheeks imprinted on the leather chair.

CHAPTER 24

River

"Boss, they've been waiting for over thirty minutes," Michael says as we walk back toward our table. Patrick is glaring, clearly not impressed. But he's not alone. No, he has Amanza, his sister, with him. She lights up when she sees me, and I notice Anya's curious gaze.

"Do you know her?" Anya asks me as I pull out her chair for her to sit.

Anya is very good at reading people, and nothing ever gets by her. Before I can answer, Patrick stands and reaches his hand out to me. "I don't enjoy waiting."

"Apologies. An urgent matter popped up that I had to attend to." His skeptical gaze shifts to Anya. He and Amanza sit to my right, opposite Anya.

When Patrick pulls back, Amanza has already walked around her brother and leans in for a hug. I casually wrap one arm around her as she says, "It's good to see you again." She presses a kiss to my cheek. She lingers a little longer than necessary, as if expecting me to return the kiss. I don't. She pulls back, seeming slightly confused before she once again takes her seat next to her brother.

Patrick is a necessity in my business. He's an accountant, and a good one at that, who keeps my money clean. I've worked with him for five years now. The accountant I had before that was taking money from me. So now he lies with the dead.

"Patrick, I don't think you've had the pleasure of meeting Anya Ivanov yet, have you?" Patrick looks at Anya, and I can tell right away he appreciates what he sees because he sits a little straighter when introduced. It's not just her beauty but the demanding, entitled presence of her. She's a queen in her own right.

"No, I have not," he says, offering her his hand. She glances at it and then at me. I can imagine the eye roll as she reaches out, no smile—which is not a surprise—and shakes his hand.

"Patrick is from a small town on the coast. You don't come to New York all that often, do you?" I ask him. I purposely orchestrated this business meeting to showcase to Anya that I already have everything I need in place to work alongside her. There is no liability in solidifying business together.

"No, but I always welcome an invitation for such an offer," he says, smiling at Anya. "This is Amanza, my sister," Patrick says to Anya, waving to his sister. She smiles at Anya, and Anya just stares.

I'd be pissed if she smiled freely, considering how hard I've had to work for the few she's thrown my way.

Fuck, I really want her. The image of Anya on her knees, bound by the very belt I'm wearing now, has me shifting uncomfortably again.

I will never have enough of this woman.

"Did you two used to fuck?" Anya asks, turning to face me. Amanza gasps, but I just smirk at her bluntness. I've become used to her crude and abrupt nature. Why does a woman who literally has the world at her feet need to pause for pleasantries?

"Yes," I answer truthfully. Lying to her isn't necessary, and it isn't really something I want to do.

She turns to Amanza, picks up her glass of water, and takes a sip of it before she places it back down and asks, "Was he good?" Everyone falls silent, and Amanza opens her mouth in shock.

"I... How could you be so crude?" Amanza asks.

"It was a simple question. Did you or did you not enjoy it when he fucked you?"

Amanza gapes at me.

"You can answer her however you wish," I tell her, lifting my glass and watching Anya. She doesn't once glance my way. She's watching Amanza, and despite how confident she is, Anya has the not-so-subtle skill to break anyone's resolve.

"Yes, it was good," Amanza says, her gaze darting around the table.

Patrick seems uncomfortable as he takes a sip of his whisky.

"And are you here hoping he'll fuck you again?"

"Okay, that's a little uncalled for," Patrick interjects, and Anya looks at me.

"Your friend, or business partner, whatever you wish to call each other, intends to fuck me, Patrick, so I would like to know. Definitely if he's interested in fucking other people, because there's a room back there he might let her fuck him in."

"You're starting to sound jealous, sweetheart," I say as I grab her hand that rests on the table. She freezes at the touch and most likely the insinuation. I think the only thing Anya has ever been knowingly jealous of is if another woman gives her brother attention.

She offers a sickly-sweet smile. "Just giving you

permission to fuck others who might be able to 'take their fill,' fuckface," she adds.

I lean over, rubbing my thumb over hers. "Do I need to teach you another lesson with my belt?" I whisper into her ear loud enough that everyone can hear it.

"Sure, if you actually fuck me while using it," she replies, not bothering to whisper.

My men are staring at her. Some with awe and others with fascination. She does that—holds people captive.

"You two are together?" Amanza asks. "You said you don't do relationships," she says pointedly to me.

"I don't, so don't worry," Anya says, cutting me off from answering. "So once he's had his fun, and we sort out our agreement, he's free for all your cuddles."

"That's what you think." I smirk at Anya. She eyes me and doesn't say another word as she pulls her hand out of mine.

I clasp my hands together. "Now, shall we start with dinner? And, Patrick, if you could please tell Anya about current figures, I'd be greatly appreciative."

CHAPTER 25
Anya

Amanza has eyed me, then River, then me again throughout the last dreadful hour. I glance at the time more times than I can count, wanting this to end.

It started on a high as I rode his fingers and tongue into oblivion, and now I'm forced to sit through this uncomfortable meeting. I can tell what River is trying to do; to show me how stable and profitable his business is. It's impressive, to say the least, but I'm sure he wasn't counting on the fact that his little awestruck lover was attending as well.

I stare at my half-empty glass of water as Patrick and River discuss personal matters. I think back to River's and my kiss. It keeps running through my mind. I know sex. This other fluffy shit, however, is new and uncomfortable for me. Yet I leaned into it, like discovering a new sexual position. It was deeper than anything I tried before, and he didn't even have his cock inside me. That was terrifying.

I let him take my control away when I'm so used to doing that to others.

Whatever this thing is between River and me is changing me, yet the further I lean into it, the more curious I become. The hungrier for him I am. So much so that I was willing to throw in a freebie to suck his cock so he got off just as much as me.

I'm falling. But for what, I'm not sure.

"Dessert?" River asks me, as the most beautiful piece of chocolate cake is sat in front of him. I lean in without even thinking, and he lifts his fork, which now has a piece of the cake on it, and places it in my mouth. I close my eyes, and a soft moan escapes my lips.

The table's occupants continue to chatter away around us, but it feels like it's only us sitting here.

"Remember, it's bad if you shoot me in front of all my men. So remember that before what I'm about to say."

My gaze dips to the cake. "Then you better make sure this cake is worth it."

He chuckles as he feeds me another bite, and I

know in the way that he's staring at me, he's imagining this fork is his cock instead.

"I saw where you went today at three," he admits.

A chill runs over my body, and my gaze snaps to his. His hand locks on my knee. "Don't run away. It's just a pleasant chat."

"I don't do pleasant," I reply.

"Don't I fucking know it," he says with a small laugh. "I'm not going to tell anyone."

I don't like the way he makes it sound like it's our little secret. In fact, I don't like at all the way he knows this part of me.

"For what it's worth, in third grade, I got rejected by my first crush," River says.

I scoff. "You? Rejected? Sounds like a theme."

He laughs, but it's then I realize he might be trying to... make me feel better? Share a secret? He offers me another bite of cake, and his hand gravitates up my inner thigh, eliciting goose bumps and promises of more of what happened only an hour ago.

"Where are your birth parents?" he asks.

I chew the cake, eyeing him.

"Dead for all I know," I reply with a shrug. I look around the table, uncomfortable with the personal questions. Then I realize he probably already knows all of this. I have a file on him as well, but I find myself asking, "Where are yours?"

He fills my glass of water to the top, and I take a massive mouthful, feeling suddenly parched.

"My mother lives back home in a house I pay for." He cuts off another bite of cake and lifts the fork to my mouth. I'm not into this feeding shit, but I take satisfaction in the way Amanza's gaze is burning into the side of my head. I don't think of myself as a petty woman, but while I'm forced to sit through this, I might as well ruin someone's hopes and dreams.

When I don't continue the conversation, River asks, "Why the fascination with jewelry?"

"It's obvious, isn't it? I like pretty things that sparkle." I open my mouth, and he slides the fork in. Just as he does, Vance comes up behind me and leans down to whisper in my ear.

"Meredith called," he reports. Fuck me, the old bitch is going to be on my case now that she knows about Alek's disappearance.

"Who is Meredith?" River asks. From his reports, he most likely already knows she's my foster mother. She does, however, have two names, so he might not be so familiar with the other one.

"My foster mother," I say dismissively as I stand. I know better than to ignore Meredith. Alek and I learned quickly that the consequences of making her wait were not worth it. I'm not sure, though, if this summons has to do with Alek being MIA or her wanting to wiggle her way into this deal with River.

"Do you plan to fuck Amanza?" I ask him because I know she's listening. Maybe this will give him a opportunity to distract himself elsewhere. At least that way, I might not have this tiny nagging voice asking something else of River. Something I never want to address with any man.

"No, I plan to fuck you and only you," he replies as he stands.

I press a hand to his chest. "We aren't exclusive," I inform him. "My pussy will be your payment as discussed, then once the debt is paid, we end and are back to business only."

That arrogant smile returns as he says, "If you say so." He forks another piece of the cake, but instead of offering it to me, he places it in his mouth. I hate his boyish smugness.

Vance walks back over then and says, "She requests your presence immediately." I didn't realize Clay still had a phone to his ear. Is that old bitch still on the phone with him? "What should I tell her?"

"While this has been fun, meeting your men, and a woman you've fucked, I have business of my own to attend to," I state. I look at Patrick and give him a smile and a nod. His gaze tracks me up and down as he takes me in. I keep my smile in place as I look at Amanza before I turn to River. "Pleasure."

He shakes his head. "We're not done. I haven't finished my meeting."

"Rain check, then," I say smugly.

"I have to escort Anya. Please, enjoy whatever is on the menu." He reaches for his phone and slides it into his pocket, looking at me. "I'll take you."

"I have my men," I remind him.

"Why do you have men?" Amanza questions, and I turn to see her studying me. "Isn't River protection enough?"

I scoff. "Excuse me?" Clearly, this bitch doesn't know who I am if she thinks I need to depend on the likes of River for security.

She looks behind me to Vance and Clay. I can tell she likes what she sees, so it unfurls an ugly side to my scathing personality.

I lean over with my hand on the table, as if I'm letting her in on a secret. "Sometimes I let them fuck me with their mouths. Other times, it's for protection. But mostly, it's because I can afford eye candy instead of hiding behind an innocent girl's persona. Is that all?"

"I don't know what he sees in you," she says, shocked by my words.

"That's enough," River says to Amanza, who's stunned that she's being scolded, as he places his hand on my lower back before he steers me away.

I tentatively look at the fork on the table, and River casually pushes it away. "You're not stabbing someone with a fork in my restaurant," he whispers into my ear. It's loud enough for her to hear, and her eyes go wide.

"At least your restaurant might be known for something, then," I reply as I smile and wriggle my fingers at her to say goodbye.

"Sir, are you leaving already?" Michael asks as he stands at the other end of the table.

"Deal with the rest of the evening for me, Michael. I'm escorting Anya."

"Sorry?" I say. "Our evening together is done."

"It's done when I say it is," River says as he guides me to the entrance. The two cars are already waiting as my guards step out behind us into the cool evening air.

River opens the passenger door of his car and addresses my men. "I'll be taking her." They don't take orders from him, so they look at me instead. I internally sigh. Fuck, this asshole is determined. I don't like the idea of introducing anyone to Meredith, but who knows, maybe she'll throw a kitchen knife at him and put me out of my misery.

I give a simple nod, and he shuts my door before he rounds the hood and gets in the car.

"Where am I going?" he asks as he rolls up his sleeves to reveal his tattooed arms. I tell him Meredith's address as he drives. I look at my phone, out of habit now, hopeful that Alek might've replied.

"You were jealous," he says after a moment of silence.

"W-what?" I choke out.

"You asked about Amanza because you were jealous."

A crazed laugh escapes me. Me? Jealous? Impossible.

"No, let's not get our facts wrong. I was not jealous, Lake." I smile at him.

"If you say so, Tanya."

"I do say so," I tell him, not taking my eyes off him. "Is this whole facade a power thing? You want me because I'm powerful and you're curious how I fuck?"

"No," he says calmly. I'm disappointed that he doesn't give me more bite.

"So why?"

"It's an Anya thing," he says with a smirk. "Though, I do want to know how you fuck. I want to know how else to elicit those noises from you when cake isn't involved." He turns to look at me then, and I try to hide the smile that dares mar my usual unmoving features.

"I like cake."

"And jewels," he adds.

"Yes, I'm a simple girl with simple pleasures," I say, and as it leaves my mouth, it sounds like a lie.

"You are far from simple, Red. I doubt you have a simple bone in your fucking body."

CHAPTER 26

Anya

I lick my lips as I look away from River and see Meredith's mansion come into view. As soon as we pull up, the front door opens, and the old bitch is on her porch in a silk robe, hair in a messy bun, with big-ass earrings hanging from her ears, waiting impatiently.

I open the car door before River has the chance, and when he gets out of the car, she narrows her gaze on him. Perhaps it wasn't such a great idea to bring him after all. Wishful thinking and all, she might still sic the dogs on him.

My eyebrows knit in confusion at the spatula in her hand.

"You didn't care to tell me Alek's galivanting around the countryside after some dancer? It's better if he ends up dead," she seethes as she points the spatula in my direction.

I walk two steps ahead of River as she pins him with a glare, her lips pressed into a thin line. She looks him up and down before her gaze rolls back over to me. "And you bring me back a boyfriend? Have I taught you and your brother nothing?" she scoffs, then turns back to head into the house, waving the spatula for us to follow her inside.

Into the lioness's den we go. Because the old bitch is nothing if not unpredictable when in a bad mood. I know because she raised me to be the same.

When we close the door, I take my heels off at the door, and River removes his shoes too.

"She seems..."

"Crazy," I finish for him. "But you're not allowed to say that. Only I am. And besides, you insisted on coming along."

In all the years I lived here, and those after, not much has changed. The old bitch took a liking to traditional Japanese housing design and so built her own modern version with paper sliding doors for all the main gathering rooms. She also liked the idea of everyone taking their shoes off at the door, which made for a wicked time for Alek and me as we stole guests' shoes from time to time.

Meredith has a thing for consistency. It's why everything about her regal ass hasn't changed one bit. I'm pretty sure if I were to walk into my old bedroom, it would be untouched. I often wonder if Alek is the way he is today because of her, with his no-touching thing. Perhaps because she was so peculiar on cleanliness and where items were placed that he formed his own aversion to filth. But I doubt that, and never really dug deeper because I understood that was his issue, no matter how close we are. All I know for sure is that the way she molded us left a distinct impression.

I follow the smell of something burning in the kitchen.

"For fuck's sake," she curses as she throws a tray of muffins on the oversized island. Not once have I seen her in here. And her skills show it.

"Are you trying to burn the house down?" I ask.

"Very funny, smartass," she says in her thick Russian accent. "The doctor said I should take up a hobby. It'll be good for me, she says." She lifts a cigarette to her mouth and takes a drag, then blows out a cloud of smoke.

"I'm sure the doctor could recommend cutting some things out," I say pointedly. *If you don't want to end up dead,* I add to myself.

The old bitch looks at River and then me. "Where

are your guards?"

"They're not needed in order to visit you, are they?" I ask diplomatically. But I know it's the foreign man in her kitchen who she doesn't trust. I know better than to introduce River, because Meredith prefers when people make way for her. She says you can read a lot about someone in the way they introduce themselves, and I don't make the mistake to do it for him.

She opens the top drawer, pulls out a gun, and places it on the counter.

I roll my eyes. "Meredith, I don't think that's necessary."

Her eyebrows shoot up. "No? Because right now your brother is missing because he's chasing pussy, and you seem distracted because of..." She waves her hand toward River and loses her words. "He's beautiful, I'll give him that. But you two have lost your ever-fucking minds."

"He and I are nothing," I'm quick to say, denying her insinuation about me and River. But River barges past me and holds out his hand with a cunning smile.

"The name is River, ma'am." I cringe at his use of "ma'am," and he doesn't miss it either. He just looks at me and shoots me a small smirk.

"Oh, would you look at that... it speaks," she says

condescendingly as she takes another puff, ignoring his outstretched hand.

He smiles. "You two are more alike than I expected."

"Flattery won't get you anywhere here, boy," she snarks back.

"Who said it was a compliment?" he replies sweetly.

Her eyebrows shoot up, and she turns to me. "I can see why you might've caught her attention," Meredith says over the counter as she pours herself a glass of whiskey and then a second and hands it to River.

I've only ever seen him drink scotch, but he accepts it.

You can't be serious? There's no way he can win over this old bitch.

"River who?" she asks, properly appraising him.

I roll my eyes and sit on a stool at the counter. River remains standing at the edge, closest to the door, and I hope it's an intentional exit strategy, because he might need it.

"River Bently," he tells her.

Meredith looks into her whiskey as she swirls it with a cigarette hanging from her fingers. "Born and raised in Los Angeles, mother is a widow, and you run one of the largest gun selling businesses worldwide. Am I missing anything?"

Oh, I forgot to mention her photographic memory.

"Yes, but how did you..." River says, tensing his shoulders.

"Meredith has a photographic memory, and she keeps tabs on anyone of importance who steps into town," I inform him.

"Meredith..." River says, brows pinched, and it's rather nice and unusual watching him only figure out something now. "I know that name."

Because if he looked into Alek's and my foster papers, he would've seen a Miranda Petrov signed on the dotted line. What's not on the records is the handsome price she paid to ensure we were handed to her.

"I'm sure you do, kid." She nods.

River looks at me then.

"You were raised by Meredith Fork," he says, eyeing me. "I get it. I get why you are who you are." He looks back at Meredith, a new revelation sparking in his eyes. "You were known for your high-quality, no-nonsense bullshit. Cutthroat and one of the first and only women to run drugs and ammo. I heard rumor of you when I first started, but that your business was taken over by the Ivanov siblings."

"Taken over or handed down, depending on what intel you choose to believe. If someone like me was taken down by the siblings, then they were someone not to be trifled with from the very start," she says to him. "I gave them the perfect head start."

She pins me with a stare. "It's not easy being a woman in this line of business. You have to be more ruthless than any man. You'll be wise to remember that, girl."

"Meredith has retired," I inform him, ignoring her not-so-subtle dig.

I'm reconsidering whether I should've brought River here at all now. Meredith has had lovers. Men at her beck and call. But having a man in your life permanently was a weakness to her.

I don't know why she would look at River in any other way.

"Big shoes to fill," River says in salute as he takes a sip of the whiskey.

"It would appear this generation gets distracted easily," the old bitch tosses out, specifically for me.

"I'm pretty sure there's been no complaints about the retirement fund you sit on and the monthly income you receive to give you all the time in the world to bake and burn fucking muffins," I say back.

"I'm surprised, Anya, how quickly you've replaced

Alek," she purrs, flicking the ash off her cigarette. "What's it been... three, four months since Alek disappeared? You've never learned how to be alone, have you?"

"I've only ever known how to be alone," I snap. And her cold, calculated gaze is fixated on me. The rest of the sentence goes unsaid. *I've only ever known how to be alone because of you.*

She offers a sharp, antagonizing smile. "Yes, so I passed my business down to these two. Who have been doing great before I found out about Alek," she says through clenched teeth to River. "So you can't blame a mother for being concerned if the empire is going to shit."

"Everything is fine," I grit out.

She hmphs at me and takes a sip of her whisky. "So he decided to chase the dancer after all? Stupid, stupid boy. I told him to stay away."

She pulls out a bag of flour and a new bowl.

"You know about her?" I ask, my eyebrows knitting in confusion.

River has since put his whiskey down and gravitated closer to me. I don't know if he thinks it's some kind of comfort, but I make sure to be out of arm's reach in front of Meredith. Any type of touch, attachment, or endearment is viewed as a weakness.

I have only myself to blame for letting him come, but I'm not sure I could've stopped him either.

"Of course I do. You think I don't still have my own informants? I don't know much about the girl, and frankly, I don't care. She's a nobody." Her accent slips out thicker. It always does when she's scolding me or thinks someone has underestimated her intelligence.

"You think I don't notice when one of my children becomes besotted with something or someone? I never thought he'd be stupid enough to actually chase after her. She's most likely been sold, and he presumes with all his money and power he could buy her back. Little does he know the market in Russia is deadlier than here." She shakes her head.

"Do you know her name?" I ask, thinking of the photo I received from the orphanage. Could it be the same girl?

She scoffs. "Of course I do. Cinita Aetos."

I shake my head in disbelief. "She was a girl from our orphanage."

The old bitch rolls her eyes. "Nothing good came from that place, I swear. I don't even know how they got back in touch."

I don't bite back at her underhanded comment. Because Alek and I would never be good enough. She's harder on me because I'm a woman in the man's world she stepped away from for reasons I don't entirely understand. Someone as power- and money-hungry as Meredith does not simply slip away. Or perhaps I've never truly understood Meredith at all.

"Do you plan to do anything about it?" she asks me. "Or do you plan to fuck your boyfriend here and pretend everything is okay in la-la land?"

"Boyfriend does have a nice ring to it, doesn't it?" River says, ignoring her insult. It further pisses me off.

"He's an acquaintance, nothing more," I remind him and her.

"Nothing more, huh?" River says with a smirk. The old bitch is watching us like a hawk, and I can tell she doesn't like what she sees. I'm not sure I entirely do either. I stand and push the stool back.

"Of course I'm trying to find him. You know more than anyone how difficult it can be to find Alek when he chooses not to be found."

She scoffs at that, probably remembering how Alek and I were as mischievous children and ungrateful teenagers.

"Since I don't have anything to update you about Alek, we're leaving. Good luck with your muffins."

"You may be a boss, Anya, but you will treat me with more respect," she scolds. "Don't think you are untouchable."

I offer a sharp smile. "Mother, that almost sounds like a threat."

"Don't think you're too old to not have your ass handed to you," she quips.

"I'd like to see you try," I reply as I lean across the counter, a flash of adrenaline coursing through me as both our gazes dip to the gun between us.

"Have a good evening, Meredith," I say as I push off the counter and turn my back to her. River quietly follows, and it's strange in the way he was silent for most of the conversation. Then again, that shouldn't have been a conversation he was a part of. It's no secret Alek is missing. But I wonder if he will exploit me with the knowledge of who my foster mother truly is.

We put our shoes on and walk out the front door.

"Is it always like that between you and Meredith?" he asks.

"Sometimes we throw knives at a target for sport. You don't do that with your mother?" I ask, and I can tell he doesn't know if I'm joking or not. I'm not.

"So, are you going to fuck me now so we can be done with this arrangement?" I ask.

He chuckles as he opens the car door for me. "Don't get your panties in a twist at me, Red. I told you to stay at dinner, didn't I?"

CHAPTER 27
River

I take her back to her place. She eyes me suspiciously as I stop the car but make no move to get out.

"I didn't agree to my place," she says.

"I know."

"So why are we back here?"

"Because I'm dropping you off, not fucking you."

"Fuck me, you're worse than a woman. Can you just make up your mind?" She whips her seat belt off. She's been in a sour mood since leaving Meredith's. All the snide remarks and digs the woman tossed Anya's way were obvious.

Anya having a man in her life is obviously frowned upon. It's viewed as a weakness, and I have my work cut out for me helping her unlearn all the conditioning that has kept her safe in this world for so long.

Those gorgeous eyes glare at me through narrowed lids as she says, "This is over. You didn't accept payment, and I owe you nothing." She turns to open the car door without waiting for me to speak.

I grab her wrist. "You do, Anya. You so fucking do."

"I don't get it with you. I've attended your business meetings, so all that's left is to fuck. You say you like the taste of my pussy, but what? Can't you get it up to fuck me?" Her face goes solemn. "Are you using me to get to Vance and Clay? Is that it? Because I'm totally okay with you fucking them as long as I can watch."

I grab for her cheeks, but she slaps my hands away. "Don't fucking touch me."

A lock of hair falls out of her tight bun, and she pushes it to the side to ensure her immaculate appearance doesn't have a fault.

I want to smack the brat out of her. She has no idea how much of a chokehold she has on me. Has had from the very first day. I'll play this game for as long as I have to until I finally wear her down. Until, little by little, she lets me in and sees me as her equal. I want to discover every bit there is to know about this woman and her beautiful, powerful mind and body.

I lick my lips. "Do you know what I want, Anya? The real you. Not the woman you present to the rest of the world. Not just parts of you. *All* of you. And not just for sex."

She scoffs and then looks at me again. A cynical expression crosses her features, and I notice Vance approaching the car in the glow of her front porch lights. "You can't be serious, River. It was only ever a business deal. Don't tell me you're actually falling for me?"

"What if I am?" I ask pointedly.

She laughs, deranged and lethal. "I don't do this shit." She waves her finger between us. "I do sex, money, drugs, auctions, and everything between. But a relationship? You're out of your goddamn mind."

"You're the only one out of your fucking mind, Anya. You're crazy and beautiful and intelligent. And icy as all hell, but I fucking love those things about you."

Silence fills the car, and she turns a paler shade. I realize too late what triggered her.

"Anya, I said I love those thing about you, not that I—"

She lifts her hand up and points her finger gun at

me as I reach for her, and I can see Vance pull out his gun and aim it in my direction. "Don't touch me, River. You don't know me. And if you won't fuck me, then there is nothing else between us," she says in a clipped tone.

"I won't abandon you like your brother. If you'll have me—" I cut myself off abruptly. If looks could kill, I would be dead.

"You have no right to speak of my brother. We're done."

She opens the car door, and I reach for her again. "Anya, stop being a brat and let's talk about this like adults."

She slams the door shut, and my knuckles turn white over the steering wheel. I'm so furious with myself for being open with her. I should've kept my mouth shut. What's even more infuriating is how powerful this woman is, yet how quick she is to crumble with the thought of what others might think if she were to give us a chance. No, not others. Meredith.

I roll my window down. "I'm not done with you, Red."

"Get off my property!" She plucks the gun from Vance's hand and points it in my direction.

I'm livid as I carve up the stones on her driveway

when I start to pull away. Then I hear a bang, and my tire pops before another shot goes off.

Fucking crazy bitch.

She's my undoing and everything I still fucking want.

I drive, swerving uncontrollably down her driveway.

I'm fucking furious as I grab my phone and send a text to Will.

Me: I want everything on Meredith Fork. Hurry the fuck up about Alek Ivanov as well. I'll double your payment.

I don't like the old bitch who was able to crumble my she-devil, whether Anya likes to admit it or not. Something is fucked up about this foster shit, and I don't think it's dumb luck that the two were taken in by someone as cunning as Meredith Fork.

CHAPTER 28
Anya

I haven't heard from River for a week, and I'm grateful for it. I've concentrated on my work and finding Alek, which should be my only focuses. Not entertaining some gun dealer.

I'm in the main room at one of my auction sites. It's usually my favorite auction, but I have nothing to be excited about despite the thriving first half of the evening. I weave through the seated patrons, anticipating the second half as my waitstaff tends to their needs.

I find myself looking over to where River sat last time, half expecting the arrogant asshole to be sitting there. He's not. The person sitting in his spot looks baffled as to why I'm looking in his direction.

I turn and head for my private room. Clay and

Vance trail behind me and enter the room. "Have they found something more on the dancer?" I ask, hopeful.

"Yes and no, miss," Vance says. "Much like your brother, the dancer seems to have gone off grid. In fact, she hasn't been seen for five months now."

I plop into my chair behind my desk and throw my hands up in bewilderment. She can't be found because she's most likely dead.

The only reason why I care even a little about this dancer is because if I find her, I'll find Alek, right?

"Why is this so fucking difficult?!" I demand from them, slapping the new file on my desk. "I don't need outdated information. I need to know where the fuck my brother is!"

Clay steps behind me and begins to massage my shoulders. I'm riddled with knots and tension. "Miss, it's most likely because Alek knows how your men operate and how to avoid them. He'll come home."

I laugh, almost half crazed. "It's a fucking cry for help if you're giving me sympathy, Clay."

He says nothing as Vance drops to his knees in front of me. "We can help release your tension, miss." And he almost looks hopeful. It's like a cold wash of reality because why the fuck don't I find my men attractive anymore? River Bently, that's why.

Fuck.

"I just need to be alone for a few minutes," I tell them. They look at one another but take the hint and leave the room. I hear the second half of the auctions begin as I put my head in my hands.

What the fuck am I doing?

My phone rings, and my specific ringtone for Alek startles me into sliding the screen more than once to answer. Alek's name appears on the screen, and my heart beats through my chest.

"Alek," I say in a rushed breath as I answer.

"Call your guard dog off, Anya," he growls into the phone.

I'm still so stunned that it's finally him that all I can say is, "My what?"

"I'll kill him. Call him off now. I don't care if you have feelings for him. If he fucks up what I'm doing and gets her killed, I will kill River Bently," he says and hangs up. I'm shocked and confused. And now the room is quiet. What the fuck?

I hit call, but he doesn't answer. I call another three times.

On the fourth ring, I get his voicemail, and I unload.

"What the fuck was that, Alek? Are you serious? The first and only thing you have to say to me is a fucking threat? Do you realize the shit I've been going through here to keep this business afloat, and you can't even give me a proper fucking explanation? I hope your dancer does fucking die. In fact, I might put a hit on her myself so you're done with this stupid puppy love shit."

I hang up and do everything I can not to absolutely lose my shit. But it's not enough. I need an outlet. The first thing I grab is the keyboard, and I fling it across the room. The next is a glass that explodes against the wall. Anything I can manage to grab explodes in one way or another as I do everything I can not to cry. I will turn this room upside down and burn the building to the ground, all to prevent myself from fucking crying.

No man will make me cry. Not even Alek.

A tap comes on the door. "Fuck off!" I scream.

But it opens anyway. I grab the gun from my drawer and point it in the direction of the door, licking my lips. I don't give a shit who it is. I just need a release.

"Well," Meredith says as she looks around the room, unfazed by the gun. "Put that gun down, girl, before you hurt somebody with it."

I consider her for a moment, and she raises an eyebrow in warning.

"What the fuck have you done to this room?" she

asks as she steps in and closes the door behind her. "Another tantrum?"

My temple throbs. "There was a bug. What are you doing here anyway? I didn't get a call or an ASAP demand." I lean back in the chair.

Meredith is wearing a long, loose dress that's bright red. Her hair is up in a bun, and I wonder if I adopted her styling along the way. I must have. My hair is always up, I'm only ever in red or black, and I'm sure I have her attitude. Even if she isn't my biological mother, she's the only mother we've really known.

"Can't a mother check on her daughter's business?" she asks as she dusts off a part of the seat across from me.

I narrow my gaze on her. *Daughter's business*. I'm not her daughter.

"No, she can't. Aren't you supposed to be baking muffins or something in your retired life?"

"About that. I think it's time I pick up the reins again and try to straighten out this fiasco," she says.

"I'm sorry, what?" I ask, trying to figure out if I heard her right.

"You're a mess, sweetheart. I thought you might be able to do this without Alek, but it appears it's too hard for you."

My eyebrows furrow in confusion. "You're fucking

with me, right? What part do you think is going amiss? Everything is still running as smoothly as ever. I make sure it does."

She gives me a patronizing stare. "Not if you're galivanting around with a man who is clearly only using you to benefit himself. Anya, darling, how many times have I told you not to fall for a man?"

I lick my lips, trying to moisten my dry mouth. "Not that it's any of your concern, but the same man you're talking about is the very same one I shot at through his car a week ago."

Her gaze is piercing as she says, "You said you shot *at* him, not that you actually shot him, Anya. I know how good your aim is. You've become soft."

I choke on her accusation. "Are you serious right now?"

"Your man has put feelers out on me. He's trying to investigate a gun deal that went wrong way before I took you and your brother in. I don't like people trying to bring up the past. So either you deal with him, or I will."

I'm in shock. Because both she and Alek have said the same thing.

River's obviously snooping where his nose doesn't belong.

"I'll deal with him. I don't need your assistance," I state.

She raises her eyebrows again, mockingly. "I've heard that before. Have you heard from Alek yet?"

I lick my lips as I reassess the old bitch. Something's off. Whether it's because of River or not... something is different.

"No, I haven't," I lie. "I'm still trying to track down the dancer after you gave me her name. You?"

"When was the last time that boy called me, even when he was in town? Tell me if he makes contact."

"Is that all?" I ask, but she just stares and stares, that patronizing gaze unraveling my last fucking nerve. How dare she come in here and think she can so easily take over once again. Ten years later and she thinks she's in charge because she says so. I haven't worked my ass off to simply hand it over.

I *am* the Ivanov auctions.

I will bury someone for it.

"What?" I demand when she continues to stare.

"Sometimes I worry I carved you too closely to mirror me," she muses. "Then, at other times, I realize you're still that needy child inside. You've always been so reliant on Alek. It makes you weak."

"He's my twin," I remind her. "And part of the

reason you were able to retire in such a lavish lifestyle, so respect is due."

"Yes, but now there is only you, dear. I suggest you remember that," she says, a hint of warning in her tone.

"We are all each other had. I know Alek. He'll return."

Sitting back in the chair, she places her hands behind her head and gives me a pitying look. "If you say so."

I want to reach for the letter opener right now and lodge it in her throat. Instead, I turn away to calm myself. She always knows how to trigger me, as if daring me to lay a finger on her. She pushes me to remind me that her word is law. Or so she thinks. "Being a woman in this business is always difficult, Anya. You should know this. How many attempts on our lives were there?" she says.

My lips curve up into a tight smile. Hers wasn't the worst foster care home we'd gone to. But overall, she'd been the most twisted.

"Why would you bring kids into a world like this?" I question. It's something I never wanted an answer to before. When I walk through the hallways of the orphanage, I can never think about bringing them into this world. As heartless as I might be, I'm not that cruel.

"Hmm. Truthfully, I thought children would work in my favor for a few of my business dealings. The Italian Mafia are big on family. I was a single woman. If they saw I had a family, they might have been less inclined to kill me and persuade business deals because they thought we had common values." She smiles. "It worked only for one deal, and then I was stuck with you two."

"At first, you were both annoying, but you learned and adapted quickly; you more so than your brother. He followed in your footsteps not long after," she says. "And I saw my empire grow. I saw potential in you."

It doesn't hurt like it should. I'm not at all surprised since I didn't expect anything maternal from her whatso-ever, but it's the ease with which she states it that's unset-tling. We may be alike in so many ways, but there was a line I would not cross. I would not take the innocence of a child for my gain in any way. Especially considering how my brother and I were stripped of ours far too soon.

"That's fucked up," I tell her.

"Yes, I suppose it is." She shrugs. "But look at you now."

"Yeah, look at us now," I mumble angrily. My

brother is God knows where, and my first real contact with him in months was him yelling at me. Not once did he ask about me, let alone our business. And the business is just as important to him as it is to me. At least that's what I always thought, but maybe I was wrong about that as well.

"Take it over. It was always meant to be yours, Anya. Announce your brother's death. Let him live his fantasy chasing some dancer. Your brother only ever stayed because of his loyalty to you, and now that's shifted."

My head whips in her direction. "What do you mean?"

"He hated the business, hated that you lit up every time you learned something new."

"He did not." He would have told me.

"But then he discovered the ruthless side of it. Not just the drugs and other things, but his first kill when he was a teenager and how he enjoyed it. That's why he stayed."

I remember the first time he killed someone. Afterward was when I noticed he started wearing gloves. I don't know exactly what happened, but he changed after that.

One thing I know is that Alek and I have one another's back, no matter what.

Even amongst all this shit, we have each other.

"The business was meant for you. It's time, Anya, for you to grow up and claim it. Or I will take it back."

"He *will* come back," I promise her, and it goes unsaid that she'll never lay a hand on our auctions. She had her business in the past, but these auctions are ours.

"But he may not."

I never thought the day would come when Alek would abandon me. The voice telling me that he'll return grows smaller as time ticks by. The old bitch is right about most things. But not that. Alek won't leave me forever, will he?

"Get rid of your 'not' boyfriend. He's a problem," she says as she stands.

Why is River looking into my family?

Maybe it's as the old bitch says; perhaps he's been using me this whole time. He's made it clear he wants in on the business, so did he think fucking me was the only way to get it? But if that were the case, then why hasn't he fucked me yet?

Deep down, I know River isn't after that, but I can't help but be hindered by the self-doubt Meredith lays there. It's a dangerous world we work in. Lies and trickery are a constant. What if I'm betraying my own instincts to make room for River? What if Meredith is right?

When did I allow myself to have a high enough opinion of him that I could... trust him? No, absolutely not. I shut that thought down. I can't put myself in any vulnerable position.

"I'll be watching you carefully, Anya. You can't trust anyone but me, remember that." Her tone is far more bitter than the sinking feeling in my gut at the thought that River might be tricking me. But I know that's not the case. Isn't it? Or am I only being a fool? *He is nothing to me*, I remind myself.

She walks out without a goodbye, not that I expected anything more from her. I never have.

CHAPTER 29

River

My phone buzzes, and the profile picture that appears with her ringtone pops up. My cock immediately goes stiff at the image of her lifting her top, revealing those perfectly pierced nipples and the earrings I bought her.

I ignore her call and focus back on the papers.

"It might be dangerous looking into Meredith Fork's history," Michael suggests, yet again. And I ignore him. Again.

I know it is, which is why I sent a fake tip-off so she thinks I'm looking into something so trivial as a gun deal that went wrong, because that's not what I'm interested in. What I'm interested in is the photo I'm looking at right now.

Meredith, with a drink in hand, as she sits with a

Mr. and Mrs. Ivanov. I don't find it a coincidence that she fostered them from the orphanage. It took Will a week to uncover this photo among thousands of other images and dealings she's had in the past. Now he's working to figure out their association.

A woman like Meredith doesn't have a heart or a care in the world for children, so why did she take the twins in? And where the fuck did Anya's parents go? She's always so flippant about their whereabouts.

"Sir, if I may. Your obsession with Anya Ivanov might be putting you at risk," Michael says.

"Michael, are you really set on pissing me off today?" I ask.

"No, sir. I serve you, which means I also offer my council. Either the Ivanovs allow you to do business here and further integrate into their auctions or they don't."

"They will."

In silence, he nods.

My phone buzzes with a photo of Alek Ivanov, dated today.

I smile. *Finally, I've found him*, I think to myself. Until a message follows.

Will: He gave me the slip, but I'm on his tail. You better triple my rate. This guy shot at me twice, and I had a bullet pulled out of my shoulder because of it.

Close. I'm close.

Never in a million years did I think I would be searching halfway around the world for another man.

Fuck, maybe I really am whipped. And all I've had is a taste.

CHAPTER 30
Anya

I f the fucker won't answer his phone, then I'll go to him. When I walk into the restaurant, the hostess tries to stop me but is quick to trip over her own feet as she realizes who I am and evidently sees the expression on my face. I am *not* fucking around today. Vance and Clay flank me, half the restaurant watching on as I ascend the stairs.

"Excuse me, you can't be up there," she says from behind me. Unless she plans to put her hands on me, I don't see how she'll be able to stop me.

I spot River right away, in the same way his gaze gravitates to me. Next to him is his accountant, Patrick, plus the very charming Amanza. Great, another reason to fucking hate this place.

The few men he has sitting at his table make no

attempt to stop me as I approach, and I feel everyone's eyes on me. I stand at the opposite end of the table from where River is sitting.

There are a few new faces here, and one of them daringly smiles as he says, "Why don't you come and sit on my lap, princess?"

I arch an eyebrow and raise my finger to River before he says anything. "Princess?" I say, throwing my head back and laughing before I look back at River.

"Should I go and sit on your man's lap since he asked so nicely?" I ask. "Considering you can't even answer my calls or fill my pussy with your cock, maybe your man here is a better option."

Amanza chokes on her drink, and the guy who called me princess has turned a shade of green, now realizing that I'm not a woman to be trifled with.

River is staring at me, those hypnotizing eyes locked on mine. And they say so much and so little at the same time.

"C'mon, River, I can be a princess, can't I?" I coo and lean down so my cleavage is on full display for him. Not once does his gaze wander from mine.

"I wonder if he'll call me a princess when I walk over there and bite his fucking lips off," I whisper across the table. His jaw tics, and I stand at my full height again. I need his bite. Something to attack and make me feel better.

"Your mouth goes anywhere near another man, I will cut off their dick and feed it to you for breakfast," he growls, and everyone shrinks into their chairs. *There he is.*

"Then why don't you keep your promise?" I question, dragging my hand over each one of his men's heads as I stride alongside the table until I come to a stop at River and loom over him.

"You seem to be in a mood today," he says casually.

I cock an insincere smile. This man has done nothing but patronize me for the past few months, and now he's giving me the cold shoulder. Why? Because I shot a few bullets at his car? Boo-fucking-hoo. Buy a new one.

"You have no idea. We need to talk," I say.

He grabs me and tugs me onto his lap, his hand wrapping around my throat. "You need to stay for dessert first."

"So many promises with such little follow through," I spit. But my core floods from his scent and touch. All my wrath and fury begin to slip, but I cling to them desperately because they're the only things I feel safe in. And River brings up unknown feelings and desires.

River addresses the table. "I shouldn't have to repeat myself, but if anyone is to go near this woman, I'll feed you to my dogs," he growls out.

I lean in to whisper in his ear, "It's a bit of a lame threat, considering you don't even have dogs."

"I do have dogs, actually. They arrived last week," he says. "And I don't need to hear lame threats coming from you, someone who just promised to bite someone's lips off."

"Wait, so you do have dogs?" I ask.

"Are you joking?" he asks me. "Are you really fucking joking right now? That's what gets you to smile? My fucking dogs?"

I school my features. I had no idea I was even smiling at him. This is bad, yet I find myself saying, "Yes, I love dogs."

Fuck, what is this man doing to me?

I remove his hand from around my throat, missing the touch, but I need to claim my power again. I came in here planning to wreak havoc, yet I'm sitting on his lap like some kind of fucking good girl. Yet there's something comfortable in it that I don't understand.

"We need to talk," I tell him again.

"You can wait until we've had dessert."

Fine, if he won't do as I say, then I'll give him no other choice but to excuse himself.

I pin Amanza with a stare. "Hi, Amanza, have you fucked River lately?"

She chokes on her drink again and stares at me wide-eyed.

"You can answer truthfully," I say to her. "I promise I won't go crazy." I make a cross sign over my heart at the words. She just eyes me like I'm crazy.

Okay, maybe I am a little crazy.

"No secrets among this table, right? Because people get killed for that, don't they?" I say pointedly to River.

"Anya, I know what you're doing," River says.

"I'm just asking a question, girl to girl. Have you two fucked yet?"

"No. No, we have not." She shakes her head. "You're a bit of a bitch, aren't you?"

I laugh, surprised that this little mouse actually has a backbone. "I've been called worse. Just so you know, you can have him. He's been giving me nothing but limp dick vibes."

River's hand goes to my pussy and he grabs me there, hard. "Do you really think of yourself as a clever girl for saying these things in front of my men?"

My body rolls into his touch, grateful for the thin fabric I wore today. I realize, despite how angry I am at him, I *have* to fuck River Bently. I need him out of my system so I can put a bullet through his brains for the havoc he's causing me.

"Do you think you can just give me away?" he says into my ear, and the others at the table avert their gazes.

"Well, since you aren't fucking me, I guessed you were getting it elsewhere."

"Oh, we're going to fuck, Red. You still have a debt that's owed," he growls.

"Maybe Amanza wants to watch?" I purr and turn to Amanza. "Do you want to watch? I mean, he's told me he would fuck me before and left me high and dry, so you may end up disappointed like I was." I smirk.

"That's it." He stands, and as he does, he picks me up and places me on my feet, keeping hold of my waist.

"Michael, you can finish up here. Seems someone needs a cock in her fucking mouth to learn to keep our business private."

I drop the good girl charade and pull out of his grasp. "Finally, we can get to business. I need to speak with you."

The hostess avoids my gaze as we walk out the front door.

"Get in the car," he growls. "And it's not a suggestion. And no, your men aren't going to be following us," he says as he opens the passenger door. I signal to my men to stay back.

I can handle River Bently, even if this goes bad.

I slide into the car and wait for him to get in on the other side.

"We're getting this fucking blackmail shit out of the way, and then we need to discuss my brother—"

He angles my head toward him and slams his lips against mine. Hard, impatient, and unrelenting. His tongue slides easily through my parted lips, and I melt into him. One week was too long. No, I shouldn't be craving this part of him. This isn't what I came for. Yet my body acts on its own, pulling him in closer by the collar.

Am I actually crazy?

Have I really fallen?

No. It's not possible.

Who had I ever kissed before River Bently?

I don't even remember.

But his kiss makes up for all the ones I don't recall.

Just as I go to slide my hands through his hair, he pulls back, that gaze telling me more than I can understand in words.

River Bently is a dangerous man because he doesn't just want my business.

He wants *me*.

I can't betray my family for him, can I?

"You took too long to return, Red."

"I don't chase," I say as I lean back, trying to sort through my thoughts.

"Last time I saw you, you were shooting holes into my car. So that gives room for a little bit of groveling."

I bark a laugh. "Me? Grovel? River, are you going to fuck me tonight or not?"

"I thought you once said you do the fucking," he says with an arrogant smile. "We'll talk business after."

"And then that's it. We're done after that, right?"

He laughs. "Oh, Anya, we've only just begun."

CHAPTER 31

River

My dogs are barking the minute we pull up to my house and I park in the garage. They arrived the day after Anya successfully freaked the fuck out over a kiss, and I was so fucking happy to see both of them. Getting out of the car and moving to the other side to open her door, she steps out and follows me through the garage. She looks at my multitude of sports cars.

"You like cars," she notes.

"You like shiny jewels. We all have our vices," I tell her.

She already asked on the way over what breed my dogs are—Chow Chows. They're temperamental little fucks, but also the best.

I know she's not here just to see my dogs.

She wants this agreement to end between us, but I want it to continue.

I still don't know enough about Meredith's connection to her parents, and I've decided I won't yet say anything until I have all the facts.

"Did you grow up with dogs?" I ask as I lead her to the door from the garage into the main house.

"No, Meredith is allergic," she says, walking behind me.

The dogs' barking has shifted from the front door to the garage door, and it's only increased. They know someone else is with me.

"Don't pet them. Let them sniff you first," I instruct. She nods her head, and I can see the hint of a smile on her face as I open the door. Both dogs push past me and go straight for her. She stays stock-still, not afraid at all. I like her lack of fear. There isn't one brittle or delicate bone in this woman's body. Except a small one for her brother, one that I hope I can shift to me instead.

The dogs circle her, sniffing. She eyes them and offers the back of her hand. Barry is the first to sniff it, and when he returns to sniffing her leg, she reaches out and touches his fluffy fur. They're both due for a cut soon, especially around their eyes. Anya runs her hand down his coat, and he pushes up against her, always a sucker for a good scratch. Stan, on the other hand, can't stop sniffing her.

"Stan," I call, and he eyes me before he comes running over. I pat his back before he runs back over to her.

"These are the dogs you're going to feed one of your men to?" She chokes on a disbelieving laugh.

I arch an eyebrow. "You're lucky you're with me. If you were someone trying to break in, it would be a very different story."

"I want them," she says as she offers Stan her hand before she runs it down his back, just as she did with Barry. She seems content with animals, which is somewhat surprising.

"Well, it seems they like you," I say.

"Of course they do. What's not to like?"

I agree with her but stay silent. The last thing this she-devil needs is a further inflated ego.

"You can come in now." She looks up from petting the dogs but makes no move to enter the house.

"I didn't come for you. I came to see your dogs." She smiles. "So why would I come into the house?"

"Here." I bark out the command, pointing next to me. Both dogs come running to me, and I tell them to go back inside.

"Well, that was unfair," she says, pouting.

"Was it?" I reach for her. "Now, get your fucking ass inside."

"Why? Do you plan to shut me up with your cock in my mouth?" she sasses with a twinkle in her eyes.

"Is that what you want?"

"It's not something I often offer. But I rather enjoyed myself last time," she says, and it appears admitting it pains her.

I step into her space, grabbing her by the hip as I rub my cock against her. Fucking hell, she'll be the death of me.

"My cock is going in your mouth, and you will fucking like it," I growl. She takes a breath, and I can see her peaked nipples beneath her dress. So perfect. Always ready to go for me.

"We have to talk business first," she breathes out.

"You have from now until we get to the stairs. I suggest you talk fast," I reply as I throw her over my shoulder. She yelps at the undignified way I'm carrying her.

"It's serious stuff, River," she yells over my shoulder.

I slap her ass. "And so is me filling that beautiful cunt of yours. Do you know how long I've waited for this?"

"You were the problem in the first place," she chastises.

I step onto the first stair. "Time's ticking, Red."

"Okay. Fuck. You need to call off your men from investigating my brother and Meredith. Either one of them will put a bullet in your head or I will."

I chuckle. "I'd like to see you try."

"River, I'm serious. I will always choose my family first."

It should hurt, but I hear something entirely different. "So you're starting to take me seriously. Not just as a business prospect but as a man."

She goes rigid, and I smile with amusement. Oh, how far we've come, Red.

When I reach my room, the dogs are already in there, tails wagging, and I step on a squeaky toy.

"Out," I bark at them, and obediently, they run for the door and I close it behind them.

"Hey, that's mean."

"Mean?" I say, laughing. This cold-ass, beautiful woman is saying I'm mean? After she so elegantly just told me to put my cock in her mouth and all the other crazy things she's put me through?

I flip her over my shoulder, and her tits graze down my front. She's looking up at me with that hooded gaze.

"If I fuck you now, are you going to disappear afterward?" I ask.

"Most likely. Depends how good the sex is."

I grab her ass and push her against my hard cock pressing through my trousers. I know I can satisfy Anya's needs, offer something she most likely hasn't experienced before... relinquishment of control.

But I want something else from her. A guarantee that she's here for the same reasons I am. I want her and inevitably will have her.

I knew the moment I saw her, I would make her mine. A woman as powerful and strong willed as her is a spectacle to see, and I plan on drinking her in every day. Mesmerized and charmed in the same way I was when I first laid eyes on her. Fucking her into submission is another perk.

"Call off your men," she demands.

"What will you do for me if I do?" I ask as I graze my thumb against her cheekbone and to the back of her hair, where I find the little pins that keep it in place and remove them one by one.

"I won't blow your brains out," she says matter-of-factly. Her breath is shallow as she watches me pluck each pin out of her hair.

Her vibrant red locks fall around her face. It's long

with shining waves. Beautiful. "I like it when you wear your hair down."

"Shut up and just fuck me, River," she sneers.

I grab the back of her neck and pull her into me, sliding my tongue against hers. This time, she doesn't fight me. Instead, she melts as her hands desperately pull me closer.

My hand wraps around her throat as I deepen our kiss.

She licks her lips, and I reach for my belt, pull it free, and undo my button before I slide the zipper down. My cock springs free, and she eyes it hungrily. "Anya."

"Yes, River?" She says my name but doesn't look up at me as she does.

"I suggest you get on your knees."

"Okay," she replies with ease. I watch as this powerhouse of a woman drops to her knees, coming to eye level with my cock. She reaches for it.

"No touching until I say." She opens her mouth as I push my fingers into her hair, enjoying the silky-smooth feel of it. Everything about this woman is fucking perfect. I grab hold of her hair and move her head toward my cock. She opens for me, but as soon as I feel her tongue, I pull her back and back some more. She darts out her tongue and licks the tip of it. "Bad girl," I tell her, stepping back and dropping my hold on her hair. "Now, crawl up to the fucking bed and pull that skirt up over your ass."

"So demanding," she purrs with a sinister smile but wiggles the skirt up over her ass. And for my viewing pleasure, she has on no underwear. I just knew she didn't.

"Move it," I command, and I can tell from the way she smirks that she enjoys being told what to do.

My bad, bad girl.

CHAPTER 32

Anya

"Why are you stopping, Anya?" He says my name with a drawl, almost like he's teasing me. I'm halfway to the bed, and I know he's watching me. I can feel his stare all over my body. "You look so good, so wet for me," he croons, and I feel him come up closer, and his hand caresses my ass. It's been a while since I let a man control me like this. Actually, I think this is the only time I've let a man have this much control over me.

This is no different from when I let him bind me at his restaurant. I understand the psychology between dominant and submissive. I sell it. But I never thought I would find myself crawling on hands and knees because a man said so.

But River is different. I don't know why, but with

him, I don't have to constantly fight. I can just relinquish control, even if just for a few minutes. And it makes me feel alive.

Deep down, I must trust River to a degree, and I don't trust anyone except for my brother.

Ever so slowly, this man has carved his way into my space and maybe more...

I push that thought away.

I can't focus on the more.

I only have now.

I'm not even sure why I'm giving him the power, but fuck, his cock tasted good.

I want another taste.

His hand moves to my other ass cheek before he leans over me from behind. I can feel his breath near my ear.

"How wet?" he asks me.

"Very wet."

"Hmm," he hums, his hand sliding down between my ass cheeks until it reaches my pussy and he slips a finger between my folds. I moan at his touch, and am aware of its disappearance the moment it leaves my pussy. When I look over my shoulder, I watch mesmerized as he puts his fingers in his mouth, sucking them with eyes closed before opening them with a smile. "I think you should taste it."

I nod my head, eager for whatever it is he wants to give me. But he grips my ass with both hands, and I feel him at my entrance. His cock teases me before it slides inside, and it's like heaven, eliciting a moan from my lips. One I can't contain. But the minute I feel full, he pulls away, leaving me empty and desperate.

My eyes spring open, and he lazily walks around me and sits at the end of the bed. He looks down at me and indicates with one finger—the same one he tasted me with—to continue crawling to him. I do as I'm told, my eyes on his very hard cock. It glistens from being coated in my wetness.

When I reach him, he puts a finger under my chin and lifts my head. "Now, up."

My gaze doesn't want to move from his cock. It's beautiful. He's perfectly manicured, veins in all the right places, and it's large. And, fuck, does it feel good inside me.

"Taste," he says as he reaches for my hair yet again and brings my head down to his cock. I wrap my mouth around him and take him as far down as I can go. I can taste myself on him.

He moans, but I can't take all of him in; he's too large for that. Lifting my head up and down, I go again. When I reach for the base of his cock, he stops me and pulls back. "No. My bad girl needs something a little more. You can stand now."

I sit up on my heels, my dress still up around my waist, as I watch him pull something from a drawer. I see it's something made of leather. "Undress."

I've seen almost every sex contraption and toy imaginable, so I leave it as a surprise as I reach for my hem and follow his directive. I'm usually in charge in the bedroom. I don't let a man lead, but here I am, listening to every command he gives.

Why?

Because it feels fucking good not to be in charge for once in my life.

"Anya." I focus on him and not what he's holding. Because it doesn't matter what River uses on me or does to me. I understand now what he's been training me for this entire time. The kisses. Intentionally forcing me to hold out on sex. It's about trust and connection. Something I've never had in the bedroom unless I controlled it. Have I ever enjoyed sex like this? No. I thought I had, but it will never compare. I now realize it was always lacking, and perhaps that's because I've never desired anyone like I have River.

"Don't think, just feel," he commands. I nod at his instruction. It's nice to focus solely on his voice and, for a split second, not think, not second-guess. Just do.

Sliding my dress all the way off, I keep my heels on. He smiles, and when I reach him, he turns me around so my back is facing him. He then places the item over my head. A ball goes into my mouth, and it straps around to the back of my head. He reaches for both my hands and straps them in as well, locking them behind my back. When I try to move my restrained hands, my head yanks back. Everything is connected.

He tugs on the contraption, pulling me up and onto the bed, still on my knees.

He drops to his knees in front of me, my hands behind my back, unable to move.

"Maybe I should use a gag on you more often so there are no complaints," he says with an arrogant smile.

I try to tell him to just fuck me, but it comes out muffled, and his smile grows.

He grabs a handful of my ass and twists, the painful awakening throbbing at my core. He lies down on his back and positions me over his face, the view of his perfect cock in front of me.

He raises his mouth to my pussy, and he wastes no time before his tongue darts out and slides straight between my folds. I moan but can't say anything around the ball gag. My body trembles over him, wanting to so badly reach for him, but I'm unable to while my hands are bound. He slides his tongue up and down, teasing me and making me want to touch him. But I can't. He dips a finger inside me while his tongue works absolute magic. Up and down and slow circles around my clit until I can feel myself tightening around his finger. Just as I'm about to come, he pulls away. He repositions himself on his knees beside me, and when I begin to curse and complain, he pushes me so I fall directly onto his bed face-first.

Thank God his bed is soft. I don't have my hands to break the fall.

He pulls me back before I feel him at my entrance again. I wiggle into him, begging for him to fill me. I'm due my release. I've never needed or wanted anything so desperately. If I didn't have this gag on, I would more than likely beg.

And I have never begged a man in my life.

So I'm thankful for the gag. I would hate to inflate River Bently's ego.

He chuckles and slides straight inside me. As he does, I feel the instant relief that I was searching for. He stays still for a few moments before he finally moves in and out of me as he winds my hair around his knuckles and tugs my head back.

He leans over and whispers into my ear, "Wear your fucking hair down more often." I shake my head, but it's hard to do with it being restricted. He pushes it away and keeps on thrusting. He doesn't stop, pumping slowly and steadily into me. And it's like reaching up for the clouds and then thinking you have a hold of something, but it gets pulled away.

I wish my hands were free. I would turn around and fucking climb him so I could have my way.

Instead, he tortures me with his slow and steady pace until I feel myself tighten, and everything in me feels like it's about to burst.

"That's it, baby, suck my fucking cock with your cunt."

I can't stop it. It just builds and builds until even around the ball gag I'm screaming as his thrusts get faster and faster until my body can't take it anymore and shuts down. River slaps my ass, and I suck in a breath.

Holy shit. Holy fuck. What is happening?

Just when I think I can't come again, he picks up the pace, and something else keeps building inside me, not slowing down. He fucks me until we both come. He's jerking inside me as my pussy milks him, and I don't want this high to ever end. I want this man to forever throw me around at his whim. Breaking me ever so slowly into a sensual bliss I've never known.

There's fucking.

Then there's this...

River Bently.

When he's done, he pulls out of me and lies beside me. Smiling, I'm barely able to keep my eyes open as he brushes back the hair that fell in my face before he says, "I'll be marrying you very soon, Red, because you were fucking made for me."

My heart rate picks up, and if I wasn't just fucked into submission, I might very well slit his throat.

CHAPTER 33
River

I leave her like that until the fire in her eyes dies down. I knew she would go livid when I told her I was planning to marry her. It's just how she is. Spectacular. That's really the only word I have for her right now. Because my cock is already getting hard, thinking it can go for round two.

She makes a noise, and I get off the bed, untying her hands and removing the ball gag from her mouth. She instantly gets up and turns to me, swinging, her fists flying. She clocks me in the jaw, but before she can get a second hit in, I capture her wrists. I then block her legs from kicking me in the appendage that intends to slide back into her.

"Anya."

"I'd release me, River." Her words drip with

venom. I smile as I stare down at her, knowing it'll piss her off again. She hates to admit that she loves my arrogant smile.

"But I intend to fuck you again, my sweet," I croon, which just makes her angrier.

She leans forward, teeth bared, and goes to bite me. I jerk my head back, but when she does it again, I stay where I am, holding her in place as her teeth come down on my lips. I let her bite me until I taste my own blood, and still I don't release her.

"Sweet, just like you," I murmur against her lips before I kiss her. At first, she doesn't kiss me back, but when I slide my tongue into her mouth, she does. Her tongue meets mine, and I taste a mixture of her sweet pussy and my own fucking blood.

She pulls back and tries to free herself, but I'm not having it. I can tell she's ready for me again, because when she kisses me, her body rubs against mine.

And her sweet, sweet cunt is drenched.

Made for me, she is.

She struggles in my grip as I step forward, moving her back until her legs hit the bed. She falls back onto the mattress, pulling me down on top of her, and I go willingly as she leans up and kisses me again. I release the tight hold I have on her, which was pinning her arms to her sides, and the minute I do, she flips me to my back and climbs on top of me. Then she smacks me hard across the face. Her wild red hair cascades down over her perfect tits, and from my position, I have an unobstructed view of the ink that wraps around her stomach.

Perfection. That's another word to describe her.

"You think you have a hold of me now?" She laughs, and its evil. Her hand goes to my throat, and she wiggles her hips back until she is on my cock. I'm not inside her; she's sliding back and forth along the shaft. "You think, what, because I let you fuck me, make me crawl to you, that you can own any part of this?" She looks down at where she's rubbing against me, then she lifts her hips, and my cock slides straight into her.

Exquisite.

"I'm going to tell you a secret, River." She leans down, her sharp nails scraping along my chest, drawing blood as she goes. "I like letting you fuck me, but don't for a second think it's anything more than that." Her hips start rocking back and forth, back and forth.

Fuck.

Bewitching. That's what she is. She's fucking bewitching me.

"I don't need you to know you're mine. Not yet at least," I tell her, leaning up, but she pushes me back down with her hand that's digging into my chest, marking me.

"I'll never be yours, River." She grins down at me as she continues to ride my cock. "Because I am *mine*."

Fuck, that's hot.

Gripping her hips, I rock her faster. Her hands go to her hair, and she pulls at the beautiful strands, her tits begging to be touched as she rides my cock.

Obsessed. That's what I've become.

I'm fucking obsessed with this red-headed she-devil who could tear my world down, and I would still stand there and ask her if she liked me yet. All the while knowing she'll tell me to fuck off. But then my heart will pitter-patter faster, and I would burn down whoever or whatever she required.

How does she have me so hooked already?

It can't be just her sweet pussy. I mean, it is my absolute favorite thing to be buried inside of. No other woman will compare, and I feel I'm ruined for life now.

She has ruined me, and couldn't care that she did so.

No, I'm pretty sure out of the two of us, it's me who is going to be fucked.

My coldhearted ice princess is made of stone.

Luckily for her, I like to break things I'm not supposed to.

And I plan to break all the way down to her core till she lets me in.

Even if I have to beg.

That's how much I want her.

My men call me crazy. Fuck, she may even kill me in the process.

My mother will most likely not approve of her. *Too cold*, she would say. *What can a woman like her give you?*

Her. That's all I want from her. Nothing else, and I will take it in bits and pieces if I have to.

Anya Ivanov will be mine. She just needs to wake up and smell the roses to realize there will be no me without her.

I'll let her fuck me to feel like she's regaining control. Meanwhile, I'll be trying to think how I can prove myself to this fucking she-devil, and show her that she needs me as much as I need her.

CHAPTER 34

Anya

The moment I come, I climb off him.

He says my name, but I'm already pulling my dress back on.

"I gave you a bonus-round fuck. Lucky you," I say as I slip one of my heels on.

I need to get the fuck out of his house. If I don't, I'll stay here forever. It's starting to feel like its own little oasis from the outside world and all the bullshit that's happening. I can't depend on him for this.

"I didn't use protection," River says, turning to his side on the bed.

"I won't fall pregnant, so unless you have a disease..."

"No. I haven't fucked anyone for months, and I

used protection. Before that, I was checked." I slip my other heel on. "Why won't you get pregnant?" he asks.

"I fixed that situation years ago," I reply.

I turn to leave, but he grabs my wrist. I try to free myself, avoiding his gaze. "We're done now, right? Your blackmail didn't work. I want you out of the city."

"Look at me," he says, and tries to navigate my chin toward him, but I pull away. "Look at me," he says again, and it's the same tone he used when he told me to crawl to him. And as I did then, I listen.

"Live a little for yourself. You're spooked because I told you I want to marry you. Is that it? Is that all it takes to crumble the mighty Anya Ivanov?" he prods.

"Don't pretend you know me," I spit.

"I'm learning about you, and that's what terrifies you. Run all you want, but I will always find you. I'll prove to you over and over again why we're so good for each other."

"So you can have a slice of my business and money? Isn't that all you've wanted?" I seethe, and I realize they're not even my thoughts or words anymore. They're Meredith's.

His eyebrows furrow in confusion. "You think I'm only here for the business? Let me assure you that if that's all I wanted, I would've stolen it from you the moment I arrived here."

I scoff as I yank myself free. "Our debt is settled."

"Not in the slightest, Red," he calls out behind me as I storm out of his room. "Didn't you say we had to discuss business? Or are you just going to run off again as soon as it all gets a little too real?"

"Fuck off." I flick him my middle finger as I dash down the stairs. As I hit the last step, Barry and Stan run up to me, tails wagging. I look over my shoulder and see River isn't following me.

Thank fuck. I realize now that when I storm out, he gives me space. Other times, he's entirely over-bearing.

I crouch down and quickly pat the dogs. "You're lucky you guys are cute," I say quietly because I just can't help myself. I might be pissed off at their asshole of a fur dad, but not them.

"Anya." I hear him call out from the stairs, but I hurry out the door to the garage before he can catch up, grabbing his car keys on my way. I go straight to his car and start her up.

I'm reversing out of the garage by the time he reaches the door. He stands there, naked and smiling, arms crossed over his chest, shaking his head with disbelief. I flick him the middle finger again.

"Leave me the fuck alone, or I'll use this car for target practice next!"

I zip out of the garage and onto the main street, all to enter the next driveway.

Me? Married? Is River out of his goddamn mind?

Marriage has never been part of my plan.

The mere thought of it implodes my brain.

He's after something. Has to be. Men like him only want to take.

I'm confused as to why I've given him more and more these past few months.

I can't even say I hate him anymore because I naturally gravitate back to him.

When I arrive home, I find Vance and Clay waiting for me.

"Miss, you were gone longer than we anticipated," Vance says.

"I was at River's, and I was fine," I tell him as I throw Clay the keys. "Make me some tea. Then after that I plan to sleep and not wake up for a full day." I go straight to my room and undress.

Although I left River, I can't get him out of my mind.

Pregnant? I scoff.

That could never happen. When I was twenty-one, I paid a private doctor a lot of money to fix it so I could never have a child. It was money well spent. I would never want to bring a child into my world. It's already fucked-up and dangerous enough for me, and I'm a full-blown adult who knows how to use a weapon.

I strip down to nothing and beeline for my shower. I wait until the hot water steams up half the bathroom as I stare at myself in the mirror.

I didn't even ask River why he was looking into my brother and Meredith. I just literally went over there and had my brains fucked out. *I crawled to him.* And the memory elicits goose bumps to pop out over my skin and stirs another pounding in my core. But fuck, it felt good. Every part of it. And him.

Running my hands through my hair when I step into the shower, I'm furious about giving so much of myself to him. He doesn't deserve it. And when I tried to take it back, he just laughed and decided to make me come instead.

And damn, it was good.

So fucking good.

I know for certain that when I sleep tonight, my dreams will all center on him, and that annoys me so much more than I can say.

Running my hands down my body, I remember how he tied my wrists behind my back, how he stopped me from talking by gagging me.

Everything was somehow so perfect.

He seems so sure of himself, so arrogant in the way he assumes that I want anything more from him than sex. But it was only months ago that I said I'd never let him touch me, wasn't it? Now it's all I crave, and it's becoming harder to remain mad at him.

He wants to marry me one day? I don't want marriage; that's the last thing in this life that I would ever want. Why would I want a man to control me or have any type of hold on me? I am my own woman and boss.

Yet when he does stifle my control in the bedroom, I feel free for the first time.

Fuck, my head's a mess as I consider Meredith's words. Is he using me?

But hasn't she done the same all my life?

Or am I simply making an excuse for a man who I've undeniably somehow let slither a tendril into my heart.

Fuck. I've really fucked up.

My phone rings, and I ignore it. Usually, I would run to it, hoping it would be Alek. But tonight, I don't want to know.

I don't want to hear the outside noise or opinions of others on how I should live my life. It was perfect only months ago, and now it feels like it's falling apart, no matter what way I try to direct it.

Besides all my riches, empire, and power, do I want anything more in life?

I've never really thought about it before. But now I am.

CHAPTER 35
River

The only thing keeping me tied to New York is Anya. And I fucking refuse to give up on her.

She's avoiding me—I know she is—but she can't avoid me forever. I know all her little ins and outs now. I know the night she works, the days she goes out to shop. And the days she doesn't leave the house.

It might've only been a day since I saw her last, but I'm done with this back-and-forth runaway shit. I'm certainly not going to wait a week like I did last time. Little by little, I'll wear her down. Not because I want to see her fire dim but because I want her to admit that she's made for me. I just need to make her realize I don't want to take her power or empire away. I just want to be in her world.

Some may call it stalking, but I call it being efficient.

I want to maximize every opportunity I have with her, which is exactly why I'm walking into Cartier, her favorite jeweler, again.

When I step inside, Clay and Vance are standing stoically near the back of the store. She's definitely here.

The sales assistant eyes me, evidently recognizing me from the last time I was here.

"Do you have an appointment, sir?" she asks, and makes a pointed look at Michael, who looms over my shoulder.

"Yes, my soon-to-be wife is seeing someone in here," I say.

Her eyes light up. "Who is your fiancée?"

"Anya Ivanov."

"Oh, Miss Anya never told us she was engaged. Would you like to join her?" she asks, a lot less frightened of our intrusion, which says wonders if she thinks so highly of my she-devil. Then again, she's probably one of the most frequent patrons here.

"Sit. Stay. Drink champagne, and don't scare

anyone," I instruct Michael. Anya might think business between us is done, but it's not.

And she still has my fucking car.

The saleswoman walks me to a back room, Anya's pair of guard dogs not overly impressed to see me. The feeling is mutual. Anya twists in her chair, and her eyes narrow as the jeweler showing her some diamonds looks up, surprised.

"Anya, sweetheart, you didn't wait for me." I step inside and lean down to kiss her cheek. She doesn't pull away when I do, and I linger a second longer than necessary.

"Please, have a seat," The jeweler says, seeming surprised that Anya has any friends, let alone a male one. I take the chair next to Anya. I eye her hand, thinking of grabbing it, but she pulls it away, as if reading my thoughts. I hold in a chuckle.

"More diamonds?" I ask her, leaning over to look at the tennis bracelet she's currently eyeing, only to see she's wearing the last gift I sent her.

"Yes, more diamonds," she says through gritted teeth, clearly not happy I'm here.

"Miss Ivanov is deciding which she likes from our new collection, so I'm laying out the options."

I lean forward to have a better look. Next to the

tennis bracelet is a ring, which has a flower on it made from diamonds.

"We'll take both," I say, smiling as the woman from the front comes in and offers me a glass of champagne. A glass of water is positioned in front of Anya, untouched. Raising the glass to my lips, I take a sip as her beautiful eyes narrow at me. "Yes, sweetheart?"

"That's great. I'll get these two wrapped for you. If you'll excuse me for a moment," the jeweler says, then gets up to leave. As soon as she's out the door, Anya turns to me fully.

"You," she spits. "Why are you here? Was I not clear enough last night? We're done."

"You still have my car," I point out. "And I was hoping we could finish our discussion regarding your brother and Meredith. Also, blackmail aside, I was hoping for a repeat." I wink at her before I down the rest of the champagne.

"A repeat? So you think by buying me jewelry, you'll get laid outside of our already completed agreement?" I can hear the laugh in her voice.

"A man can hope, right?" I say. I turn her chair so she's facing me. "Anya, what do I have to do so you let me in? You can say it's all just sex. If you had friends, I wouldn't mind if you told them that's all it is. But you and I both know this runs deeper than that."

"You think too highly of yourself," she scoffs.

"Why do you think we get along so well?" I retort. "Help me understand yesterday. You come in, guns blazing at my restaurant because you want to talk business. You ask me to stop following up on your brother and Meredith, which, by the way, I'm trying to find your brother to help *you*. Then we have sex and you split."

"You just want to know where my brother is so you can deal with him instead," she seethes.

"I don't want to do business with anyone but you, Anya. I won't apologize for my ambition in wanting in on the auctions and territory. Personal feelings aside, we will both profit if we work together. But I'm here for *you*, Anya. So what did you want to say to me yesterday?"

She turns away, and I wait. And wait. And wait. Getting this she-devil to open up is a nightmare. But when the silence becomes too great for her, she looks to the snake watch and says in a clipped tone, "My brother finally called me. You need to back off. Whatever you're doing, stop it. He'll kill you if he has to. The same goes for Meredith."

"Sooo, you're trying to tell me you care about my safety?" I ask, grinning.

"No," she snaps, abashed by the insinuation.

I chuckle, wanting to place my hand on hers but knowing better right now than to touch the prickly bitch. Anya will come to me again in her own time. And if it's not within a week, then I'll break into her fucking house to make it happen.

Chivalry be damned when she likes to be fucked like a whore.

"You want Alek found, don't you?"

"I don't. Now, leave it."

"It's all you've wanted since he disappeared, Red. I couldn't care less if he threatened me. If finding your brother is what will make you happy, then I'll make it happen."

She goes to speak, but the jeweler walks in. I hand her my credit card, and she swipes it with no issue before I sign for it. Reaching for the bag, I hold it as we stand. Anya eyes it but doesn't say anything as we walk out.

"How about lunch?" I ask.

"I've already eaten," she says, still not reaching for the bag in my hand.

"How about dinner?"

"I'm sure I have plans," she bites back.

And just when there's a glimmer of the vulnerable woman she can be, the she-devil comes back out.

"What can I get you to do for this jewelry?" I ask, holding it out of her reach.

"You can keep it. I'm sure it will look amazing on you." She turns and walks off. I watch her go, dressed in a different red dress today, her hair up in her usual bun, and wonder what I have to do to make her scream my name next time I fuck her.

Because there *will* be a next time.

I have no doubt.

I just need to pull out more of the Anya I've seen glimpses of hidden underneath that tough exterior.

As I stand here and watch her ass swaying back and forth, all I can think is... When did I become so whipped?

CHAPTER 36
Anya

I do what any sane woman does when she comes across a dilemma, and what one might consider emotional turmoil. I go shopping. River has seriously pissed me off. Not only is he tracking me, but he also took my fucking jewelry with him.

Clay and Vance walk behind me with multiple shopping bags. For the first time in a long time, I felt like casually browsing instead of booking appointments.

My eyes light up as I see one of my favorite stores. "Vance, you take the bags back to the car. Clay, you stay with me," I instruct as I joyfully listen to my heels click against the pavement.

I stop short, my joy stripped away, when Amanza

walks out of the store, blocking my view of the pretties inside.

"Anya?" she says, surprised. Why does this bitch keep popping up? Shouldn't her brother be done with his business here so he can take her sorry ass out of the city? I mean, there are other ways I could ensure she leaves New York, but they'll be messy and will require a body bag.

I bite the inside of my cheek. If I were to do that, it would royally piss River off. Then again, I might get punished. The kind I like.

No, stop thinking of River, I reprimand myself internally.

"Amanda, what a surprise." I purposely say her name wrong, and I can tell it's immediately pissed her off.

She appraises the excessive number of bags Vance walks by with before she looks back to me. I'm not sure what she wants me to say; I came here for some retail therapy, and usually no one recognizes me. Well, I should say no one has the balls to come up and talk to me. But this little blonde does for some reason.

"You're shopping; doing normal stuff." She laughs as she points at my bags. Again, I say nothing. "I'm kind of glad I've run into you, though. Look, you and River..." There it is, the real reason she wants to talk. "I get the attraction you have. Hell, I even get the appeal he has for you. You are stunning and powerful, but you two are both crazy. And two crazy people don't mix. He needs someone calm, you know? To be his safe place when he comes home."

"No, I do *not* know." And I don't. Not only for the fact she thinks she's right in this scenario, but because she thinks she can tell me what to do.

I don't take orders unless you plan to fuck me, and even that was an exception, and only for River.

"He has a life outside of this place. A mother he cares for deeply, who will not approve of someone like you."

My eyebrows shoot up, and I'm actually shocked by how ballsy she is. Perhaps I underestimated her, or she mistakenly confused me for someone else. I raise my designer sunglasses so I can look her in the eyes as I say, "I'm sorry your pussy didn't cut it for the man's needs. I mean, I'm not attached to your momma's boy, but you clearly are, and he still rejected you. It must be painful."

I hit home as her gaze fills with fury.

"But since his indifference toward you isn't completely clear, let's call him, shall we, so there's no room for misinterpretation? I'm often praised for my communication and problem-solving skills, you know," I say, because this actually makes me want to fucking laugh.

If this woman had any idea or sense as to who I am, she would've run the other way.

"You don't need—"

I cut her off. "No, I insist." I press call on his number. It rings once and he answers. I put it on speaker, not even caring what he says.

"I knew it wouldn't take long. Ready for that sweet cunt of yours to be filled to the brim again? What time should I come over, sweetheart?"

Amanza's eyes go wide in shock.

"I'm here with your friend, and you're on speaker," I say once he finishes speaking.

"I don't have many of those, so be more specific," he says.

"Amanza, who was just warning me off you and insisting that we're not a perfect match," I tell him. "I just thought I would call and get your opinion on it. You know, since you were balls deep in me last night and all. Everything seemed to fit quiet perfectly then."

Amanza is absolutely appalled, and I'm certain this is the last time she'll ever approach me again.

"Is she there?" River asks.

"Oh yes, she can hear you." I smile at her, and she looks around as people walk by, but I couldn't care less.

She's the one who pulled me to the side like she had some claim on him. She can fucking have him for all I care. But I don't take kindly to someone telling me what I should and should not have.

I suppose the same rings true regarding Meredith's warnings about River Bently.

"Amanza," he says pointedly.

"Yes. I'm here," she replies as she pushes back a lock of her hair, and I try my hardest not to roll my eyes so hard at her in public.

"I'd suggest you don't speak to Anya again if you wish for your brother to keep on breathing." Her eyes go wide at his threat, and it fills me with an unfamiliar smugness.

"But—"

"But nothing. We fucked, and it was fun."

"I'm sorry, what? It was fun?" I scoff. Amanza looks to be on the verge of tears from his words, whereas I want to strangle him.

"Take me off speaker, Anya," he requests in the tone he uses when he orders me to bend over and do as he pleases.

"Fun," I say, shaking my head, irked for some reason. What about this little pipsqueak could be fun? She looks like she's about to burst into tears, and that alone should give me satisfaction. So why doesn't it?

"Anya, we need to discuss last night," he starts.

"No, thank you. Our agreement is *over*. Go and have some more *fun* with someone else." I hang up.

He calls right back.

I don't answer.

I run my hand over my hair, ensuring it's still perfect. Amanza looks like her world has crumbled, and I don't even need to threaten her, which is greatly disappointing. I almost feel sorry for her if she truly thinks River is as crazy as me. I step around her and walk into the store without another word.

CHAPTER 37
Anya

I'm fucking furious, and I have no idea why. But I think it has something to do with River saying how much "fun" he had fucking Amanza. That doe-eyed bitch? In what century? It'd be as good as fucking a blow-up doll.

"A fucking blow-up doll, I tell you!" I say as I throw a knife and hit my target dead on. "Shopping is meant to make me feel better, so why the fuck am I angrier?" I throw the next knife and it hits slightly off center. I scream, self-imploding.

It's been a while since I made my way to the back of my mansion for target practice, but there's a lethal edge I need to try my hardest to smooth over. Otherwise, I'll probably go after the doe-eyed bitch. And some part of me, that's never made itself known before, thinks that would be unreasonable.

"Fuck," I grumble and then pick up my tea as I look over the well-manicured backyard. Vance stands off to the side at a distance, and I lick my lips. Why do I have so much pent-up rage inside me when I was fucked to within an inch of my life yesterday?

I grab my phone out of habit. This time, River is the most recent call. I frown at that. Alek has always been top of the list.

I hit call on Alek's number.

It rings, and I wait for voicemail, not even hopeful anymore that he'll answer.

I sigh when I hear the recording, then start to speak. "Do you remember when we were kids and we started throwing knives?" I ask, reliving the memory of the old bitch teaching us to hit dead center. I idly flip a knife in my hand.

Our lives have never been easy, but at least we had each other. Or so I thought. I throw the knife, and it fills me with satisfaction. "If memory serves correctly, I was a better shot initially." I know how much that statement will piss Alek off. Even though I'm calling him, distance and time have taken away my need to hear his voice. At least I know he's alive.

I think about River, and wonder if he's being

honest when he says he's looking for Alek for my sake. "Anyway, I told River to stop following you. I don't know why you're mad at me about it since you were originally the one who dumped him on me. FYI, I still think I'm going crazy. I think I might like him, but not in a bright and shiny way. In the way where I don't want anyone else's dick inside me. I mean, I fucking hate him right now... but I've never experienced this. Is this what you're feeling for your dancer?" Fuck, I don't know what I'm saying anymore.

"Please come back. The old bitch is getting ahead of herself too, thinking she can take it all back. I need you."

I hang up and stare at the phone for longer than necessary. Did I really just ramble to my brother that I like someone? The very same someone I imagine throwing knives at because he think's fucking someone else was "fun"?

God, I want to claw at my own chest. Is this what jealousy feels like?

"Delivery, miss." Clay walks out holding a bag, and I know what it is right away, because I picked it all out. Even if he paid for it. It's mine. This fucker actually thinks sending me my own jewelry is going to make up for that bullshit on the phone.

I toss a knife into the air, considering if it'll make

me feel better or worse if I kill River today. I'll be sad to say goodbye to his cock, but at least if he's six feet under, I won't have to deal with this uncomfortable, uncontrollable rage.

"Miss," Clay says, shaking me from my thoughts. I look up at him. "Now that your agreement is over with Mr. Bently, will you require our extra services again?"

"No," I say automatically. I won't. Not only is my need for River still very raw, but I don't want another man's hands on me right now.

It comes out so quickly that we're all slightly taken aback. I had been reliant on these two for so many years to bring my stress levels down. And now I only want River, because what? He says so?

"Did we do anything wrong?" he asks, and I'm surprised by the vulnerability in his tone.

"No," I answer.

"Okay, miss," he says and then enters the house again, leaving Vance behind to stand stoically.

Everything went to shit as soon as River Bently came to town. I cut the knife through the air as I hit call on River's number.

He answers on the first ring. "Sweetheart. Two calls in one day; we're making leaps and bounds."

"Fuckface," I sing back at him.

"Oh, she's spicy," someone says on his end. I think

it's Michael.

"You're on speaker in the car."

"That sounds like your stupidity, not mine."

"Pull over," he orders to someone.

"Sir, we're on a highway," Michael says. It's unusual that Michael's driving.

"Fucking hell," River grumbles.

"Do you think sending me more jewelry is actually going to put me in a good mood or let you touch me again?"

"I'm gonna pull over," Michael says.

"Yeah, I think that would be a great idea," River snarks before I hear honking and then his cool, silky voice is directed back at me.

"Sweetheart, is that any way to talk?" he growls, and I want to throw my phone. "No, I didn't send it to you for a fuck, but if you're offering, I won't say no. I also want to say how unreasonable you're being about the Amanza thing, considering you walk around with your two guards who you used to fuck two months ago."

Rage ignites in my veins. He wants me to be reasonable? Oh, that shit ain't going to fly.

"You like diamonds, I like you. It's a simple fix," he says, and I can hear the noise from the background, cars driving by.

"I don't like you," I tell him.

"Yeah, I kind of think you do. Since I have the scratch marks to prove it." He pauses. "Oh, and in case you were wondering, my lip is all healed, ready to taste your sweet pussy again. When would you like to arrange that?"

"You're awfully cocky," I say. "Do you know what I'm doing right now, River? I'm flipping knives for target practice and imagining your fucking face on the bullseye."

"Well, I couldn't imagine you'd be aiming at my cock since you like it so much. My cockiness involves my cock being buried deep inside you, Anya. Preferably sooner rather than later."

"And our agreement?" I repeat.

"How long are you going to hide behind that? You and I both know this has nothing to do with me blackmailing you."

"I fucking hate you. Don't call me again."

"You called me, Red," he says.

"Fuck off, Lake."

He's chuckling as I hang up on him and throw the knife, hitting dead center.

Fuck, I hate it when he's right. I hate that I'm calling him just to pick a fight so I can hear his voice.

I'm losing my fucking mind.

CHAPTER 38

River

Fuck, this is just what I need; her angry with me just after I tried to patch things up. I may like it in the bedroom, but not when I can't touch her.

"You really do know how to pick them," Michael says, laughing in the driver's seat.

"Yes, it seems I do," I say, shaking my head. And I suspect any moment now she's also about to receive the lingerie sets I paid to be delivered today.

But what's the worst that could happen? Jewelry and lingerie... surely, those will lift her mood.

The car comes to a stop out front of the airport, and I spot my mother right away. She's tiny, her head, with its light-blond curls, only coming up to my chin. She waves with a kind smile when she spots us.

Michael and I both step out of the car as I walk around to give her a hug. Her arms go around my waist, and she pulls me into her. Michael grabs her bags and puts them in the trunk.

"My boy. Gosh, I've missed you," she says as she gives me a once-over.

She always tells me I remind her of my deceased father. She never re-married, and as far as I know, she hasn't dated anyone for a long time. Which means I'm her world, so I make sure to make her mine. I send her money, even though she tells me to stop. I bought her a house when I got my first real money, and while I don't outright tell her what I do, I suspect she knows it's not all legal. No investor makes this much money, unless it's dirty somewhere along the line.

"It's good to see you, Mother." She pulls back, taps my chest, and smiles at me. "A little more notice next time might give me time to properly prepare."

"A mother doesn't need to give notice or a good excuse to visit her child. Besides, I miss the dogs," she says, and appraises Michael, who she thinks is my personal assistant.

She reaches for him to give him a warm hug, one he begrudgingly accepts.

"We just finished with a business meeting," I explain to her as I get her settled in the car. Michael sits behind the wheel, and I join my mother in the back. I almost always choose to drive, but it'd been months since I last saw my mother.

She immediately begins to interrogate me. "So, why are you staying out here? Big business venture?" she asks. "I was surprised when you said you'd bought an estate here. I didn't think you liked it in New York."

Michael looks through the rearview mirror, and I can sense he's probably laughing internally right now. How do you tell your mother you're addicted to a woman in the same way a druggie is to crack?

"I've met someone," I say simply. "But, yes, also a business venture."

Her jaw drops. "You know my girlfriend told me you might've met someone, but I didn't believe her. She must be such a sweet girl. Tell me about her."

I try not to choke on the assumption of her being a sweet anything. Unless you liked your treats dipped in poison, that is.

"She takes some getting used to and is stubbornly headstrong." I smile thinking of Anya and how she just chewed me out over the phone. I can't help but find it all charming.

"So when do I get to meet her?" She reaches into her purse and pulls out a bag of cookies. She makes them for me every time she sees me. It's like our little ritual. I accept the one she offers.

"It'll depend on her work schedule," I hedge. I want my mother to meet Anya, but with the current mood she's in...

My phone begins to ring and automatically goes through the car system. Mention the she-devil and she will call.

Michael stares at me through the rearview mirror.

"Is that her?" my mother asks. The screen shows "She-Devil," and I'm grateful Michael and my mother can't see the photo I have of Anya as my screensaver.

"It would appear so. Think she got my package?" I say to Michael with an arrogant smile. Because Anya is most likely going to be explosive right now.

"Sir?" Michael asks.

"Answer it. She doesn't take it well when I don't," I say, already amused by the outburst that's about to happen.

"You piece of shit. How dare you send me lingerie as well as a fucking diamond collar. You think this will make up for your bad behavior of saying you liked to fuck her? You think I'm going to get on my hands and knees for you just because you say so?!" I smile as she yells. My mother, on the other hand, has wide eyes and is staring at me like I've lost my mind.

"Sweetheart," I say with a smile, just imagining her livid expression.

"Don't you sweetheart me. I earn just as much money as you, asshole. I can buy my own fucking jewelry. And how about you wear this collar while I shove something up your ass for a change?"

My mother gasps. "Oh, her language."

There's a pause.

"You have another woman with you? Are you fucking kidding me?!"

"Jealousy sounds good on you, sweetheart."

"I am not fucking jealous! Fuck you! I'm pouring gasoline on your car and torching it. Once I'm done with this car, I'm going over to your house and torching the others. And then I'm going to—"

For my mother's sake, I hang up through my phone before Anya can tell me she'll put a bullet in my brain.

My mother's absolutely shocked to the core. "That was her?" she asks almost breathlessly.

I crack a smile. "I might've upset her a little today. She's a bit of the jealous type."

"A bit?" My mother gulps.

"Michael, go to the Ivanov estate please. On the way, please drop my mother off."

"She's not really going to set your car on fire, is she?" my mother asks with a hand over her heart.

I casually shrug. "It's been a rough day. We have a few trust issues at the moment."

But at least I know how to provoke her so much that she'll call me three times in one day.

My mother looks stricken with fear but attempts a fake smile.

Well, shit.

* * *

Michael drives me up Anya's driveway after dropping my mother off. Her guards are out front, but I see no sign of her. One of them greets me as we park in front of her home.

Smoke is billowing on the front lawn from what appears to be one of my favorite cars up in flames.

"Tell her to get out here, now," I demand.

"I'm sorry, sir. She requested you not enter the premises," one of her men says. I don't know or care which one he is.

"Get out here, Anya, before I break their legs!" I shout.

The front door flies open, and there she is, dressed in red, as usual. Her hair is pulled into a bun, as it always is, and her face is makeup free. She still looks like perfection... and royally pissed. She smiles evilly and flings my car keys in my direction. I snatch them out of the air.

I don't even care about my car.

"As much as I like you livid like this and want to fuck you while the fire burns in your eyes, you're acting like a psychopath right now."

I knew it was a good call not to bring my mother around right now. Because the truth is, I fucking love the psycho in Anya.

"You like them old now?" Anya taunts. I try to hide my smile, because in a million years I didn't believe Anya's jealousy could be this unhinged.

"The woman you heard in the car is my mother."

Anya doesn't seem fazed. She just eyes me.

"I would like you to meet her."

She scoffs. "I didn't agree to meet your mother. Now, get the fuck off my property." She turns and walks back inside, and her guards step in front of me, blocking my path to her, as she slams the door. I lick my lips. It's obvious my little she-devil will have to be broken in other ways. I'm going to have to fuck the brat out of her. And I have every intention of breaking into her home tonight to do just that. Preferably after my mother falls asleep.

CHAPTER 39
Anya

I wake to unusual noises, which is weird considering everyone in the house should be asleep. Sitting up in bed, I notice my bedroom door is open, and my men know not to enter without a knock.

I open the drawer of my bedside table and reach for the gun I have stored there, but before I can touch it, a hand covers mine and pulls it away.

"Now, that's no way to treat a guest in your home." River's voice echoes through my room, and before I can think better of it, I throw myself at him and hope to God I hit him. My room is almost completely dark; blackout curtains block the light from outside, and the only illumination comes from a dim light down the hall that seeps in through the doorway.

"You're feisty tonight," he says. I try to hit him, but he just chuckles, and somehow we tumble off the bed. On the way down, he turns us so he takes the worst of the fall, ending up on his back beneath me.

"I see you were waiting for me," he growls as his hands slide up and down my naked body. I pound on his chest, but he doesn't seem to care. Then I lean forward to bite him, and the lights suddenly go on.

"Miss," Clay says, and River flips me so he's covering me with his body, and my head hits the floor.

"Get the fuck out," River growls, and I can't help the laugh that escapes me at his boldness; as if he has any right to tell anyone what to do in my home. When his gaze moves back to me, he leans in. "Tell your men to leave, *now*."

I keep my smile in place as I answer him. "No."

He reaches for something, and I don't take notice until I hear a gunshot.

"Did you just shoot at my men?" I question, trying to see over his shoulder.

"Next time I won't miss. Now, tell them to leave."

"Get off me."

"No, you're naked." As he says it, his other hand slips between us and to my pussy. "Tell them before I shoot again." His eyes are on me but his gun is pointed at my men. "It's become apparent to me today that I have to fuck the brat out of you. I have a feeling they won't like how I'm about to handle you."

"Leave," I tell them.

"Are you sure, miss?" Vance asks, concern lacing his voice.

"She's sure. And when you hear her screaming, do not come back in."

"Bit cocky there, aren't you?" I taunt.

He leans down and bites my bottom lip before he takes it in his mouth and sucks it. When the door shuts, the gun he was holding drops and he lets go of my lip before he pulls away, his body leaving mine as I lie on the floor with him now above me.

"You've left a lasting impression on my mother, and not in a good way," he tells me, his gaze tracing my body. I can feel my nipples harden at the attention. "That was very, very bad of you." He pulls his belt free from his trousers, and with his other hand he flips me over so I'm on my stomach. And before I can say a thing, his belt comes down hard on my ass.

A grunt leaves me, but I don't scream. And I have a feeling he was hoping I would.

I'm still fucking furious with him, even if I am

being unreasonable, yet my ass raises, begging for more.

"Do you fuck her the same way you fuck me?" I hiss, silently begging for the belt across my ass again.

"Who?"

"Don't 'who' me." I go to get up, but he holds me down with his boot on my ass, pushing me back into the floor.

"Who, sweetheart?"

"Stop calling me that."

"Why?"

I go to move again and he pushes me back down.

"Because I am anything but sweet."

He leans down a little.

"To me, you *are* the sweetest because you taste the sweetest."

"I bet you said the same to her."

"I hear jealousy, my sweet, but that's okay. I can show you why you're the only one I dream of." His boot disappears from my ass, and before I can even think to move, his belt cracks over my ass again. I turn over and he offers me a hand to help me up. As I glare up at him, I notice his pants are undone, his cock hard and ready, and his shirt is half undone from our struggle.

"How do you want it? In the ass or in your sweet

cunt?" I slap his hand away and stand on my own. He smirks at me. Those eyes twinkle as they stare back at me, full of mischief.

"You aren't welcome in my ass."

"I will be, it's just a matter of time. But for now, I'm happy to take whatever it is you'll give." He steps closer to me, the belt still in his hand and a sinister smile on his lips, and I take a step back. "Why, my sweetheart, do you look scared?" His head tilts to the side. "I'd never hurt you. Well, not in a way you didn't like."

He winks and pushes me back with one hand, and I land on the bed. He pulls his trousers off followed by his shirt, exposing the scratch marks I left on him last time. He glances down at them. "War wounds. I'd happily go to war with you any time."

"How romantic," I reply sarcastically.

My body yearns for him, and all the rage and fury I want to unleash on him, fuck into oblivion.

"I thought so. You didn't like my presents?" he asks as he crawls over top of me. He spreads my legs with his own and gets down close. He drops the belt and reaches between us, his hand sliding down my stomach and to my clit. "I picked those just for you." He smiles at me.

"Did you?" I raise my hips, and he pushes inside

me, ever so slowly, as his hand leaves my clit.

"I did. Would you like my own jewels?" he asks with a smirk.

"Your jewels?" I scrunch my nose at his words.

"My balls. The family jewels. They're all yours."

I roll my eyes. "You can keep them," I say as my hands move up around his neck, forcing him down to kiss me. I like kissing River Bently, as much as I hate him. He is a damn good kisser, and he knows it. He knows that no matter how much I fight him, I will always give in.

I hate to want him.

And want to hate him.

It's a tug of war that I'm not winning.

He gives a little thrust, and all the fight in me completely melts away. I give in. Because I want him to make me forget all the bad things. I want to find that pure bliss I know only he can give me.

"There she is," he says as my arms wrap around his back and I cling on as he fucks me slow and steady.

He's doing it on purpose—fucking me as if he means it. He wants me to know what power he has over me. And I'm too tired to fight him on it.

My phone rings, and my hands pause their exploration of his back. It's my brother's ringtone.

"Ignore it," he says, and I want to, I really do. I'm

almost there, to the place where my mind goes blank and all I can think about is pure bliss.

But that singular ringtone has me pushing at his chest, and he looks at me, confused, but pulls out and rolls off me when I push again. I crawl over him to reach for my phone.

"Alek," I say into the phone, but he doesn't answer. Pulling it away from my ear, I see I missed the call. Pressing redial, I call back right away, but he doesn't answer.

Fuck. When the hell did I start putting River first? I hang my head off the bed as I feel River come up behind me. He rubs a hand down over my spine and then pulls me back to him.

It's all a mess. I want River more than I let on, and I want to stop fighting him. I want to let him in.

But it feels like I'm giving up the last of my power. Handing it over to him on a silver platter.

"You can leave now," I tell him.

His hand pauses on my ass.

"I'll stay," he counters.

"No, you can leave." I go to get out of bed, but he tightens his hold on me.

"Go to sleep, I won't fuck you again till morning."

"I don't like to share my bed," I tell him.

"Good, we aren't sharing. We're sleeping until I

306

can fuck you again, and your anger calms down from hating me for making you miss your brother's call. Let's just call it a truce for today, Red. Aren't you tired of fighting me all the time?"

Not in the slightest, but also yes. I'm exhausted from fighting how I feel about this man. I can't form words right now. Instead, I let him pull me down to the mattress, our naked bodies touching as I hold my phone in my hand, not letting it go. Not daring to let it go in case Alek calls back.

It feels like I have to choose between the two of them.

Alek is the only person I've ever cared for. What happens when he returns?

Will he disapprove of River like the old bitch does?

"I hate this snuggling shit." I lie because the truth is... it feels nice. Unusual in the way that I don't think I'll be able to sleep. But nice. I feel like with River beside me, I won't have to sleep with a gun in my top drawer. That no matter what, I'm safe. And that's a dangerous notion in itself.

"Good night, sweetheart." River kisses my shoulder, and I curl further into myself. I'm acting like some lovestruck girl. And maybe a small part of me is... in love with River.

And it's terrifying.

CHAPTER 40
River

She is the most peaceful sleeper I have ever encountered. It's as if she's dead. If it weren't for her chest rising, I would think she was dead. Not once does she drop that phone from her hand. I brush her hair from her face, pleased by the length of it freely cascading over the pillow.

"It's kind of creepy to have you staring at me," she says, still not opening her eyes.

"Tell me something about you and your brother."

She turns to face me, our lips so close that I don't have to lean in very far to taste them.

"Why would you want to know anything? You're just here to fuck me."

"Which I didn't get to do. So entertain me," I say, my hand stroking through her shining red hair.

"Hmm." She considers me. "When I was six, our first foster father tried to touch me," she says, her eyes locked on my face to see my reaction. I keep stroking her hair. "By that time, Alek didn't like to be touched, but when he walked in to see our foster father trying to get in my bed... Well, let's just say that's when Alek changed.

"He ran at him. We were so small, so the man thought nothing of it, but Alek ran, and when he got close enough, the man put a hand out. Alek kicked him between the legs, making his hand drop to clutch his cock. Then Alek got closer and dug his fingers into his eye sockets." She smiles at the memory.

"I'm a minute older than him, but somehow he always protected me until I could do it myself. When I was a teenager we returned to the man's home and I finished what the six-year-old version of me couldn't do."

My hand pauses mid-stroke, furious that I wasn't around back then to protect her. Although I despise the hell her brother's putting her through now, I'm grateful he looked after her up until this point. Until she was rightfully in my arms.

"Sounds like you two had a very special bond," I say.

She pulls back at my words. "Not *had*. We still do."

"I didn't mean..." She shakes her head and goes to pull away again.

"You should leave. This"—she waves between us—"is nothing more than great sex. Thanks for the gifts. Go home and see your mother."

I sigh, exasperated by how closely she clings to her sentiment. That it's so hard for her to be honest with me because she's used to years of engrained self-preservation. Sometimes I find it cute. Other times, it's annoying as hell.

"Will you come and meet her?"

"That's a no. Why would I want to meet your mother? That's weird." Her nose scrunches up, and I find all of these expressions no one else gets to see, cute.

"It's not weird," I protest. "It's what happens in a normal relationship."

"One, we aren't in a relationship. And two, what impression did I give you that I was normal in any way?" I lean in to kiss those lips. She doesn't pull away, and I can't help but smile as I kiss her. "You are so weird," she says, feeling my smile and pulling away now.

"Come back so I can fuck you into submission." She laughs as she walks to her bathroom. I hear the water run before she walks out with a cup in her hand and throws it at me. Freezing cold water splashes me on the chest. "What the fuck?"

"Get out of my bed and get dressed. I have to prepare for an auction today."

"You always have an auction," I grumble, throwing the fucking saturated sheets off me. Her eyes fall to my very hard cock as I stand, and I run my hands down my chest to wipe off the water, and when I look up, I see her eyes on my chest.

"I like to work. It keeps me sane." She shrugs.

"I have something else that can keep you distracted." I cup my cock, and she licks her lips. *Got her*. Just as I step toward her, she walks back into the bathroom, refills the cup, and walks back out.

"If you throw that at me, I will bend you over and blow out your back by fucking you so hard. Do you understand me, sweetheart?" Just as I let the last word leave my mouth, she throws it straight at my face. I reach for her, gripping her by her hair. She yelps, but I pull her to me, slam her back into my front, and let my other hand run down the front of her until I cup her cunt.

"I warned you," I growl, slipping a finger through her folds to make sure she's wet. Pulling my hand away,

I push her forward, bending her over. I don't loosen my grip of her hair as I position her in just the right spot before I slide into her.

She moans, and, fuck, she feels good. It's like fucking heaven. Her cunt was perfectly made for me.

"That's it," I breathe, sliding my other hand back to her clit while I fuck her from behind. She moans, and I apply more pressure to her clit. Her hand covers mine and moves with me. She directs my hand, showing me what she likes. I follow her guidance because I want her to want it as much as I do. I want her to come as hard as I know I will.

"Tell me who fucking owns you," I say into her ear before I bite it. I can feel her tightening, her walls milking my fucking cock.

What a good girl.

"Anya," I growl.

"I do," she pants, and I can't help the smirk that touches my lips. She comes, and I'm right behind her.

Fuck.

This fucking woman.

We're breathing heavily together as she straightens and slides off my dick, then walks into her bathroom.

"Promise me you'll meet my mother while she's in town," I say.

She walks back out with a sickly-sweet smile on her face and throws another glass of water in my face.

"Now, leave."

CHAPTER 41
Anya

It's a dick fest in here tonight. At least that's what Alek used to say when it was only men who attended an auction. That didn't bother me in the slightest. What does bother me is that Alek never called me back last night. And I wish he had. I'm mad that I was too distracted to answer his call. Alek isn't someone I compromise for.

Ever.

Yet I'm letting River sneak in more and more.

I don't know if it's selfish to ask River to stop searching for Alek. Would it be for Alek's sake or for mine? Have I fallen into a habitual stupor that this workload and lifestyle without him might carry on for longer?

I never thought the day would come when I would consider Alek's and my separation—ever.

"It's a full house tonight, and the crowd is eager to buy," Vance reports after I return from momentarily slipping into the private office. I'm watching the stage from the side as the auctioneer presents the last woman for the first half of the auction.

I would expect no less from any of our auctions. It just always seems peculiar on the nights when it's only men buying. Like I give a shit. Money is money, after all, no matter whose hand it comes from.

"Anya, you're looking as beautiful as always." I turn to find Rick Cansis approaching me. He must've spotted me from his table. He isn't much older than me, maybe in his early forties, and is a kingpin in sex trafficking. It's rare to see him come to these events personally, though he's been a loyal customer for quite some time. And while he's here to buy the women, he always tries his luck with me, even after being rejected multiple times.

I turn to look at him with no smile on my face whatsoever, as I sense this will be no exception.

"Anya, you can smile. It won't crack that beauty." He winks, and still, I say nothing. "What will it cost?" he asks, leaning against the same wall I am.

"Excuse me?"

"To buy you," he says matter-of-factly.

I'm almost having déjà vu. I huff out a small breath.

"Name your price. You know I have the money." He moves in a little closer.

"You couldn't afford me, Rick. It's best you get back to the auction now." I wave a hand in the direction of the stage.

"You know, rumor has it you're looking to settle down," Rick says as he leans in, as if it's our little secret. "That's why I thought I'd come to you first. You don't want any of these average-income-earning men."

My temple pulses. None of our patrons are "average-income-earning," but that's a bold fucking statement about me looking for anything.

"I'm sorry, what?" I scoff, tempted to ask Vance to bring me my knife.

"Meredith and I had lunch a few days ago. She said you were ready to settle down."

What the actual fuck?

"So how much?" he repeats.

My phone dings, and I look down at it. *Payment received.*

"That's enough, right?" I turn toward River's voice.

"You just sent me twenty million dollars. Is it

enough for what?" I say, trying to gather my thoughts about Meredith suggesting to a sex trafficking kingpin that I'm looking for anything.

River smiles, dressed in an all-black suit, his gaze sharp as a knife.

"A date," he replies, then looks at Rick. "You should leave before I pull out my gun or Anya gets her knives. She has a nasty habit of carving out people's eyes."

"For your information, that only happened once, and I much prefer cutting off dicks now."

Rick sizes up River, but when his gaze cuts to me, his shoulders sag slightly. "I must be mistaken. I didn't know you found someone so quickly."

He's quick to walk away and back to the auction.

That old bitch is trying to cause havoc now, but why? Considering how she feels about relationships, why is she trying to put fuckers like Rick onto me?

"I didn't need your help," I growl at River.

"I wasn't helping you. Since you refuse to wear a ring, it's obvious I have to make my ownership known."

I gasp. "Are you fucking kidding me? Calm your macho shit down."

He breaks out in a smile. "That's the first time you haven't outright denied that you're mine."

317

I roll my eyes and cross my arms over my chest. He's lucky he fucked me so well this morning that I'm in a good mood. "You have a habit of showing up when you aren't welcome," I tell him, turning back to the stage as the last woman steps out.

"You see her?" I point at her. "That is what your money will get you, so go and bid."

"And have you throw gasoline on another one of my cars? No, thank you. You might actually be gaslighting me right now," he suggests with an arched eyebrow.

I try to hide my smile, because it was a lot of fun setting his car on fire.

"Thank you for your generous contribution of twenty million. I'll take your payment as good faith for future opportunities."

"No, you will take that payment for a date. Now, come." He reaches for my hand and pulls me behind him.

Vance seems almost used to the exchange, as he doesn't even bother to interfere.

I sigh. Technically, I don't need to be here. I have enough people trained for this job, and I could easily leave. But it's the question of *should I?*

"I think you forgot who you're trying to boss around." I pull back.

"Fuck it." He grabs me, lifts me up, and throws me over his shoulder. "Dinner. With me. Now," he barks, carrying me out the door and past Clay, who is now just as used to River coming in and taking me when he wants to. I'm amazed he hasn't been shot yet. Maybe I'll have to be the one to rectify that.

"So demanding. Are you this demanding with your other women?" I ask as he carries me out to a new car that I haven't yet seen. He puts me down, careful that my dress doesn't ride up.

"That was jealousy, sweetheart. I can admit it, unlike some," he says, wiping something from my black dress. "How about this?" he croons, his fingers now on my lips. "I'll hike up your dress, taste that sweet pussy, and you can take a photo. And if you feel the need to get jealous again, you can look at it. Fuck, you can even send it to whoever you think you need to be jealous of." He winks.

"Just get in the car," I tell him, opening the passenger door for myself. He smirks as he waits until I'm inside, then he closes the door for me and walks around to sit beside me.

"You didn't like my idea. I thought it was rather clever." He smiles as he starts the car.

"You just want to go down on me again."

"Fucking truth," he says, stepping on the gas and

tearing down the driveway and onto the main road. Someone beeps behind us, but he doesn't seem fazed.

"It's not the correct way to ask for a date," I chastise him as I look at my nails.

"It's a half date," he corrects me.

"What even is a half date?" I ask, confused. If I've learned one thing about River Bently, it's that he's about as unpredictable as I am.

"It's where my mother is also joining us."

"Fucking hell, River." I throw my hands in the air. "Parents don't like me. It's just the nature of the beast. They hate me, and why would I want to sit awkwardly with your mother?"

"Because you two are the most important people in my life. I want you to like her, and her to like you."

His honesty catches me off guard. Am I really that important to him?

I'd usually flippantly think *"why would I care,"* but the thought doesn't rear its ugly head.

I like the way it sounds, but it doesn't change the fact that I don't do well with parents. Not that I've ever tried. But considering my own estranged relationship with Meredith, I don't do first impressions well.

"What if she doesn't like me?" I ask. "Because that's a high possibility. Mothers hate me."

"She won't once she gets to know you," he says

with unrelenting confidence. "She's only here for a short while this time, and I've already spent most of my time with you."

"Breaking into my house, I might add."

"Yeah." He smirks.

"How did you even get past my guards last night?" I ask, baffled. Anyone else who tried—and there were only two previous attempts—was shot dead before they even made it past a window or door.

"I have my ways." He winks. "That and I hacked all of your security cameras and had a key made for your front door."

My jaw drops open. "You just used a key to let yourself in?"

"Yes, Anya. It's how people used to do it back in the day. You should try it someday," he says smugly. "I'm not against you firing your bodyguards, though."

"I'll get rid of you before them," I say defiantly.

"I feel much the same way about my dogs," he says with an arrogant smile. "My mother loves Mexican food. I hope you're okay with that?"

I sigh. I'm out of my fucking mind actually doing this. But it might be an interesting distraction to watch how a normal mother interacts with their adult child since mine is currently trying to fuck me over at every turn now that Alek isn't around.

"I'll be sure to bring my sombrero," I say, exasperated.

He chuckles as he grabs my hand, rubbing his thumb over it.

I stare and stare and stare.

I really have gone mad.

CHAPTER 42

Anya

"It seems strange you're not forcing your mother to your god-awful restaurant," I say as we pull up in front of what looks to be a popular Mexican restaurant. I wouldn't know because I rotate between a select few that I already know I like.

"It doesn't hurt to try different things, Anya. Besides, we ate there last night," he says, rather smug. "You're going to enjoy it."

"Lucky me, because we all know how much I love margaritas." I roll my eyes as we get out of the car. He locks it and places his hand on my lower back as the valet comes to take his keys.

"Let your hair down," River orders.

I stop walking and look at him.

"This won't work if you tell me what to do."

"I love your hair down, and you always have it up. Put it down."

"It takes a lot of effort to get it like this," I say, pointing at the bun. It's slicked back and got a lot of product in it.

"And while it's beautiful, I prefer it down," he growls, and it's that tone that promises sweet, sweet pleasure. I bite my bottom lip.

"Don't give me that look, Red," he says, his voice gravelly. "We can at least say hi to my mother first."

"And after that?" I ask innocently as I start to unpin my hair. He watches me intensely. I hate those eyes, how they stare into me, make me forget who I am, and get me to do whatever he wants. That is way too much power for my liking.

"After that, I'm going to break into your home and fill that sweet little cunt of yours. I'm going to tie each of your limbs to a bedpost and torture you into oblivion," he says. My pussy throbs and floods at the visual. "Since you're behaving like such a good girl."

Once my hair is free, he places both of his hands at the back of my head and pulls me in for a kiss. We stand in the middle of the walkway, two people oblivious to anything around us. His tongue slides in my mouth and takes over. I moan into his mouth, and he pulls me closer. I can feel his hardness through his pants, proof of how badly he wants me.

I want him just as much.

"River." He pulls back at the sound of his name, then stares at me and wipes my lips.

"I'll just be a second, Mother," he says, and he gives me his best charming smile. "I smudged your beautiful lips." I let him try to fix it, but I can sense his mother's stare on the back of my head. "Perfect," he whispers, then steps back and grabs my hand as if he thinks I'll run.

I may run.

I just haven't decided where to yet.

"Mother, you remember Anya from the phone call?"

His mother, petite and blond, stares back at me.

"Yes, I do." She nods, and River keeps a hold of my hand as he leans in and kisses his mother's cheek.

"You took longer than I expected today. It was just me and the dogs. Where have you been? I come to visit, and you don't even make time for me," she accuses, and I know it's because of me.

"I had work."

"I'm sure you did," she says, her gaze darting back to me.

She looks small, kind, and everything opposite to

me. There is no judgment in her tone or gaze, but I feel it just the same.

"Shall we eat? I'm starved," River says.

Again, I stay quiet as we walk into the restaurant. The hostess immediately escorts us to a table. River makes sure he takes the seat next to me, and grips my leg under the table. He starts massaging my bare thigh while his mother looks over the menu, and I can't but help think how precarious this all is.

If she knew I was just selling sex for profit, would she be so inclined to enjoy a meal with me?

Then again, River mentioned his mother doesn't know what he does for a living. I sell people, and he sells the tools that help kill them. Wouldn't that just rock her world?

"Anya, was it?" she asks, and I realize I'd spaced out. I nod. "Do you have a preference for wine?"

"Anya doesn't drink," River interjects. "But order the red. I feel like red tonight." As he says it, he squeezes my thigh.

"Oh, apologies. I didn't know. Can I ask why?" she says sweetly.

Small talk. Great. Not my strong suit.

"One of my foster fathers was a drunk. That man was as bad as they come, in more ways than one. Every time he attempted to do bad things to me, he was drunk," I say, no emotion in my tone. "So I just decided I wouldn't let that happen to me. Nothing to inhibit my thoughts or impare my judgment."

His mother goes quiet at my words and just stares at me with her mouth slightly open.

Small talk. Still not my forte.

"Anya is a very strong woman," River says, and leans in to kiss my cheek.

"I can see that," his mother replies and then calls the server over. "We'll just have water, please." I don't say anything, but think she's done it to somehow win me over. But isn't it supposed to be the other way around? When the fuck did I start caring about what people think?

The server stops at the end of the table, pen and pad ready as she waits expectantly for the food order.

"Do you know what you'd like, Anya?" his mother asks. "I was here for ten minutes before you arrived, so I may have already decided, and I know River frequents this place for takeout."

My eyebrows lift in surprise. The normality of this situation is so peculiar that I almost want to laugh. If Alek saw me right now, he would too.

"I'm not overly hungry," I confess. "Can I try some of yours?" I ask River, knowing that if I don't order something, he'll force me to eat anyway. "I don't usually have a big appetite," I find myself saying. *Why the fuck am I still talking?*

River and his mother place their orders, and she offers me a smile. "So, Anya, tell me what you do for a living? You come across as very well put together and powerful."

"Anya sells exotic jewelry," River is quick to say. I hide my smirk.

"I didn't realize you'd gotten into the habit of speaking for women," his mother scolds.

Oooh, I like her.

"It's as River says. I sell exotic jewels and such. My brother and I took over the family business from my foster mother."

"Well, that's most impressive. Do you get along well with your brother and foster mother? Is it the same home where the alcoholic gentleman lived?" she says.

"No, he's definitely in the grave now. My brother and I are very close, twins actually. My foster mother and I have a very unique relationship, but I'm grateful for how she raised me."

"Oh, wow, you have twins in your family as well? River has cousins who are twins. If you two were ever to have kids, it might be a possibility for you as well," she says excitedly.

River's hand stills on my leg. Before I can speak, he does. "Anya and I have no intention of having children. Isn't that right, sweetheart?" he asks, looking at me.

I fall for him a little harder. I never told him specifically about my surgery, but I made it known I will never birth a child into this world. "Yes."

"Oh." She seems disappointed but takes a sip of her water. "Well, lucky your niece keeps me young," she says with a little laugh. I realize now that River really is her everything. I thought most women would want their children to be parents. That it would be another reason she would want to set me to the side, but instead, she accepts me because of him.

The server walks over and sets plates full of food on the table. Without words, River pushes a portion of his rice dish onto a small plate for me.

"I've been dying to try these enchiladas." His mother squeals with excitement. "So how did you two meet?"

I take a sip of the lukewarm water. "Coincidently, River bought the house beside me, and well, we just hit it off, didn't we?" I say, amused.

"So that's why he wasn't gone for long yesterday when he went to retrieve his car," his mother says. "Sorry your phone call came through the speaker. I was nervous you actually did torch his car." She laughs.

My mouth curves into a smirk, and River squeezes my thigh again.

"So you've seen his home. It's beautiful, isn't it?" she says proudly.

"Exquisite," I reply, then take a forkful of the food. I'm surprised that I enjoy its flavor.

"It's the dogs that make her smile, so I've been avoiding bringing her back until I can elicit the same reaction."

"Dogs are a good judge of character," his mother says pointedly.

My phone buzzes, and I look down to see Clay's name. He knows where I am and would only call in an emergency. "Excuse me." I slide out of the booth and walk to the front of the restaurant.

"Did something happen at the auction?" I ask immediately.

"No, miss. Meredith is here," he says.

"At the auction house?" I look at my snake watch. "It's over, and patrons should have left now. Why is she there?"

"She said she's here to see you and she's not moving until she does."

I curse. *What the fuck is the old bitch up to?* "I'm on my way."

"Vance is already on his way to pick you up."

I hang up the phone and walk back into the restaurant.

River and his mother are laughing, and it feels intrusive to ruin what looks like a wholesome moment. I never had this growing up. I've never yearned for it either. It's simply interesting to watch.

"Something came up at work," I say.

"You have to go?" his mother asks.

"Yes."

"I'll drive you," River says, wiping his mouth.

"Vance is already on his way to pick me up. He'll be here any minute."

"Then I'll walk you out," River says as he slides out of the booth.

"It was lovely meeting you. If you have time, I would love it if you could come to River's while I'm still visiting," his mother says earnestly.

Surprised, I offer a nod as a goodbye.

"Is everything okay?" he asks.

"It's Meredith. She's at the auction house. Looks like she and I need to have a discussion about boundaries."

"Do you need anything?"

The question catches me off guard. "When would I ever need anything from anyone?"

He gives me a pointed look, and I sigh.

"Well, if you do, let me know. My mother likes you, by the way," he says, surprising me.

"No, she does not. If you believe that, then poor judgment is hereditary, it seems."

He leans in and kisses my cheek. "She likes you, and so do I."

My car pulls up, and I see Vance in the driver's seat.

"Ask her if she still likes me when she discovers what I really do," I say with a haughty laugh.

"Should I tell your brother the explicit ways you crawl to me in the bedroom, sweetheart? Let's agree that some secrets are best kept between us," he taunts with a smug expression. He tries to grab me again, but I'm already climbing into the car and putting my hair back in a bun.

"I'll see you later, River. Don't be late tonight. I might even leave my window open," I tease.

CHAPTER 43

Anya

I'm back here again. Why? Because she called.

And when she calls, I come. No matter how much I don't want to. That's what you do for family. Or so I've been led to believe.

Lately, however, the old bitch is getting her nose out of joint, and she's about to hear some hard truths.

When I arrive at the mansion where the auction finished over an hour ago, only a few lights are on. The door to the office is open, and she's comfortably sitting in my chair.

"You're looking awfully fucking cozy," I say as I walk in.

Vance and Clay remain outside the door. I don't have to worry about anyone overhearing this conversation.

"You're still seeing him," she says with disgust.

"Do you really think I would stop seeing someone because you said so?"

"Your brother always listened better than you," she scoffs.

"Yeah, so you always tell me. But who is the one you always call?"

"That's because your brother never fucking answers," she snaps. "Avoiding my calls, that little shit."

"He's avoiding all calls," I remind her. "Not just yours."

"I told you to stay away from River because he's bad news."

"Yes, I remember, but you want to know what?" I raise a brow as I pause. "I'm worse." She shakes her head and stares at me.

"Stay away from him. Do you want the business that we built to go up in flames? Because that's what will happen. Men like him like to be in charge. Do you think he will let you remain more powerful than him?" she sneers. "Powerful and greedy men don't like to let women rule."

"Alek lets me," I remind her.

"Your brother is different."

"Why? It was only a week ago you were telling me to announce him as dead."

She slams her hands on the desk. "Because he is. He was raised by me," Meredith says, as if that's point enough.

"You didn't raise us from the beginning, Meredith. Remember that."

"If I had my choice, I would have."

"What do you mean by that?" I ask, stepping in closer. She picks up her glass and leans back in the chair.

"Exactly what I said. If I had a choice, you would have been with me since you both could walk. Then I wouldn't have to deal with this vigilante shit." She shakes her head and mumbles, "Fucking foster system."

I laugh. Vigilante shit? She was the very person who dragged us into this world.

"Do you even know their names?" I ask. "Our parents. Do you know their names?" Alek and I only looked into our family once. With something as common as Ivanov for a last name, we didn't get far. But that's because the moment Meredith found out, she was a raging storm, and she forbade us to focus on anything past her domain and rule.

"No, why would I?" She huffs, but the way she says it makes me question her honesty. She pulls a cigarette out and lights it with the gold-dragon-engraved lighter. "You two have been fucking up every-thing I've created these last few months."

"Are you fucking kidding me?" I snap.

"Watch your tone with me!" Her eyes narrow.

"Or what, Meredith? You're going to fucking shoot me?"

"Don't think you're an exception, girl," she says in a threatening tone, and it provokes my own lethal edge.

"Don't forget you're becoming senile, you old bitch. None of this is yours." I sweep my finger in the air. "This is what Alek and I created. So you had a few standing ovations at the auctions you had in your day, but you could have never built it to what it is today without us. This is none of you and all of us."

She scoffs. "You'd be nothing without me, you ungrateful brat."

I laugh again. "Is this why you sent Rick to me, to try to control me? Have you truly lost your fucking mind? You think because I'm seeing someone that it's going to destroy everything I've built? How weak you've become if you're so easily shaken by any man's presence."

Her hand slams on the desk. "I fucking made you, and I will take you out of this world just as quickly if you do not obey me!"

I choke on a laugh, and silence fills the void. I shouldn't be shocked, but I am.

"You wear his jewelry like some branded whore," she accuses. "What happened to your loyalty to your brother, Anya? Seems short lived since you've taken your men off tracking him. Where's your loyalty to your family?"

I don't need to tell her that Alek called me days ago to call off the search for him. I didn't want to, but I chose to. For him. "You wanted me to announce Alek dead only days ago, and now you're using him against me and telling me I'm not loyal." I flash a wicked grin. "My, your manipulation is getting rusty, you old bitch."

Her teeth grind.

"I suggest you leave," I say as I approach my desk and stare down at her. I grab the gold lighter she always carries and light the flame. "Before I torch this mansion with you inside."

"You wouldn't dare. You love your auctions too much."

I grin. "I have other auction houses. And I can rebuild any mansion whenever the fuck I please. I will continue to grow this empire. You can either stand in my shadow or crumble with a small piece of it."

"You'll come to your senses real fucking soon, girl.

You will beg for my mercy," she snarls as she stands. "You're nothing without me."

"I don't think I will. Now, get the fuck out."

I drop the lighter, and she snatches it up, her chin raised high, not bothering to look at Clay and Vance as she leaves.

"Are you sure it's okay to let her leave?" Clay asks.

A weight shifts inside me, and for some reason, I feel stronger. More powerful. "Yes. I think it's quite all right. This is my empire now. Entirely."

"If Alek comes back?" Vance asks.

"He grovels," I say, leaving no room for argument. I don't want to do this without my brother, but I sure as hell can. "Then I'll see which leg I'll break first before I let him back in."

I might be heartless, but I don't want to lose the only two people I've ever been able to call family in one night.

CHAPTER 44

River

I spend the rest of the evening with my mother. She has a dog on either side of her, their heads on her lap, as she sits on the sofa in the living room. She always spoils them. I'm sure coming to live with me again was a pain in the ass for them.

"I see you're breaking the rules of the house." She turns and smiles. The dogs don't even bother moving. Supposedly, the dogs aren't allowed to lie on the sofa, but I have yet to see that rule actually be enforced.

She's reading a book and sets her tea down. "I love this tea, River. I'll have to grab some before I go back home," she says in way of changing the topic.

"It's Anya's favorite," I say as I sit on the couch opposite her.

"Anya is an interesting choice," she says carefully. I

give her a pointed look as I fish my phone out of my pocket.

"You like her, don't you?" I ask. Whether my mother approves or not, there is no me without Anya.

My mother nods, and it fills me with pride. "Not really who I thought would be the first woman of yours I'd meet. She certainly has a temper, but I'm sure you can handle her."

"You've met other women," I remind her, and her saying Anya has a temper is an understatement.

"None that you couldn't keep your hands off of or that you were smitten with," she points out as she stretches her legs. The dogs jump off as if only just now realizing I'm in the room.

"I'm not smitten," I counter as I unlock my phone to the screensaver of Anya and her beautifully pierced tits on my screen. I can't wait to break into her home tonight, and break her in as well.

"No, I think you're in love," my mother says as she stands. I don't confirm or deny it. "Just be careful with that one. It sounds like she went through her fair share of hardships growing up. She may have never been loved before, and I'm pretty sure she will do everything in her power to push it away or sabotage it."

"I'm very persistent," I reply with a smile.

My mother just laughs and nods her head. "Don't

I know it. I'm going to bed now. Enjoy your evening, River, and don't be out too late," she says as she summons the dogs behind her.

"Whatever could you mean?" I ask innocently, and she gives me a knowing look. Now that she knows Anya and I are neighbors, she knows exactly where I'm heading tonight.

My phone buzzes, and it's a message from Will. My eyes widen at the onslaught of information. Though I might've called him off Alek Ivanov for the time being, it didn't take away my curiosity around Meredith Fork.

For good reason. *Fuck.* My instincts are always on point, and as I read the information he's sent through, they prove correct once again.

There's no way Anya can possibly know this.

An alert trips on my property's perimeter alarm and notifies me through my phone.

"What the fuck?" I say as I switch out the screen and look at my security cameras. There's nothing on screen, but I know better than that, considering I used the same tactic on Anya's premises last night.

Someone's on my property, and it's most likely someone who shouldn't be. If it were Anya, there would be no sneaking. She'd kick in the front door unapologetically.

I stand and peek out of the living room and up the

staircase. My mother is in her bedroom now, and the dogs are with her. If someone is trying to get in, then their first choice is most likely through the garage. Because that's the first place I would break into.

Michael would have been alerted about the intrusion as well, and he'll be minutes away.

I open the wooden cabinet in my living room and shift three of the books. I grab the pistol hidden there. In the book beside it is the silencer, and I combine the two. My second sensor alerts me through my phone, closer to the house now. The cameras aren't relaying that detail to me, but as expected, they're heading toward the garage, so I do the same.

Who the actual fuck has enough balls to target me in my own home? Especially while my mother is upstairs trying to sleep. I crouch behind one of my cars in the dark, then purposely override my security system to unlock the door. Why make it difficult for them when this is exactly where I want them to walk into?

A small noise grabs my attention, and with laser focus, I narrow my gaze on three people wearing all black. Three? Is that all that was sent? What a fucking insult.

They have guns raised as they walk in, black masks covering their faces. They look for the door into the house and head in that direction. Before they even make it to the door, I shoot two in the back of the head. The final one I shoot in the back of the knee and then the hand holding the gun.

He screams, the only noise heard among the ordeal as I come up behind him and press my hand to his mouth to muffle his screams.

"I'm giving you one fucking chance to answer me or I will murder everyone you love and force you to watch. Who sent you?" I say calmly, a wild storm beneath as adrenaline courses through me from the kills.

The intruder is slick with blood as I hear barking. *Fuck*. My mother's most likely heard the noises. I glance between the intruder and the door. If she comes in here, she's in for a startling reality check.

"Rick Cansis," the person squeaks.

The sex trafficker? I angle him away, put the gun to his head, and blow out his brains.

I run to the door, closing the garage door behind me, and remain in the dark as my mother calls out from the staircase.

"River, is everything okay? I heard screaming," she says. My dogs are barking as they run to me. They growl at the door, and I signal for them to return to her.

"Everything is fine. I just stubbed my toe on the

TL. SMITH & KIA CARRINGTON- RUSSELL

coffee table again," I call out to her.

Headlights streak across the front windows. "Michael's coming over for a drink. We'll be quiet. Go back to sleep, Mother," I say. "You might want to shut your door. You know how clumsy he can get after a few too many drinks. Don't want him stumbling into your bed again, do you?"

"Dear God," she mumbles as her door slams.

Michael comes into the garage as I switch on the light. Another two men are behind him, guns raised as they walk in.

"What the fuck happened?" Michael asks.

I raise my finger to my lips. "My mother is upstairs, and I would like for her not to discover the three bodies here. Arrange a cleanup immediately."

"Who the fuck put a hit on you?" Michael asks, snapping his fingers for the other two to start busily making this place appear brand fucking new again.

They begin to drag out the bodies as I say, "Find me Rick Cansis's address."

Michael's eyebrows shoot up. "You want to go after the sex trafficking kingpin?"

I offer a crazed half smile, my blood pumping with the thrill. "He came after me first. Besides, I don't like how he parted his hair anyway. Oh, and he also made a pass at my woman."

CHAPTER 45

Anya

I'm fucking furious. Not only did River stand me last night with undelivered promises, but now he's summoned me to his restaurant. No, not summoned. He demanded it when he called, assuring me he has something I need to see immediately.

I rejected the thought of coming here because I'm not at his beck and call, yet somehow, I still had Vance drive me here. I never thought I would want to be in a relationship, and even now, I don't think I want to put labels on anything. But if you were to ask me how I'd feel if he slept with someone else...

I would say murderous.

And that's putting it politely.

I don't know if it's monogamy that I'm after, but

it doesn't mean I can't be pissed about him leaving me high and dry last night.

His restaurant isn't open for once, but Michael stands at the door, waiting for me. He has dark circles under his eyes. "Rough night?" I ask, not really caring about the answer. I know Michael doesn't like me, and the feeling's entirely mutual.

"Like you wouldn't believe. He's waiting for you inside," he says. The restaurant is still lit up but seems oddly spacious without the tables being fully booked out as they usually are. Clay walks in behind me while Vance waits at the car.

When I ascend the stairs, I see River sitting at the end of the table, broody and handsome.

"You better give me the name of the woman you were fucking last night because I'd like to pay her a visit," I say. He doesn't smile as his knuckles go white.

"Sit," he instructs. "No time for games today, Red."

I scoff. "I thought that's why you like me."

I sit across from him, and he stands and walks to me. Unusual since we usually push and pull until, eventually, I go to him, preferably crawling. He slaps a folder onto the table in front of me. I then notice part of a bandage underneath his black shirt around his wrists.

"Are you hurt?" I ask.

He flicks his nose. "A shallow knife wound. It'll heal."

I jump out of my chair. "What the fuck? From who? Only I'm allowed to stab you."

"Sit," he commands.

I warily look over my shoulder at Clay. River's tone is lethal, and I know if ever the time comes that I have to instruct one of my guards to shoot him, they will. Though it's more likely I'd pull the trigger myself.

I do as he says.

"Last night, three men broke into my home. They're obviously dead now. They were sent by Rick Cansis."

"Rick?" I ask in disbelief. He usually sticks to his own internal fights. "Why?"

River makes a pointed look at the file. "Let's just say Rick won't be attending your auctions anymore."

"You took down Rick Cansis last night?" I'm shocked. Honestly, I never liked the guy or his trade—I enjoy willing participants in my auctions. It's not to say I haven't dabbled in other things, but I didn't like it as a full-time income. But I certainly wasn't going to judge any of the crooks in this business. "Is this because you were jealous?" I breathe out.

A dark, haunting laugh escapes him. "Not *my* jealousy, Red." He flicks open the folder for me. Images of me and Alek as children come into view. My eyes grow wide at the two people sitting behind us. The woman has the same red hair and porcelain skin as me. Beautiful. The man looks like a slimmer version of Alek.

I know who they are without even asking. "How did you find these photos?" I see their names. Date of births. Birthplaces. Everything.

"It's not a coincidence Meredith ended up with you and your brother, Anya. She knew your parents. Well."

I flip through the images that show Meredith in her younger years, stoic-looking as she sits with my father and mother. My eye catches on the gold-dragon-engraved lighter. The same one Meredith always carries.

"Your parents were only here for a year and were neighbors to Meredith Fork. For an unknown reason, even before selling their house, they purchased four tickets to return to Russia. But they never made the flight."

I stare at him in disbelief. "Are you saying Meredith has something to do with their disappearance?"

He shrugs. "You tell me if it looks from those photos like they're two parents who want to abandon their children. You might not understand love, Anya, but that's what it looks like."

My stomach drops. There's pain in my chest as I try to wrap my head around this information. "You're lying," I whisper.

"Am I?" he says without remorse. "Then why did Meredith have a sex trafficker put a hit out on me last night? The same day she tried to have him make a move on you?"

My eyebrows furrow. "Meredith is good at many things, one of them being manipulating men and curling them around her finger. But this is a stretch."

"I haven't removed Rick's body from his home yet. I didn't want to tip Meredith off. So this is a courtesy to you. Either you deal with Meredith or I will."

"You can't just—"

"My mother was at home, Anya!" he snaps. "I do not forgive those who threaten what and who I love. And that includes you. Either you deal with this or I will."

I feel numb, but a wild, unrelenting pain stretches from my stomach. All these years, she told me we were unlovable. Abandoned. A nuisance. We could only become important if we learned how to lie, murder, and grow an empire.

So we did.

I've been so blind this whole time. But wasn't this some form of love? That you expect the people closest to you to be the ones to protect you... not hurt you instead.

I stand at the end of the table and take the folder. "Don't call me," I say to River.

"Anya," he says behind me, but I have Clay stand between us as the numbness slowly drains from my legs, and I find my strength again.

I had literally been holding that gold dragon lighter last night.

All this time...

All these years...

And it's on my shoulders alone because Alek still isn't here.

CHAPTER 46

Anya

Vance drives me to Meredith's as I silently flick through the photos.

When I was a teenager and first looked into my parents' disappearance, Meredith found out quickly and squashed the delusion of searching for them. Even when I did—behind her back—all I came up with was dead ends.

The house beside her had been burned down and was nothing but barren property that she'd bought by the time we were brought into her home.

This entire time, everything was there, and Alek and I were too brainwashed to realize. Too young to understand. Not anymore, though.

I pull out my phone and hit call on Alek's number.

I feel like I'm in a calm fury, something I'm not used to.

It rings.

And rings.

And rings.

Until his voicemail picks up.

"Hey, Alek, I'm about to do something pretty stupid," I say and lick my lips. "I don't know what you're going to say about it, so before I proceed, I want you to know that I love you. Even if you hate my decision right now. You're all I have left. I mean, I like River too, which is rather surprising since he's an asshole. You're both kind of the same in that regard, which is why I know you'll hate each other."

I shake my head. "I digress. Alek, please don't be mad at me. I'm not mad at you for leaving me with this decision on my own, but it looks like I have one more loose end to clean up for us."

I hang up the phone. Vance looks at me in the rearview mirror.

"Are you sure about this, miss?" he asks.

"You can stay in the car, Vance. It's going to be messy. Family arguments always are, aren't they?"

"No, miss, we'll come with you," Clay says from the passenger seat. "We're here to protect you no matter what."

I let out a heavy breath. "I appreciate you both. But this, I have to do on my own."

Meredith's driveway gates come into sight, and I'm not surprised to see them open. As if she's expecting me to show up and grovel and apologize. But it's most likely for an entirely different reason.

"I want you two to take care of her guards. Leave Meredith to me," I say, and that unfurling anger rises as I look at the pictures of my parents one more time.

My heels hit the pavement as I step out of the car. I look up at the home in a new light. I've always hated this fucking house. I turn to the left, knowing a smaller home once stood there. Where a family of immigrants from Russia lived, and the woman next door was powerful enough to wipe them out overnight.

One of the maids opens the door with a smile, her stomach swollen in pregnancy. I glance down at it and whisper quietly into her ear, "If I were you, I'd make myself scarce."

My tone is lethal. She turns pale and nods. "She's in the kitchen."

I smirk as I walk to the kitchen, enjoying the click of my heels against the wooden floors.

"How many times have I told you to remove your shoes?" the old bitch's voice rings out.

"You were expecting me, were you not?" I ask as I

come around the corner. She has a cigarette hanging out of her mouth as she stirs some poisonous concoction that's possibly supposed to be muffin batter.

A cold, bloody fury pumps through my veins. But I'm calm. Collected. Stalking. I've killed for money. Killed for power. But never have I killed for the satisfaction I'm about to receive now.

For those in their graves who cannot defend themselves. For two children who had no idea the monster who had shaped and molded them was the very thief of joy they could never touch or understand.

"Come to apologize?" she says. "It better be in the way of money and assets. And I'll be dealing with half of the auctions now."

I smirk. She watches me skeptically. She and I both eye the assortment of knives on the counter. Beside them is the very lighter my father once owned. It was a trophy to her, and I'd been so blinded, I never realized it was under my nose the entire time.

"I'm not the one with a need to apologize." The voice doesn't even sound like my own.

Realization dawns on her, and tension crackles in the air. She lunges for a knife, but I'm already on top of her, so she reaches back and grabs the gun from beneath her jacket. I push her hand that's holding the gun out of the way, narrowly missing being shot, as she thrusts a flip knife from her pocket toward my stomach. I dodge it and slam her wrist against the edge of the counter, satisfied by the snapping noise.

She screams as I snatch one of the other knives and plunge it into her gut. She's shocked, hunched over me as she tries to grapple for my face. I lean back as I fight her for the gun and shove her back.

She's holding her stomach now, glaring at me.

I look at the gun and then her. "No worries, I didn't pierce anywhere you'll bleed out immediately. You taught us well, after all."

"You ungrateful little bitch!" she says with shallow breaths. I drag the set of knives away from her reach and place the gun beside me.

I grab one of the knives and flip it in the air. "I only came for an explanation."

"You're choosing that fucker over your own family?" she seethes.

My eyebrows shoot up. "No, actually, I'm choosing my family. My *real* family, which you took away from me."

She seems to go a shade paler and then that scornful, twisted expression appears. "I knew I should've killed that fucker the moment I realized he was looking into me."

I throw another knife into her leg, and she screams

as she drops to one knee. She pulls it out and throws it back at me. I dodge it, and it impales the wall behind me.

And we both know if she pulls the one out of her stomach, she'll bleed to death.

"It would appear that you've become senile in your old age after all. Why did you kill our parents, Meredith?"

She stares at me, a smile blossoming on her lips, and then she tries to laugh. It's short lived as she coughs in pain. "You both always thought you were so clever. But you were just two traumatized little kids who couldn't even remember your parents' faces.

"I didn't lie when I told you it was only so I could do dealings with the Italians in town. No deeper meaning at all. Your parents simply moved into the wrong house and caught my attention, so I befriended them. Killed them. Took you two ungrateful shits in. The only reason I handed the auctions over to you was because I'd found myself in some strife, forcing me to step down. So I thought, why not have you two take my place and flip me a fortune." She sneers. "Not as mysterious as you were hoping?" She chuckles, and blood leaks from between her lips.

An inner turmoil twists in my stomach, but I'm past the point of acting on it or questioning it. I'm sure to most it's painful to hear, unbearable to know. But I have been empty for a very long time. Becoming an orphan will not change that.

Meredith is a predator.

Unfortunately for her, the cubs that she trained have far surpassed her.

"I think this is the most honest you've ever been," I say as I flip another knife and then smile. "How I'm going to cling to your every scream, you old bitch. Try your best to haunt me for the rest of my days and hinder any kind of happiness I might have like you already have."

I step closer, pocketing my father's lighter. Because once I'm done with this old bitch, this place is going up in flames.

For the first time in my life, I see a sweep of fear cross her expression, and it fills me with satisfaction.

"It would appear, Meredith, that you've lost your touch."

CHAPTER 47
River

I watch through the security cameras as Anya's car comes up the driveway. When it stops and she steps out, I'm grateful Michael has taken my mother out to buy groceries for dinner.

I'm down the stairs and opening the door as she stops in front of me, covered in blood and soot. She looks like she's crawled out of hell itself, but knowing her, she was the one who caused the havoc.

But she came back to me. She looks empty almost, that lethal resolve evaporated from hours ago. Her showing up as bloody as this fills my heart because she came here first.

"Meredith?" I ask as I stand in the doorway. Because who knows, she might be here to put a bullet straight in my brain afterward.

"Who?" she says, that little bit of bite in her tone.

"You're not hurt?" I ask, and feel stupid for asking. As if anyone could hurt this she-devil. Her face scrunches up as she looks at my sleeve that's hiding the bandage.

"Unlike some, I know how to handle knives," she says. She's still her. I break out of my frozen state and crush my lips to hers.

It was a gamble exposing the truth to her. She might've turned on me, but she's nothing if not a truth seeker, even if she liked to twist it at times for her own benefit.

Her arms wrap around my neck, and she hikes up her dress so she can twine her legs around my waist. Her kiss is desperate and soul-sucking all in one.

I grab her bare ass, slamming the door behind us in case her men are watching. We fall onto the sofa in the living room as she grabs at my belt desperately. I pull off her dress, my nose flaring at that beautiful fucking body of hers. There's still blood on her arms and legs, but she pushes me down as she grabs my throat and kisses me so deeply that I'm impressed by her strength.

I want to flip her over and fuck her as I promised, but it's a gentle dance with my she-devil. She needs this, so I'm happy to let her ride my cock into oblivion.

Her sweet pussy glides over my shaft as she sighs in relief and begins to bounce.

A bark interrupts us but doesn't stop her pace. I click my fingers at Barry and Stan, who are staring at us, wide-eyed.

"Fuck off," I say to them between kisses. She's milking me as she groans into my mouth, riding the pure bliss.

"Did you hold out for me, sweetheart?" I ask, because I know what it's like to ride a high after a kill.

"Shut up, Lake," she breathes, and my hand goes to her throat in warning because I know she said my name wrong on purpose.

"Bounce harder, Tanya," I order, and her pussy clenches around my cock. *Fuck.* This woman. She undoes her hair as she bounces, and it's mesmerizing as she rides me, filthy and covered in blood.

This woman was built only for me.

"Say you're mine," I order as I crush her cheeks together.

"Let me get off," she replies.

"Anya," I growl. I can tell she's close to climaxing, and fuck me if I'm not holding on for dear life as I watch her.

"Yes," she breathes as her pleasure grows. "Maybe.

Oh fuck!" she screams as she crashes over the edge. I blow into her as her pussy contracts around my cock.

I fist her hair and yank her head back. "Say you're mine," I growl.

Her piercing green eyes hit me through thick eyelashes. "How about you take me upstairs and wash me first?"

"How about you crawl up those stairs like a good girl, I fuck you hard again, and then I'll think about washing you before my mother comes home wondering why my woman has blood all over her."

She laughs—actually fucking laughs—and it's the most beautiful thing I've ever fucking seen.

"Let's start with the crawling, shall we?"

CHAPTER 48
Anya

I'm lying on top of River's chest as I trace the tattoos on his arms. His mother is downstairs, most likely cooking again, since apparently that's what she likes to do. I haven't left River's home since arriving two days ago. I pushed back meetings and I switched off my phone, honestly just needing space from the world.

"You look good in my shirt," he says as he brushes his hand through my hair.

"I look good in everything," I say as I raise onto my elbow and look down at him.

"It feels weird that you're being so nice, Tanya."

"Fuck off. And don't expect it in front of others," I say, and he chuckles. I love the way it vibrates against me.

For the first time in a long time, I feel free.

"Do you know what else will look good on you?" River asks as he gets out of bed. I appreciate the view.

"I swear to God, if you're trying to sell me guns while we're in bed, I'm going to shoot you with it."

"Not that." He chuckles again.

He pulls out a red box. I get excited and clap my hands at the present. Cartier. My favorite.

"It matches the set I bought you," he says.

"Which one?" I ask as I open it, and my heart stops. It's a Paraiba tourmaline from the set of matching earrings and necklace he gave me, but it's a ring. I snap the lid shut.

"What the fuck?" I grit out.

"Calm down," he says, and I fight every instinct not to run out that fucking door. "I'm not asking you for some fancy ceremony or even a marriage certificate. I just want every person on this fucking planet to know that you're mine, and that if anyone makes a pass at you, then I have free rein to shoot them in the head."

My breathing is erratic.

"I'm not the only one here who gets jealous, Anya. I need the world to know you're mine."

It's the earnestness in his tone that has me looking between him and the box. "And what do I get?"

His eyebrows raise. "Besides an expensive, shiny fucking ring?"

"I have plenty of those already. I'll make you an deal. I'll wear this fucking ring if you get my name tattooed on your forehead."

He chuckles as he lies back beside me. "That's a big fucking no."

"Then no can do," I say but find myself opening the box again and studying the ring because it's fucking beautiful.

"What if you thread it through a necklace and wear it around your neck as a collar until you come around to the idea?" he says as he grabs the back of my neck and pulls my face to his.

His voice vibrates over me and gives me tingles in their promiscuous promise. "It better be a really nice necklace."

"Don't you have a beautiful necklace from the set I'd bought you that you haven't yet worn?" He challenges.

"I want another one." I say trying to hide my smirk.

His lips crush mine as he smiles. "Anything for my queen."

CHAPTER 49

Anya

I'm not surprised by the lack of people who attend Meredith Forks' funeral. It's a ceremony only—no viewing or casket—because I know all they were able to get out of that house were her bones. Such a tragedy that half of her décor was paper walls. Went up in flames within minutes, the reports say.

I watch from a distance as someone pays their respects and leaves. River's hand is on my lower back as I begin to move toward her photo. When I stop at her grave, I spit on it.

River's eyebrows arch. "You came all this way to spit on someone's grave?"

"In the same way you make me wear a fucking engagement ring around my neck when we're not getting married. We all do what others might consider unnecessary."

He laughs as I stare at the grave for a little longer. I hate this woman, but she was still the person who built me into someone capable of running an empire and an army.

I have mixed feelings, and they're not something I wish to delve into.

The snapping of a twig wakes me from my stupor, and I turn around, ready to pull out the gun concealed on the inside of my jacket. River already has his pointed as he stands in front of me, guarding me.

My eyes go wide in disbelief. "Alek?"

He's shaved his red hair since I last saw him, and he looks like he's bulked up a little. He adjusts his gloves as he eyes River, who slowly lowers his gun.

I walk up to him, and where most might expect an embrace and joyful reunion, I punch him in the face. "Are you fucking kidding me? You left for six fucking months and then turn up as if nothing has changed."

His face grows red as he grinds his jaw. "The last voice message you sent sounded suicidal."

My eyes bulge in disbelief. "You're crazy if you ever think I'm taking my own life. You have a lot to make up for."

His gaze catches on the ring around my throat, but he says nothing. He's always been a man of few words.

River steps up beside me. "I'd like to say it's a pleasure to finally meet you, but that would be a lie. If you ever hurt her like that again, I'll put a bullet in you myself."

Alek's arrogant smile blooms with the threat. Some things haven't changed, but he seems different. Off, even.

I know Alek and River have most likely spoken over the phone but they've never met in person.

"This is River Bently, Alek. He's coming into partnership with us," I explain.

"And fucking my sister, so I hear," Alek says as he steps around me and looks at Meredith's photo. He leans over and spits on her grave.

"I should've been there with you," he says quietly.

"Yes, you should've," I reply as I put my hands on my hips. "So where is this fucking dancer you left me for?"

Alek's jaw grinds as he walks past me and gives River the once-over again. "Good luck competing with her jealousy," he says and stuffs his hands into his pockets. "Don't worry about the dancer. I'm back now. That's what you wanted, wasn't it?"

I go to press him further but am held back by

something. As regal as Alek appears, there's something off about him, and I can't put my finger on what it is.

I might be his twin, but there's a part I'm realizing now that I may have never understood or even touched on.

After six months of hell, this is all he has to say to me?

"Should we spit on her grave together just for good luck, Tanya?" River says, distracting me from my brother. "C'mon, your brother's back now. You can ask him all the questions when you're back home. But this... this is a onetime opportunity," he says as he points at the grave with his gun. "And I must confess I like watching you spit. Preferably on my cock."

I can't help but smirk at his vulgarness, even at a funeral.

"It seems like we're both going to hell, Lake," I say as I push back my hair, which I've been wearing down all week.

"If that's where you are, then that's where I'll be as well," he says as he holds my hand. I feel torn as to whether I should follow my brother or stay with the man who has filled a space in my heart I never realized was empty.

"I think I might like you a little, Lake," I say as I rub my thumb over his.

He chuckles. "Well, I know I'm absolutely in love with you, Red."

I try to hide the smile.

Then to hell we go.

Together.

CHAPTER 50

Anya

"Put the ring on, red," he tells me. I look down at it as we walk out of the courthouse. We just got married.

I finally agreed to marry him, but the ring still hangs around my neck.

It took over a month for me to get here, but here I am. Dressed in a simple black dress and my red heels. I've left my hair down because that's how River loves it.

It's not your average outfit for a wedding, but we eloped at the courthouse and didn't tell anyone. I didn't even tell my brother, and I tell him everything.

I have come to realize I was too reliant on him, but that comes naturally when you grow up and only have one person you can trust. I love him with every fiber of my being, but I love this man in front of me more.

They are different types of loves.

And this one is shaping up to be my favorite.

I also wonder sometimes if my parents had this type of love.

But then I quickly banish the thought.

Looking down at his hand, I see his ring on his finger.

"You are my wife," he says, and I fight a smirk. "Red, put the fucking ring on, now." My smile breaks free as he reaches for the engagement ring and my hand, and puts it on my finger himself.

I let him. He is my husband, and I agreed to this.

Even if that ring means more to him than it does to me.

"Everyone you pass will know you're mine."

"Will they?" I ask, fighting the smirk on my lips. He steps forward as our driver pulls up, and lifts my chin with the hand that has my ring on his finger. Yes, I did pick it out and made sure it had diamonds in it. At first, I expected him to tell me he wouldn't wear diamonds, but all he did was kiss me senseless and fuck me till I screamed the night I showed it to him.

To him, my buying the ring signified that I was all

in. I'm pretty sure it could've been bright pink, and he still would've been happy. After all, he's getting everything he wants, and I guess in some way I am as well, even though I didn't realize this was what I wanted.

It's amazing what love can do to change your brain chemistry.

"Do not take it off. My ring will stay on your fucking finger. Even in death. You will be buried with this ring on your finger. Do you understand me?"

I want to laugh, but somehow, I also think it's very romantic. See, we're two peas in a pod, and both a little fucked-up in the head—one of us more so than the other—but I think that's what makes us work so well.

"If you say so, husband." His eyes go wild at me calling him husband, and before I can say anything else, he has me in his arms with his hands around my waist as he pulls me to him and slams his lips to mine.

He kisses me more passionately than he did when I said "I do," and trust me, this man knows how to fucking kiss. His hand starts to wander, and our driver coughs behind him. I go to pull back, but he just pulls me back into him. I feel how hard he is as he presses himself against me. Which makes me want to get home to fuck as soon as possible.

"You can say that again tonight, wife, while I have you tied up in the bedroom." I only nod my head because I love it when he ties me up. Hell, I love it when he does everything to me.

As one of the terms of us getting married, I made him sign a prenup. There was no way I was going to marry him without one.

Do you think I'm stupid? Ha! Hell no.

He may rival me in terms of wealth, but my money is also Alek's money, and as he's my only family, I will do everything to protect that.

I also told him I would be keeping my name. He didn't seem pleased at first, and I'm sure one day he will try to convince me to change it, but he didn't push.

But now, when I buy guns from my husband, I just have to suck his cock for a discount. It works well in both our favors.

"I'm looking forward to it, husband," I purr, pulling away so he can't grab me again, and climb into the car.

My husband.

River Bently.

Once I'm settled in the car, I text Alek. To tell him I'm married.

He doesn't reply. No, he's still trying to find that fucking dancer.

I wish I could find her and kill her myself, but at

least he's back home now.

Also by T.L. Smith

Black (Black #1)

Red (Black #2)

White (Black #3)

Green (Black #4)

Kandiland

Pure Punishment (Standalone)

Antagonize Me (Standalone)

Degrade (Flawed #1)

Twisted (Flawed #2)

Distrust (Smirnov Bratva #1) FREE

Disbelief (Smirnov Bratva #2)

Defiance (Smirnov Bratva #3)

Dismissed (Smirnov Bratva #4)

Lovesick (Standalone)

Lotus (Standalone)

Savage Collision (A Savage Love Duet book 1)

Savage Reckoning (A Savage Love Duet book 2)

Buried in Lies

A Villain's Lies

Moments of Malevolence

Moments of Madness

Moments of Mayhem

Connect with T.L Smith by tlsmithauthor.com

Also by Kia Carrington Russell

Insidious Obsession

Mine for the Night, New York Nights Book 1

Us for the Night, New York Nights Book 2

Stranded for the Night, New York Nights Book 3

Token Huntress, Token Huntress Book 1

Token Vampire, Token Huntress Book 2

Token Wolf, Token Huntress Book 3

Token Phantom, Token Huntress Book 4

Token Darkness, Token Huntress Book 5

Token Kingdom, Token Huntress Book 6

The Shadow Minds Journal

T.L. Smith

USA Today Best Selling Author T.L. Smith loves to write her characters with flaws so beautiful and dark you can't turn away. Her books have been translated into several languages. If you don't catch up with her in her home state of Queensland, Australia you can usually find her travelling the world, either sitting on a beach in Bali or exploring Alcatraz in San Francisco or walking the streets of New York.

Connect with me tlsmithauthor.com

Kia Carrington-Russell

Australian Author, Kia Carrington-Russell is known for her recognizable style of kick a$$ heroines, fast-paced action, enemies to lovers and romance that dances from light to dark in multiple genres including Fantasy, Dark and Contemporary Romance.

Obsessed with all things coffee, food and travel, Kia is always seeking out her next adventure internationally. Now back in her home country of Australia, she takes her Cavoodle, Sia along morning walks on beautiful coastline beaches, building worlds in the sea breezes and contemplating which deliciously haunting story to write next.

Made in the USA
Monee, IL
01 November 2024

69120576R00216